COAL SACKS

FOR

CURTAINS

JONI POWLING

Copyright © 2013 Joni Powling

The moral right of the author has been asserted.

Apart from any fair dealing for the purposes of research or private study,
or criticism or review, as permitted under the Copyright, Designs and Patents
Act 1988, this publication may only be reproduced, stored or transmitted, in
any form or by any means, with the prior permission in writing of the
publishers, or in the case of reprographic reproduction in accordance with
the terms of licences issued by the Copyright Licensing Agency. Enquiries
concerning reproduction outside those terms should be sent to the publishers.

Matador
9 Priory Business Park
Kibworth Beauchamp
Leicestershire LE8 0RX, UK
Tel: (+44) 116 279 2299
Fax: (+44) 116 279 2277
Email: books@troubador.co.uk
Web: www.troubador.co.uk/matador

ISBN 978 1783061 983

British Library Cataloguing in Publication Data.
A catalogue record for this book is available from the British Library.

Typeset in Aldine401 BT Roman by Troubador Publishing Ltd

Matador is an imprint of Troubador Publishing Ltd

COAL SACKS FOR CURTAINS

This book is dedicated to my sister Lily Morgan for her unfailing faith in me as an author. Also to my nephew Colin Morgan for his expert help.

Special thanks to my son Peter … you can be a hard task master, but you supplied the discipline that I required to finally get Coal Sacks for Curtains *out there.*

Last, but not least, my good friend Lesley McEwan, of North Carolina … those 2-hour transatlantic calls supported me when I was struggling to stay focused. Thanks, Lesley, it meant a lot to me.

Chapter 1

3rd September 1939

A mournful wind blew over the marshes, sending puffs of billowy grey clouds scudding across the sky, while the tall trees that skirted the long, lonely road leading to the village of Higham swayed and danced in unison as the wind caught their willowy branches. Josie shivered as she stood gazing out of the window. Everything looked normal – she could see Mr Dawson's sheep in the far meadow happily grazing. The occasional flash of white bobtails as rabbits hopped nervously about – but something was wrong – very wrong!

Her grandparents, Uncle Sid and Auntie Doll, and a few of the neighbours had been gathered around the radio in the front room for what seemed like hours. Suddenly the chimes of Big Ben signalling eleven o'clock echoed from the radio, and a man's voice came over the airway, his voice trembling with emotion as he announced 'THIS COUNTRY IS NOW AT WAR WITH GERMANY'.

Josie didn't quite understand what was going on. For days everyone had been talking about the possibility of war! What was war? How would it affect her? She shrugged her slight shoulders and turned towards the old stone sink. One thing she knew for sure! There would always be washing up and, it always seemed to be her job! She heard her grandmother give a gasp of horror and disbelief as everyone started talking at once, then her uncle's deep voice rising above the rest as if trying to gain some control of the situation.

'Now it's no good getting into a panic about it, that won't do any good. Let's all have a nice cup of tea; I'm sure we all need one, afterwards we'll have a talk.' There was silence for a moment or two then, as if an afterthought, he continued. 'Where is Josie? She should be in here; it will affect her as much as anyone.'

Josie stood resolutely by the sink. What did her uncle want to talk to her for? Whoever wanted to listen to her anyway? No-one in the past had ever been interested in anything she said or did. Raising her hand she brushed a lock of brown, unruly hair out of her eyes and gave a deep sigh. How she hated washing up; the steaming bowl of hot soda water that her grandma insisted she use made her hands red and sore. Suddenly she felt a hand on her shoulder and she swung quickly around to find her uncle standing behind her. His face was pale and troubled.

'Josie, leave that, lovey, and come into the front room. Did you hear the news? It's a terrible day indeed ... we are at war!' He put a comforting arm around her and shook his head sadly.

She looked up at him and a slight frown crossed her face. 'Yes, I heard, Uncle, but what does it mean – will we all get killed?'

He ran his fingers through his mop of brown, curly hair.

'No, Josie, it's not like that. Unless, of course, you are in the forces, that's a different story then, but I don't think you will need to worry too much about it. After all you are only twelve years old! It'll be over long before it can have any effect on your life.' He handed her a small towel which was hanging on the old wooden kitchen door. 'Dry your hands now and then we'll go into the front room; your grandma wants to talk to you.'

Josie dried her hands on the worn tea-towel, then, shivering slightly, followed him into the front room and sat on a small stool next to her grandmother.

She gazed solemnly around the room and for a moment her eyes focused on the fire that was burning in the grate. The yellow and red flames danced fiercely and noisily as if in anger. Even the aspidistra that once stood proudly in front of the window on grandma's old sewing machine looked forlorn and dejected while Auntie Doll dabbed the corner of her eyes as she stared intently at the floor. Everyone looked so serious – the talking had died away and it seemed they were all engrossed in their own private thoughts.

Grandmother spoke first. 'One thing is for sure,' she remarked sadly, 'Josie won't be able to go back to London next week, it won't be safe there. No! She had better stay here and go to the village school until the war is over.'

Josie stared into space as she fiddled with the edge of her apron, and her eyes filled with tears as she thought of her family – her mother, father, brother and sister – and what about Paddy her dog? What was it Gran said? London was not safe? Suppose they all got killed – she would never see them again! Unbidden tears trickled down her face as she turned to her grandmother.

'But I want to go 'ome! I want to go 'ome! How long do wars last, Gran?'

Grandmother shook her head. 'As long as it takes, Josie … just as long as it takes.'

Josie buried her face in her hands as a big sob shook her thin body.

She felt an arm being placed reassuringly around her shoulders.

'Don't cry, Josie – crying isn't going to do any good is it? After all, the war won't make any difference to you and it could well be all over by Christmas. You'll be safe enough here with me and your grandfather.'

Josie nodded bleakly – Christmas! That was two, nearly three months away. What about her brother and sister? What would they do? Would they miss her? Gran's voice broke through her train of thought.

'Come on, lovey, cheer up. Pop into the scullery and finish off those dishes.' She paused for a moment, and then wagged a finger in Josie's face. 'You know what they say, Josie, idle hands make work for the devil.'

That night she climbed the narrow stairs that led to the small bedroom, which was hers when she stayed through the long, summer holidays, and sat dejectedly on her bed.

'I wish my bruvver and sister were 'ere,' she muttered. 'They would know about war and wot is going to 'appen to us.'

She climbed into the big feather bed and lay staring at the ceiling, then with hands clasped together she prayed.

'Please God let my bruvver and sister come 'ere and bring my Paddy. 'E would like it 'ere. I know 'e would.'

She smiled as she drifted gently into sleep. She didn't care about the war as long as Paddy was with her. She thought of writing to her mother to ask if he could come and stay with her until the war was over, but then she realised that her mother never replied to any of her letters so what would be the point of it!

Josie was the baby of the family. Her sister Lucy was the eldest and brother George was the middle one. They lived in a tiny council flat near the docks in Greenwich, south-east London.

Her father had worked at the docks since he was fourteen years old and prided himself on the fact that he had never missed a day, except, of course, when he was called up to fight in the First World War. Every morning he would pack himself a sandwich for lunch, and then walk through the narrow London streets until he came to the foot tunnel that ran under the River Thames. Through the tunnel he would walk until he reached the other side, which was known as the 'Isle of Dogs'.

'Why do they call that place where you work the Isle of Dogs?' Josie had asked her father as they sat around the scrubbed, wooden table one day after tea. Father leaned back in his chair, took a rolled-up cigarette from an old tin he carried in his pocket and slowly lit it before answering.

'Well, Josie, it was like this. Many, many years ago, long before even I was born, the King of England lived in Greenwich.' He hesitated for a moment and looked at Josie questioningly.

'You know that big park you play in, Josie? The one up the hill.'

She nodded her head excitedly, anxious for him to go on with his story.

Father rubbed his chin in thought before continuing. 'Well, the park was the grounds of the royal residence, which is that big white building near the river. The King loved to hunt, but he had so many hunting dogs that there was no room for all of them at the palace, so one of his aides …'

'What is an aide, Dad?' Josie asked, screwing up her face.

'Josie, yer know well enough, it's very rude to interrupt someone who is talking. If yer do it again I won't tell you the story. Now, as I was saying! One of his aides suggested that they could build a tunnel under the river to a small island which was uninhabited at the time. Then the dogs could roam free on the island, and when they were needed by the King – well, all they had to do was to bring 'em back through the tunnel. Ever since then it's been called the Isle of Dogs.'

Josie hunched her shoulders and gave a big grin at the thought of dozens of dogs racing through the tunnel. It was her favourite story.

The sun was streaming through the open window when Josie opened her sleepy eyes the next morning. She gazed appreciatively around the room; it looked lovely in the early morning sunlight. Pretty chintz curtains hung at the window. The brass bedstead glittered like gold, while the cover on the bed lay crisp and white like freshly fallen snow. As she snuggled down further into the bed, the soft down cocooned her body like gentle fairy wings. 'I wish I could stay in this room till the war was over,' she muttered to herself. 'I don't want to go to that stupid school, it's miles away and I won't know anyone there.'

Her thoughts were interrupted by a voice calling her.

'Josie, Josie, it's 7.30 and time you were up.'

'Yes, Gran,' she replied wearily. She hastily threw the covers back and went over to the window. She stared morosely at the long, lonely road that would take her to 'that' school. Then, with a sigh of resignation, she slowly dressed and went downstairs, where grandmother was busy cooking breakfast over a roaring fire in the black, open grate.

'You had better be quick my girl,' she said, turning to look at Josie as she entered the room. 'Go into the scullery and wash yourself. We can't have them saying at school that you were not clean, now, can we?'

The scullery was a small whitewashed room, barely furnished with just an old wooden table standing flush against one wall. Next to it was an iron mangle. Many times Josie had to stand and turn the handle whilst her grandmother folded the wet clothes and guided them through the two heavy rollers. Then, while she carried them into the garden to dry on the line, it was Josie's job to empty the big tin bath which had been placed under the rollers to catch the excess water. Because there was no drainage at the old cottage all the water had to be carried down to the end of the long garden to be thrown away.

She picked up the large bar of red carbolic soap, pulling a face as she gingerly started to wash. How she hated the smell of carbolic and the feel of cold water. Carefully avoiding her neck, she finished washing and carried the bowl of water down the garden. The early morning air was cold on her face and the dew on the plants brushed against her bare legs. She shivered as she hurried down the path, stopping for a moment or two to look at the little animal cemetery that she had made with her brother the previous year. Every time they found a dead bird or an animal, they held a ceremony in grandfather's wood shed and then buried them in a little box with a cross as a headstone. She felt tears sting her eyes as she thought about her brother George. Maybe he will never come here again – maybe I will never see him again – maybe he'll get killed! She turned around and saw her grandmother hurrying up the path towards her.

'Now look here, young Josie! You had better get a move on otherwise you'll be late for school on your first day and that will never do. Hurry up indoors and get your breakfast down you. There's only a sandwich for you to take to school for your lunch so make the most of it, we'll be lucky to have any food at all if this war goes on too long.'

Once inside the house Josie quickly sat at the table, thankful for the warmth from the fire that blazed in the grate. A plate of scrambled eggs and toast was placed in front of her, and then grandmother sat down on the high-backed chair and started to pour herself a cup of tea. Josie watched her intently. She was a very precise lady, slim and only about five feet tall; her grey hair was pulled severely off the face and twisted into a bun which she kept in place with a couple of hairpins. Her eyes were her most outstanding feature: electric blue with a gleam in them that was mesmerising. She rarely smiled – her whole life seemed to be taken up with cooking and cleaning. The cottage reflected her efforts

– everything was spotlessly clean and the furniture, although old, shone with loving care.

I wonder if that's what it will be like when I get married! Josie thought as she silently ate her breakfast. It didn't seem much fun but she supposed that there wasn't much else.

Grandma thrust a note into Josie's hand just as she was about to leave for school.

'Be sure and give this to your teacher as soon as you get there, Josie, and no loitering on the way or you'll be late. Now off you go.'

With a slight push she was outside and the door of the cottage was closed firmly behind her. Josie turned and stared at it for a few minutes, feeling very alone and isolated. Then taking a deep breath she shrugged her shoulders and turned to walk up the garden path towards the lane.

'Nuffink for it, I suppose, nowhere else to go 'cept the stupid old school,' she muttered as she started up the lane, carrying her note and a small bag which contained her lunch.

To any passer-by, Josie would have looked a very vulnerable creature. She was small for her age, with light brown, wavy hair that framed an elfin-like face. Her thin dress hung down almost to her ankles, a hand-me-down from her sister. On her feet she wore a pair of black, lace-up shoes, slightly too large and down at heel; a folded wad of newspaper discretely covered holes at the bottom.

Half a mile up the road she passed the 'Red House'. It was a large, imposing building standing in its own grounds. She paused for a moment and pressed her face against the wrought-iron gates that fronted it.

'One day,' she said thoughtfully, 'one day I am gonna live in a grand 'ouse like that – I don't know 'ow but I will!'

In the distance the sound of the school bell ringing made her realise that dreams are just dreams, but reality is reality, and she had to face her first day at this strange, unfamiliar school.

She stood for a moment, and then turned to look back across the fields; she could just see the cottage in the distance. The rays from the morning sun glistened on the church spire as it stood majestically above the cluster of tiny, thatched cottages, as it had done for hundreds of years. Everything looked so peaceful! Her eyes glanced over the landscape: at the sheep grazing on lush, green grass, while, in the distance, she could just make out a herd of cows busily chewing the cud … she felt a sinking sensation in her stomach!

'Don't know wot all the fuss about a war was. Nuffink 'as 'appened. I don't know why I can't go 'ome,' she sighed, as she continued her journey with a heavy heart.

The school looked grey and forbidding as Josie stood nervously at the black iron gates. For a brief moment she was tempted to run away – back to the cottage, back to her grandmother – but she knew in her heart that it was not possible. She had been told to go to school and that is what she would do. Pushing open the gates she made her way across the playground, then through the heavy oak door. Suddenly, she was confronted by a lady wearing a long black dress.

'What do you want child?'

'Please, Miss, my grandmother said I 'ave to come to school 'ere 'cause of the war an' all that.'

'And is that letter you are holding in your hand for me?'

'Yes, Miss,' she replied, as she quickly handed her the note.

The lady took it from Josie's outstretched hand and read it intently while Josie stood silently, staring down at her shabby boots and hoping desperately that no-one would notice the holes in them. After a few minutes she was grasped by the hand and, without a word, was ushered quickly towards a door at the far end of the building. Inside she came face to face with a class of about twenty children. As soon as they saw Josie they started whispering and nudging one another at the sight of this ill-clad stranger in their midst. What was she doing here? They didn't take kindly to strangers, especially scruffy ones!

'Children, pay attention,' the teacher said, pushing Josie forward. 'Josie is from London and she will be with us until the end of the war. I hope you will make her very welcome.'

There was a sullen silence from the class.

'What do you say children?'

'Yes, Miss Taylor,' they chorused.

Josie blushed and looked down at the floor – there were boys in the class! She had never been in a mixed class before; she had always gone to a girls-only school and the thought of spending every day with at least a dozen boys who might be just like her brother George made her cringe!

Her thoughts were interrupted by the teacher telling her to go and sit at the back of the class, pointing to an empty seat next to a spotty-faced boy with red hair. Bowing her head she walked miserably towards her seat and sat down as far away from him as she could, praying that the day would soon end. She just wanted to go home – back to London where she belonged.

The spotty-faced boy watched her out of the corner of his eye – a smart kid from London, eh! They would have some fun with this one, just wait until lunchtime.

'Dirty Londoner, dirty Londoner,' shrieked a tall, blonde girl as she tore Josie's lunch bag from her grasp and started to kick it around the playground, much to the delight of the rest of the school.

Josie chased after her. 'Gimme that back, gimme my lunch.'

The blonde-haired girl smirked. 'Who's going to make me? You? A dirty, skinny Londoner like you, who can't even talk properly?'

Josie felt a great surge of anger well up inside her at this remark and took a flying leap at her tormentor, grabbing a handful of hair as they both fell wrestling to the ground, while the rest of the kids stood around cheering and taunting. Suddenly, she felt a vicious punch to the stomach and collapsed on the floor gasping for breath – the blonde girl leapt to her feet and ran off just as Josie felt a pair of strong arms reach out from the crowd and pull her to her feet, and then, unceremoniously, she was dragged across the playground to the headmaster's study.

The headmaster sat at his desk, a pair of rimless glasses perched on the end of his nose, while his piercing dark eyes stared with hostility at Josie as she stood silently in front of him.

'I will not have fighting in my school,' he thundered.

'How long have you been here? Just one half day and already you have been fighting in the playground.'

'B ... but,' Josie stammered, 'I, er.'

'No buts! I don't want to hear any excuses because there aren't any. You need to be taught a lesson girl and a lesson you will indeed be taught. We want none of your rough London ways down here.'

A slight smile of pleasure crossed his mean face as he opened a drawer in his desk and brought out a long, thin cane. Josie's eyes opened wide in horror as, with one swift movement he forced her face down across his desk, pulled up her dress, and beat her with six stinging blows, causing red, angry marks to form on her bottom.

The spotty-faced kid smirked as Josie slowly hobbled into the classroom and tried to get comfortable on the hard wooden seat.

Chapter 2

Lucy stood on the platform at Maze Hill Station, along with the other early morning commuters, waiting for the train which would take her to her job as a dressmaker in London. It was mid-September 1939 – the war had been on for two weeks and everyone was showing the strain of wondering what was going to happen. As she paced up and down, Lucy's thoughts turned to her sister. It had been three months since Josie had left home to go and stay with grandma in Kent … now she couldn't come home because of the war!

'I don't care if Josie stays with gran forever. I ain't gonna miss 'er,' said George in his usual belligerent way when mother told them the news.

Lucy sighed. George could be such a brat sometimes, but he was mother's pet and could do no wrong in her eyes.

In the distance came the sound of a shrill whistle and everyone started to move towards the edge of the platform. Within seconds the great train thundered into the station, belching huge clouds of steam from its engine. Suddenly there was a surge of bodies thrusting themselves forward, all anxious to try and find a seat where they could collapse and, hopefully, snatch a few more precious minutes of sleep.

Lucy was trapped in the corridor of the train. She had

been unlucky this time and was wedged between a large fat, greasy looking man and an equally large elderly lady. The heat was stifling, even at that early hour of the morning, Lucy sighed and gazed around her, it was going to be a long, miserable journey to Blackfriars. A petulant voice broke her train of thought and she turned to face black, piercing eyes.

'Don't know wot is up with people today, letting an old lady like me stand all the way to London while they sit comfortable as yer like. In my day we were brought up proper like. Always was taught to give our seats up to someone older than us. It's a bloomin' disgrace, that's wot it is – a bloomin' disgrace.'

Lucy barely nodded her head in acknowledgement, looking furtively around at the seated passengers, wishing she could move to another part of the train. Small beads of perspiration started to trickle down her forehead, making her auburn hair stick to her face in tendrils. She tried to find a handkerchief in her pocket to wipe her brow, but it was no good! There was not enough room even to move her arm.

The large man shifted slightly and gazed appreciatively at her, noting her pale skin and perfect features. Lucy raised her eyes and caught his gaze – she blushed furiously and turned away.

Her mother was a tall, dark-haired, angular woman who had brought up her daughters with a strictness that would have been more befitting the Victorian era. Vanity was frowned upon. Men and sex were dirty words, never, never to be discussed in the house or anywhere else for that matter!

She turned away, deep in thought as the train thundered on and on, until the screeching brakes and a sudden jolt brought her back to reality. She had arrived at Blackfriars Station in the heart of London to face another day of hard work.

Lucy hurried out of the station and walked along a few streets to the building where she worked. The tall Victorian building looked as depressing as ever as she reached the entrance. The wooden stairs which led to the narrow room at the top of the building seemed never-ending; steep, narrow and dingy they gave an air of dismal decay. Lucy sighed as she reached the final flight of stairs. If only she had another job! Working as a machinist on piece work was no fun but, of course, her mother had seen it advertised in the local paper and she had no choice.

The sound of girlish chatter greeted her as she pushed open the old wooden door to the attic room. Inside there were about forty girls of various ages ready to begin work. The morning sun was already beating down through a long, dirty skylight, making the heat in the room even more unbearable. Long trestle-type tables placed in straight rows were supporting forty machines, while fine particles of dust floated in the musty air.

'Hello, Lucy,' greeted Mary. 'Wot about the news then? A bleedin' war! Don't fancy that much, do you?'

Lucy turned and smiled at her, she had always liked Mary. She was a very pretty girl with a heart of gold, but behind her smile was a hint of sadness, almost a sense of desperation. She was only eighteen but, as Lucy had been told in confidence, she had had an illegitimate baby when she was sixteen. No-one seemed to know who the father was and Mary certainly refused to tell anyone. Apparently, she had kept the baby and worked hard to bring it up with the help of her mother. There were rumours that the father was in fact Mary's own father! Lucy shuddered at the thought and pushed it to the back of her mind.

'No, I don't fancy a war, Mary, but I really don't fink it will make a lot of difference to us, except, of course, if we get called up.'

Mary shrugged her shoulders and made her way down the lines of machines to the one in the very far corner and gratefully sank down on the hard, wooden seat in front of it. She rubbed her forehead with a damp hand; somehow, she was not feeling too good lately. Mornings were the worst when the feeling of nausea swept over her like huge violent waves. Was she pregnant again? The memory of the times, late at night, when she heard the sound of footsteps in her bedroom, then the smell of her father's beery breath on her face as his big, rough hands tore at her nightdress until she was naked and trembling in front of him. Yes! Probably she was pregnant again and no-one seemed to care! When it first started many years ago, she had screamed out in terror and pain, calling for her mother, but the house had remained deathly silent except for the heavy breathing and groaning noises coming from her father. As she got older she knew that she would never be protected by her mother, the firm closing of a door told her that. Mary's thoughts were interrupted by the roar of machinery as one by one the sewing machines leapt into life – it was time to start work!

The heat in the room became more intense as the summer sun bore down through the skylight and the air became thick and heavy. Two and a half hours elapsed until, like manna from heaven, Mrs Dowan, the supervisor, announced it was time for a tea break.

Lucy gave a sigh of relief and stretched luxuriously just as Betty came down the line and thrust a mug of weak tea into her hands.

''Ere you are, luv. You'll feel better when you've 'ad that tea,' she said with a cheeky wink, and then walked down the long rows of girls handing out the rest of the tea as the roar of machinery gradually faded away, leaving a silence that was heaven.

For a few moments Lucy closed her eyes – how she wished there was something else she could do. It seemed the only escape from this drudgery was to get married. She smiled to herself – how could she ever hope to have a boyfriend when her mother had made it perfectly clear that she would not allow 'such goings on'.

Mother was a strange, remote sort of person, she reflected, never showing the slightest emotion. Lucy thought of all the times she and her young sister, Josie, had craved for a cuddle or a goodnight kiss or, maybe even a story! But it never happened.

Her thoughts were interrupted by the sound of Mrs Dowan clapping her hands and calling for quiet. As she opened her eyes, she could see the supervisor standing at the far end of the room with the owner, Mr Goldstein, by her side. Lucy gave a gasp of surprise and the girls sat bolt upright at the sight of their boss. It was a rare occasion indeed for him to put in an appearance at this sweatshop. What did it all mean?

Mr Goldstein was a portly Jewish man, immaculately

dressed with a large Havana cigar hanging from the corner of his mouth. He glanced slowly around the room as he took a quick puff of his cigar before he spoke.

'Now, girls,' he began, 'as you know, we are at war. I have given this matter a great deal of thought over the past couple of days and I have decided that it is not a good idea to continue to trade in London. There's talk that the Germans plan to bomb it and, where would I be if all my equipment got blown up?'

'It wouldn't do us any bleedin' good either,' Mary's voice blurted out from the corner where she was sitting. Someone gave a nervous giggle as a gasp of horror swept through the room. Fancy talking to Mr Goldstein like that! How could she dare to!

Slowly he removed the cigar from his mouth and, for a brief moment, a cynical smile crossed his face. 'With your mouth, Mary, you'd be more fitting selling flowers on a street corner than working here, so I suggest you hold your tongue or, that's precisely where you will end up.'

Mary tossed her corn-coloured hair in a defiant gesture as Mr Goldstein continued with his speech.

'Anyway, girls, if I may continue without further interruption.' He glared at Mary. She shrank back in her chair. 'I have decided to move everything to Marlow, where I live. It will be a lot safer there. Everything has been sorted out and next Monday will be the date for moving. However, some of you, I suspect, will not be able to travel to Marlow, due to the cost of travel and all that sort of thing, so in that case you will have to take this as a week's notice.' He paused briefly to assess what impact his words had on his staff, and then continued. 'Those of you who think you can make the journey to Marlow every day I will see in my office after work.'

With a nod towards Mrs Dowan he turned abruptly and left the room ... she followed a few paces behind like an obedient puppy dog.

There was a stunned silence as everyone looked at each other in horror. It wasn't as if they particularly liked their job, but at least it brought in money. All of the girls came from very poor homes in the East End of London where every penny counted.

'I can't go that far to work,' protested Mary, fighting back the tears. 'By the time I pay all that train fare I won't 'ardly 'ave any money left. Wot's gonna 'appen to my little boy if I can't pay for his food and things?'

'I know wot I am gonna do,' retorted Nancy, shrugging her shoulders in a defiant manner. 'I'm gonna join the forces, that's wot I'll do.' She paused for a moment, her brown eyes alight with excitement. 'Perhaps I'll join the Air Force. Blue suits me and I think the uniform is really sexy – not forgetting all the gorgeous pilots that I could date.'

Anxious voices echoed around the room as the girls hastily tried to put some sort of plan together, to try to get order back into their lives. The clapping of hands and the sight of Mrs Dowan's piercing dark eyes darting around the room brought instant silence.

'You have had well past your tea-break. Now let's have less talking and more work out of you.'

'Old cow,' muttered Mary under her breath as they scurried back to their machines. The air was once again filled with an incessant roar as forty girls, heads bent, shoulders hunched, worked for their pitiful reward.

Lucy stared blankly out of the window as rows and rows of tiny terraced houses flashed by as the train made its way through the suburbs of London. She was oblivious to it all – her mind was too taken up with the events of the day. Soon she would be out of work. It was out of the question for her to travel to Marlow every day, the cost of the fare alone would leave precious little. As things were now, by the time she'd paid her mother for her keep and then her train fare to Blackfriars every day, there was barely any money left, and she still needed to clothe herself. She closed her eyes as if to shut out the depressing news.

The train drew to a halt at Maze Hill Station and Lucy got up slowly from her seat. From the window she could see the council flats where she lived. She knew her mother would be watching from the kitchen window and as soon as she heard the train arriving at the station food would be put on the table.

Mother's a good cook I'll give 'er that, she thought as she joined the hordes of people hurrying along the platform, everyone anxious to get home. The war had made them very nervous.

'Hey Lucy! You don't 'arf look miserable,' called a voice from her right. She turned quickly to see who the voice belonged to and came face to face with Sarah Steadman!

'You look like you've lost a tanner and found a farvin', that you do.' She grinned as she took Lucy by the arm.

Sarah was a pretty, vivacious girl with gorgeous red hair,

who always seemed to have a smile on her face. Her parents were much better off than Lucy's. They both worked in the City and Sarah was their only child. She wore expensive clothes and Lucy felt very conscious of her own shabby dress and run down shoes as they made their way through the Booking Hall.

'I've lost my job today,' Lucy said glumly. 'Don't know wot my mum is gonna say, but it ain't my fault there's a war on is it?'

'Wot you gonna do then?'

'Well,' Lucy replied, hesitating, 'I was thinking of joining up – they do take you at seventeen, don't they?'

Sarah nudged her in the ribs and pointed to a poster on the station wall. 'Wot about that then? Just right for you Lucy, you always liked funny things like cows and sheep. Don't suit me though. I like London too much to go away.'

Lucy turned her head to look at the poster Sarah had indicated.

'YOUR COUNTRY NEEDS YOU! Join the Land Army and help to feed Britain'. The girl on the poster seemed to be staring straight at her, willing her to join up. She thought of the green fields of Kent where her grandmother lived and where she had spent so many happy hours when she was younger. Now she was working she hardly ever saw her and she missed the countryside so much. Perhaps it would be fun in the Land Army! Perhaps she would give it a try!

They came to the end of the long, leafy lane where Sarah lived.

'Bye then, Lucy. Let me know wot 'appens. Perhaps you

could write to me if you do join up and let me know wot it's like. Perhaps you'll end up marrying a farmer!'

Sarah gave a little giggle at the thought of Lucy as a farmer's wife, then with a cheery wave of her hand, disappeared down the long drive while Lucy watched her enviously. If only she was as pretty as Sarah, had lovely clothes to wear and lived in a big house – what a difference it would make! She gave a sigh of resignation and continued along a narrow, dirt path which took her to the back of the flats where she lived.

Climbing the dingy steps she reached the second floor and knocked on the door. Her mother opened it almost immediately and, with just the briefest glance at her daughter, turned round and went back into the kitchen.

Lucy shrugged her shoulders, followed her into the kitchen and sat at the table... obviously mother was in one of her moods! She noticed that mother's eyes were slightly red, as if she had been crying. Her face was pale and drawn and her hands shook as she placed a cup of tea next to the plate.

Lucy got up from her chair and walked over to the table. It didn't seem a good time to tell her mother about her job. Dare she ask her what was wrong? No! She couldn't do that; they had never found it easy to talk to each other. Thoughtfully picking up her knife and fork she started to eat. The steak and kidney pie was delicious as usual but, somehow, her enjoyment of it was clouded by an air of suspense; a feeling of impending disaster that made her feel uneasy. Mother was hovering restlessly around the table until, at last, she sat in a chair opposite her and started to speak. Her voice was strangely low and quiet.

'Lucy,' she began hesitatingly, 'I have something to tell you. I don't know how you will take it but, the fact is, I am going to have another baby.'

Lucy gasped in horror – a *baby*! Her mother having a baby! After all the times she had made out that sex was something dirty – to be avoided at all costs. How could she? They hardly had enough money to live on now and the only treats they ever had was on a Friday night, when they could choose whether they wanted a little bit of real butter to spread on their bread, or a few broken biscuits from Mr Chandler's shop on the corner, but never both. How could they possibly afford a baby? They hardly had any decent clothes to wear as it was! She turned on her mother angrily.

'Does Dad know? 'Ave you told 'im?'

Mother shook her head sadly. 'No, I only found out today but I will tell him when he gets home from work.'

Lucy flung her knife and fork angrily on top of her half-eaten meal. 'Well, I think it's disgusting and I don't want to talk about it,' she cried as she ran into her bedroom and flung herself miserably onto the bed. An hour later she heard a key being turned in the lock of the front door. Her father had returned from work to face the devastating news! There was to be another mouth to feed!

Several days went by – it was Lucy's last day at work. She reflected on the events of the past week. What a week it had been! Losing her job, then the news of a new baby in the family, it was all too much, so the very next day Lucy joined the Land Army – she had taken the plunge – now there was no turning back. She didn't want to live at home anymore. It was not much fun; her mother was taking her pregnancy badly. Josie was still away, staying at their grandmother's cottage in Kent, so she wasn't able to keep in contact with her. Her brother, George, had got a job as an apprentice at a woodworking firm and she hardly ever saw him. She felt isolated and alone at the flat.

Lucy wondered how Josie was getting on. Since she left in July at the beginning of the school holidays, she had heard nothing of her, except that she was to stay with their grandmother until the war was over. Paddy, the dog, sat dejectedly on the thin rug in the front room, his dark soulful eyes gazing pitifully at anyone who would speak to him. He was missing Josie so much, their walks together, and the games they played. She smiled to herself – how on earth was Josie coping without Paddy? He was her life …

The lady in charge at the Land Army Recruitment Centre welcomed her with open arms and immediately introduced herself as Mrs Morgan.

'We need as many of you girls as we can get, my dear,' she said, taking her by the arm and guiding her into a small room at the rear of the large house that served as their headquarters. She was a lovely, motherly sort of person and Lucy took to her immediately. They sat down on opposite sides of a dark, wooden desk and started the slow, painful process of filling up numerous forms. Lucy had to produce both her identity card and birth certificate in order to confirm her age. But she had forgotten to bring her birth certificate.

'We can't have any of you girls giving us false information,' Mrs Morgan said with a grin that seemed to light up her whole face. 'Sometimes, in the past, we have had girls as young as fifteen trying to get into the Land Army. I mean, it's a lot of responsibility for the people whose farms you will eventually be sent to.'

Lucy nodded her head in agreement and, the very next day, produced her birth certificate and the final signing of papers was completed.

'There is just one other thing Lucy before you go,' Mrs Morgan said as they walked together towards the door. 'You will be sent a letter telling you where to report for your medical. You should receive it in a couple of days. All this rests on the result of your medical, of course, but, I'm sure everything will be fine.'

The formalities were over and it was time for Lucy to go home and wait until she received further instruction as to where she was to report for training. 'Be prepared to leave at 24-hours notice,' Mrs Morgan had stressed.

It was exactly twelve days later when a small buff envelope fell through the door. Lucy picked it up with trembling hands and saw her name printed on the front of it. There was no doubt that this was from the Land Army. What was she going to do? She hadn't told her mother yet what her plans were, as neither of them had spoken to each other since the outburst over the news of the baby! Slowly, plucking up courage, she walked along the dark passageway to the kitchen where her mother was busy clearing away the breakfast dishes and stood nervously in the doorway.

'Mum, I've got to talk to you – it's important.'

There was silence for a few moments and, at first, Lucy thought her mother was still angry but, slowly and deliberately, mother put down the cup she held in her hand and turned to face her.

'Well, Lucy! Have you come to apologise for your bad behaviour?'

'I ... I really came to tell you that I'm leaving 'ome,' she replied. 'I 'ave joined the Land Army and I've just got this letter.'

Quickly she thrust the letter into her mother's hand and waited while she read it. Silently mother scanned the brief letter then passed it back to her.

'It says that you are to report to the Agricultural College in Somerset in two days' time! Do you realise how far away that is, Lucy?'

Lucy shook her head. She had never been outside of London except when she went to her grandmother's in Kent – she had no idea where Bristol was, but, really, what did it matter! All she wanted to do was get away from home. Anywhere was better than this. Mother shrugged her shoulders and turned her attention to the job in hand.

'Best you get on with sorting yourself out then, Lucy … Don't expect me to help you; I've enough to do as it is.'

Tears welled up in Lucy's eyes as she turned away and walked out of the kitchen.

She flung herself onto her bed and hugged her pillow. Why didn't her mother show her some affection? How could she let her leave home without even saying she was sad to see her go? She felt as if she had been stabbed through the heart, such was the pain, and she knew that this was the

final straw. Never again would she live with her mother …
when the war was over she would find a place of her own!
She would live her own life, maybe she would even get
married!

Chapter 3

A chill wind was blowing across the marshes as Josie made her way down the lane. She bent her head as a heavy rain started to fall, whipped up to a frenzy by the wind to become like fine needles of ice as it beat into her face.

It was almost Christmas; the days were getting shorter and colder, making Josie shiver as she felt the rain seep through her thin coat and water squelched through the holes in her shoes. She hated going to the village school, she had no friends, and they all seemed to delight in making fun of her cockney accent and scruffy clothes. Angry tears stung her eyes as she trudged doggedly on.

'I hate them all, I hate them all,' she muttered under her breath. 'I'd rather be at home with me dog. I ain't gonna stand this much longer … I'll run away that's wot I'll do.'

It was almost dark when she reached the little wooden gate that led to the cottage; through the window she could see the fire burning in the grate, the flames flickering and dancing through the room. A smile crossed her cold, wet face at the sight of her grandmother busy setting the table for tea – soon she would be indoors by the fire, nice and warm and dry. Picking her way carefully to avoid the puddles of water, she walked along the narrow dirt path which led to the back door and turned the handle. It gave a loud creaking sound as if in protest at being disturbed and the sound brought her grandmother hurrying into the scullery. She looked in horror at the little, wet creature standing forlornly in front of her.

'Gracious me, Josie!' she exclaimed, throwing her hands up in the air. 'Get out of those wet clothes at once and dry yourself. Look at the water dripping on my nice clean floor. Now, be quick before your grandfather comes in, he won't be pleased to see such a mess, that's for sure. Now make haste.'

She took a towel from behind the door and threw it towards her then went back to the front room where a hot meal was cooking on the open fire.

They all sat in silence around the table. Grandfather had arrived home, just after Josie had managed to clean both herself and mop the kitchen floor. He was a big, burly man who, as far as Josie could remember, seldom spoken to her. Sometimes she wondered if he even realised she was there!

Grandfather worked on a neighbouring farm and each morning he would leave very early, taking, as Josie did, a packed lunch, and she would watch him from her bedroom window as he crossed the lane, climbed over the stile and then made his way across the wheat fields until he was out of sight. Sometimes, during mealtimes, he would tell grandma about the animals he was looking after while Josie listened enthralled. She would have loved to have asked him questions, but only grown-ups were allowed to speak at the table so she had to be satisfied just sitting and listening.

When the meal was over, Josie watched her grandfather out of the corner of her eye as he read a letter and, once or twice, she caught him glancing at her, and it made her nervous. Something obviously was going on, even her grandmother had a flushed face and her eyes were bright, as if she was bursting with some important news that she couldn't wait to impart. It was a relief when she was told to clear the table and then wash the dishes, and when she had done that she was to come straight back to the table as they had something very important to tell her!

As Josie got up and started to clear the table, she could still feel grandfather's eyes on her. What had she done to cause this tension?

After the dishes were washed she tipped the water into a bucket and carried it down the long, garden path. It was so dark! The moon was just a sliver in the sky and there was no light from the cottage because of the black-out. Josie recalled the day that she had come home from school and found her grandmother in a panic because she had been told by Mr Jackson, the air-raid warden, that all the windows in the cottage had to be covered so that no light could be seen.

'I don't know what we are going to do, Josie,' she had said. 'We only have these thin cotton ones and they'll be no good.'

But grandfather soon sorted the problem out when he arrived home from work. Without a word he went to his shed in the garden and then returned with a pile of coal sacks in his arms. 'Here you are, Ada,' he had said as he threw them to the floor. 'We'll shake these out and then nail them to the frame on the windows. You can easily tie them back in the daytime.' He had waited a second or two for his wife to respond to his suggestion of having coal sacks for curtains … but she had remained silent.

'Come on now,' grandfather had said impatiently. 'We must make haste. It will soon be dark and we have a lot of work to do.'

In the distance the hooting of an owl seemed to mock her for being so scared, while the trees that swayed in the wind seemed like great big monsters waiting to devour her. Quickly emptying the bucket, Josie ran back to the safety of the cottage where her grandparents were still sitting at the table. Silently she sat down on her chair and waited. Then her gran spoke, waving the letter in the air.

'We have had a letter from your mother, Josie. She is going to have another baby and she needs you back home with her so that you can be of some help when the baby comes.'

Josie's blue eyes grew wide with excitement – her mother having a baby! She couldn't imagine it, but if her gran said so, it must be true. Slowly a big grin spread across her face as the reality of it all began to sink in. She heard her grandmother's voice again. It seemed to come from a great distance as Josie tried to focus her mind on what she was saying.

'You must go home at the end of the week. It all seems quiet in London, no air-raids or anything. You'll be alright.' She paused for a moment for the news to sink in while Josie sat in stunned silence. 'By the way, you be a good girl for your mother or there will be trouble.'

Grandfather nodded in agreement as he noisily slurped his tea. Josie was silent, her mind racing with so many, many thoughts. No more days at that awful school, no more walking up that long, lonely lane. She wouldn't have to run away now … she was going home – home to her beloved Paddy – back to London where she belonged!

The next day Josie handed a note to Miss Taylor. It said simply, 'Josie will be leaving school today as she has to return to London to help her mother'. Miss Taylor read it and then held up a hand for silence in the class.

'Quiet now please! Josie is leaving us today to go back to her family in London. I am sure we will all miss her and wish her the very best of luck.'

The ginger-haired girl at the back of the class sniggered as Josie, her face set in a determined expression, turned to face the class.

'Well, I ain't gonna miss you lot 'cos I 'ate you all and I'm glad I'm going back 'ome.' Quickly she turned and ran from the classroom as tears of joy ran down her face. She was going home!

The next couple of days were busy getting Josie packed and organised for her trip, but soon enough she was walking up the lane for the very last time.

'Now, Josie,' said her grandmother as they walked the mile and a half to the station. 'I want you to be very careful on that train and not talk to any strangers – and don't you get off at any other station than Maze Hill. Your mother will be waiting for you in the booking hall.' Josie nodded and, with a brief kiss on the cheek, her grandmother pushed a small parcel in her hand then turned and with a wave of her hand disappeared into the distance.

The train arrived at the station, blowing out gusts of

steam as it came to a halt with a grinding of brakes. Josie looked in amazement at the soot-blackened faces of the driver and his mate, who were furiously shovelling coal onto the blazing fire. The train was crowded with people in uniform: soldiers, sailors and airmen all heading for London, every one of them hoping to find a good time in the capital before the war dispersed them to wherever or whatever the need might be.

Once on the train, Josie found herself a small space in the corner of the corridor and sat on her case, staring about her, fascinated by the different uniforms.

I 'ope this war lasts a long time, then I'll be able to wear a uniform and travel up and down on trains just like them, she thought, as they sped past fields and trees until the scene changed. The green fields gave way to small dingy streets and the sky was grey and leaden. In her hands she still held the little parcel her grandmother had given her. Gingerly she pressed the surface of the parcel – it felt like a small book! Eagerly, Josie tore the brown paper and gasped in amazement as the paper fell away to reveal a beautiful red leather-bound book, with the words 'The Heavenly Feast: A Companion to the Altar' embossed in gold letters on the cover. She opened it to reveal an inscription which read: 'Ada Collier, in remembrance of her confirmation. Higham. Lent 1873'. Tucked inside was a little note.

Dear Josie,

This little book has been my constant companion throughout my life. It has given me great comfort when I was

in need. Now, my dear, I want you to have it. Carry it with
you always and may the good Lord protect you during the
dark days ahead.
Your loving Gran

Her mother was standing by the barrier as the train pulled into the station. She looked pale and thin; her coat, which had seen many winters, failed to disguise the very obvious fact that her pregnancy was nearing its end. Josie walked up to her and stared intently into her face – had her mother missed her? Would she give a hug and say that she was glad to have her back home? But her face showed no emotion as she pulled Josie by the arm.

'Come on now, I have to get back home, your train was almost an hour late. It's such a nuisance having to waste time waiting for you.'

Josie sighed and followed her through the station and down the road towards the flats. Suddenly, in the distance, she saw a little brown, furry body hurtling towards her!

'Paddy,' she screamed with delight as she threw her case to the ground and ran towards him. He flung himself into her outstretched arms, wriggling and whining as he licked her tear-stained face.

'Oh Paddy!' she sobbed, 'I've missed you. I've missed you so much.'

Mother looked on disapprovingly at the scene in front of her. Never being one to have much time for animals, she could not understand Josie's passion for them.

'Josie, get up immediately, that dog is making you all dirty, you look like a little gypsy, that you do! I don't know how much longer we can keep that animal, not with the baby coming and all.'

Josie scrambled to her feet – her heart pounding. Get rid of her dog! Get rid of Paddy!

'You can't get rid of 'im, I won't let you. 'E's mine …'e's my friend,' she screamed as she ran off towards the flat with Paddy at her heels, happily unaware of the possible fate that awaited him.

The next few days were spent getting used to being in London again. It all seemed so different somehow. Sandbags were piled in front of shops and at the entrance to the flats. Air-raid shelters had sprung up like mushrooms on a damp September morning. Mrs Price's general store on the corner looked like a war zone, with so many sandbags piled around; it was difficult to tell whether it was a shop at all!

Josie's school had been evacuated to the country, as had most others, leaving a sense of loneliness and loss as playgrounds stood empty. The swings and slides that tempted many a child into the local park had been confiscated for the war effort, leaving the few children left in the capital with nothing to do. It seemed as if by some magical wave of a wand, the capital had lost most of its children, most of its pets and, of course, nearly all the young men and women who had been called up to protect their country. Windows were boarded up or had sticky tape criss-crossed over them for protection from any blast should there be an air-raid. It was a very different and depressing scene from the one Josie had left back in the summer.

'I'm gonna take Paddy out,' Josie called to her mother as

she took his lead, which was hanging on a nail just inside the front door.

'Don't you go far, Josie, you know I am due to have the baby any day now and I don't want the added worry of you. Now, remember! When I go into labour you are to go straight upstairs and get Mrs Lovelock, then you must stay in her flat until it's all over.'

But Josie and Paddy were already racing down the stairs and her words were lost to them.

They sat on the concrete steps at the entrance to the flats gazing out onto an almost deserted street. It was nearly tea-time and she was getting hungry but it would be about another hour before father came home and they never started tea without him, so her stomach would just have to wait. Suddenly a wave of sadness descended upon her like a huge dark cloud, causing tears to well up in her eyes as she thought of her brother and sister. They were not there when she arrived back home. The only thing she had been told was that George had been taken on as an apprentice carpenter by a small company on the Isle of Dogs. He was fourteen now and, as mother had said, 'He has gone to live with Auntie Grace because she only lives across the road from where he will be working.' She didn't really care where George was; he was a bully and was always taunting her. No, it would be more peaceful without him!

Lucy was now in the Land Army and would not be back until the war was over. It was almost a year since she had last seen her and she missed her so much. Lucy was more like a mother she reflected, as she cuddled Paddy closer to her. She remembered the times when she hurt herself while playing

… it was Lucy who patched her up and comforted her, while her mother just turned away.

She sighed deeply and cuddled Paddy closer as an overwhelming sense of loss swept over her.

'I dunno wot I'd do wivout you,' she said. 'They won't get rid of you, don't worry, I won't let them.' Paddy responded by nuzzling her gently with his soft, cold nose, then burying his face in her lap. Josie looked up at the darkening sky; it was dusted with a million stars, hanging like tiny diamonds on deep blue velvet cloth. A full moon shone, its silvery glow outlining the huge cranes as they stood idle at the docks waiting for the morning shift to start. There was a silence that was almost tangible. Josie shivered in the cool, night air.

'We'd better be going in now Paddy …' Her voice trailed away as a strange wailing sound echoed through the still night, soft at first, then becoming louder and louder until it reached a crescendo. People in the street started running in all directions. Paddy jumped up and started to bark furiously at the sky. Then, as if by magic, the noise ceased and the street became deserted. Josie listened intently, her ears straining for any sound. In the distance she could hear the soft droning of aircraft coming relentlessly closer and closer. A sudden loud explosion rocked the street while the ominous rumble of anti-aircraft guns as they opened fire on the enemy aircraft added to the noise … Paddy started howling and shaking.

'Oh my gawd!' she screamed as she gathered him up in her arms and ran upstairs to their flat. Another explosion rocked the building causing pieces of plaster and glass to shower over them. Josie felt something warm trickling down her arm … it was blood!

'Mum, Mum,' she screamed as she banged desperately on the front door. 'Let me in, please let me in.' The door opened, an arm reached out and pulled them bodily into the flat.

'Get under the table quickly, Josie, and stay there until it's all over.' Her mother's voice was trembling with fear.

'Wot will you do, Mum? Wot will you do? You must get under the table wiv me.'

Mother sat on a chair; her face pale and etched with pain, the first signs of labour had started. She shook her head.

'I can't, Josie, I just can't, and I think the baby's coming.'

Josie started to scramble out from beneath the table. 'I'll go and get Mrs Lovelock, Mum. Don't worry I'll go and get 'er now.'

'There's no need, it could be hours yet, it's not safe – just stay where you are.'

She lay back under the table and buried her face in Paddy's soft fur, shaking with fear as more loud explosions rocked the building and showers of splintered glass covered the room. Finally, after about an hour, the sound of planes gradually faded into the distance and the rumble of guns became silent. For several minutes they stayed exactly where they were until mother stirred herself into action.

'Come on, Josie, you can come out now, it's all over.'

She crawled out from under the table, staring in horror at the smashed windows and torn curtains, while Paddy stood whimpering and trembling by her side.

'Don't just stand there, Josie, go and make a cup of tea,'

mother said sharply. 'When you have done that clean this place up before your father gets in from ...'

Suddenly she bent over, gripping the edge of the table as a strong labour pain coursed through her body.

'Oh, Josie,' she gasped, 'be quick, run and fetch Mrs Lovelock, the baby's coming.'

Later that night Josie was sent upstairs to Mrs Lovelock's flat – where she lay in a strange bed, wide-awake as her ears strained for any noise ... the air-raid had unnerved her. Suppose they came back tonight while she was alone! Suddenly, through the dark silent night came two piercing screams – her sister had been born!

London was bracing itself for the Blitz. Anderson shelters were being put in every garden and air-raid wardens patrolled the streets at night, constantly vigilant for any sign of light. Shelters were hastily erected for any unwary person caught out in the street when the siren sounded and gas masks were to be issued.

Josie's little sister was named Molly in a brief ceremony at the local church. Mrs Lovelock came along as a witness and stood watching the proceedings with a self-satisfied smile on her face. She was very proud to be the one who had delivered this bright eyed, pretty baby, single handed right through an air-raid. Even her Bert was surprised when she told him what she had done, but, as he had said, 'Wot sort of world 'ave you brought that baby into Gladys? A world that's gone bloody mad, that's wot!'

Bert was right, the poor little blighter was born when bombs were dropping all around. What sort of start in life was that? But, did any of them have a life in front of them … or would they all be killed tomorrow or the next day? It would only take one bomb to be dropped on the flats!

She sighed heavily – they were all sitting targets and there was nothing they could do about it, except to take cover in those useless Anderson shelters.

A few days later Josie and her mother were trudging wearily along the almost deserted streets as they made their way to Maze Hill School, which was to act as the local distribution centre for their area. They had received a letter that distribution of gas masks was due to take place today between 9 a.m. and 7 p.m. and mother had said that they were to get to the school as near as 9 a.m. as possible so they would be near the front of the queue.

'Just look at that!' Mother gasped when she saw the long line of people, some with small children, standing patiently waiting for their turn to be issued with this possible life-saving piece of equipment. 'We'll be here for the best part of the morning, that's for sure. Let's hope we're not caught out in an air-raid,' she said, looking around anxiously as they joined the queue.

Josie looked at her little sister who was wrapped up cosily against the cold, east wind in a pink shawl that Mrs Lovelock had given her. It was second-hand, but then everything they had was second-hand.

Although Molly was only three weeks old, she had a shock of jet black hair; her features were tiny and perfect, while bright blue eyes stared inquisitively at everything around her. Josie wondered whether her mother had ever cuddled her the way she was cuddling Molly and, if she had, why had things changed? Why didn't she show her any love or affection now?

Two and a half hours passed. Josie was getting cold and fidgety, while Molly voiced her protest with short, piercing screams. Finally it was their turn and, thankfully, they made their way into the warmth of the school where an elderly, grey haired lady, surrounded by numerous boxes, beckoned to them. She looked intently at the little group in front of her and without a word dived into a large cardboard box and brought out a portable gas mask. The face had been designed to look like Mickey Mouse.

'Now,' she said, addressing Josie's mother, 'put your baby inside here and make her as comfy as possible, and then fasten it securely like so.'

Mother nodded silently, hating every moment of it; her hands shook as she put Molly inside the mask. Why should a little baby have to go through this?

'I want you to take notice of what I am going to say now – and never, never forget it,' the elderly lady said, her grey eyes boring into mother. 'You see this pump at the side here?'

Mother nodded anxiously as she leant over to get a closer look. Molly suddenly started screaming and turning red in the face.

'Quick now mother, you must keep operating the pump like so,' the lady said sharply, as she vigorously pumped the handle. 'If you stop, the baby will die – there will be no oxygen for her, you see.'

Molly was quickly taken out of the mask and it was Josie's turn. With a quick movement a small mask was thrust

42

upon her face; she felt she was being suffocated. A sickening smell of rubber made her gasp while a feeling of nausea swept over her body. Thick straps held the mask tightly in place.

'That one will do for you, young lady,' the woman said, patting Josie reassuringly on the shoulder. 'It comes in a little cardboard box and a strap to hang it over your shoulder, so you can carry it with you wherever you go.' She paused for a moment to brush a wisp of grey hair that had fallen across her face, and then continued. 'Don't leave it at home because you never know when you might need it. Remember, this is a very important piece of equipment – it could save your life!'

Two weeks later Josie left it on a No. 47 bus.

Despite the war, which had now been on for just over a year and the never-ending threat of air-raids, Josie's little sister thrived, while the Mickey Mouse gas mask gathered dust in the hall cupboard. Josie never told anyone that she had lost hers and no-one seemed to notice that it had gone.

Father was away from home more than he was in it. As well as doing his full-time job as a docker, it was now compulsory for him to report four nights a week fire-watching. The docks were a prime target for the German Air Force and it was only a matter of time before there would be a full scale attack and the men had to be trained and ready.

It was New Year's Eve, 1940, and Christmas had come and gone without much fuss. The Government tried to cheer the nation up by increasing the tea ration from two to four ounces and the sugar ration from eight to twelve ounces, but, they stressed, it was only for the Christmas week.

'It would have made more sense if they'd increased the meat ration,' said mother bitterly. 'How can I be expected to put a decent meal on the table with the little bit of meat we get?'

Josie looked up at her mother, she could see the tension in her face. 'Don't worry, Mum,' she said, 'we'll just have to manage somehow.'

The sound of shouting and screaming coming from the flat above made mother put her hands over her ears and Molly started crying. The fighting Dawson's were at it again. It was as if they were staging their own private war. Mrs Dawson was a thin, pale, feisty woman who kept herself to herself. Her husband was often out of work and, consequently, spent more time than he should in the Green Man pub down the road. Then there were the two sons: Arthur who was sixteen and Johnny who had been called up for the Army just over a week ago. A final loud crash made mother decide.

'I think I'll go over and see Auntie Grace today, Josie. I should be back before tea. I need a break from this flat, especially from that Dawson family upstairs.

'Now, Josie, be sure and lay the table and tidy up before I get back.' She hesitated for a moment. 'And don't you let that dog play up while I'm gone or it'll be the strap for you when your father gets home?'

Josie looked at her mother as tears threatened to course down her cheeks. 'But Mum, I don't want to stay 'ere on my own. Please, Mum, take me wiv you!'

Mother turned, her eyes flashing with anger.

'I'm not having that dog left behind, Josie; it doesn't

know how to behave itself. I'll have to speak to your father tonight, as soon as he gets home. It's too much worry having a dog when there's a war on, he'd be better off being put down, that he would.'

She turned and looked with disdain at Paddy, who skulked in the corner, shaking visibly … his tail between his legs.

'Don't you dare say that – I'll run away wiv 'im. You'll never see us again.'

'You're getting too big for your boots, my girl. You will do as you are told and I will hear no more of it. Do you understand?' From the bedroom came a petulant cry. 'Now go and fetch Molly for me while I finish clearing this table.'

'I'd rather 'ave me dog than a baby,' muttered Josie angrily as she went into the bedroom, where Molly was thrashing her arms and legs about in anger. 'Don't know why people make such a fuss of babies, they are 'orrible, smelly things and I ain't ever gonna 'ave any,' she said as she leaned over the cot and picked Molly up. A wet face nuzzled into her cheek and she felt a strange sensation sweep over her as she cuddled Molly closer.

'I still think you're a smelly thing, though,' she whispered as she carried her into the front room.

The afternoon seemed never-ending as Josie wandered moodily around the flat. Paddy was watching her out of one eye, hoping for some sign that they might be going out. From the flat above came the sounds of another quarrel starting. A woman screamed and the noise of furniture being thrown across the room made Josie decide – she was not going to stay in the flat any longer – mother should be home soon, she would go downstairs and wait for her on the steps.

'C'mon,' she called to Paddy as she opened the front door. He jumped up eagerly and ran off down the stairs while Josie slammed the door shut behind them. As she ran down the stairs she could hear footsteps coming towards her and she came face to face with Arthur Dawson.

'Gimme a kiss, Josie,' he said with a cheeky grin on his face. 'Gimme a kiss or I'll keep you 'ere till you do.' His face was grubby but his blue eyes sparkled as he eyed her up and down.

'I ain't ever going to kiss you, Arfur Dawson,' she replied, punching him on the arm. 'My mum doesn't like yer, or your family, and nor do I ... so leave me alone or I'll set me dog on yer.'

Arthur tipped his cap to the back of his head as he leaned against the stair rail, still grinning. 'One day, Josie, you'll see, one day you'll want me to kiss yer, but it'll be too late then!'

Josie replied by kicking him in the shin and running down the stairs.

As they settled themselves on the bottom step, silently watching people go by in the street, she cuddled Paddy in her arms. After about an hour, fine rain started to fall and a chill wind sprang up. Paddy started shivering and whimpering; it was getting miserable on the steps. She pulled him closer.

'Perhaps we 'ad better go in ....' She stopped suddenly and covered her face with her hands. 'Oh, my gawd! We can't get in, I've shut the front door!' She turned and wrapped her arms around his neck. 'Don't you worry, Paddy,' she whispered in his ear. 'Mother won't be long now, then we'll go indoors and be nice and warm.'

Desperately, she tried to cover him with the edge of her coat, as Paddy silently buried his face in her lap. A couple of hours passed, dusk started to form and soon she would be in a world of utter darkness and mother was still not home! Suddenly, out of the dusk, the escalating pitch of air-raid sirens screamed into the silence of the night. She gasped as the all too familiar droning of aircraft was heard in the distance, relentlessly coming closer and closer. The street became deserted as people ran to find a place of safety. An air-raid warden hurried by. He caught sight of Josie huddled on the steps.

'Get yourself to a shelter, quick as you can,' he shouted as he sprinted across the road. 'And you can't take the dog! Just leave 'im.'

With a final brief glance in her direction he disappeared down the dark, deserted street.

Josie sat trembling on the steps. She wasn't going to leave Paddy. He was as frightened as she was and, anyway, mother would be home soon. The ominous sound of guns filled the air as the German planes continued relentlessly towards their target. Her heart beat faster as the noise became louder and louder and Paddy started struggling and whining in terror. She gripped his collar tightly.

'Don't you worry, Paddy, I'm 'ere,' she whispered soothingly. 'It's alright.'

Suddenly, the night sky turned into day as hundreds of incendiary bombs fell from the skies and exploded on the docks. To Josie it was as if she had suddenly been transported to Hell! Everywhere she looked fires were burning, while the planes passing overhead filled the sky as they roared and rumbled like an army of angry giants.

Terrified, she flung herself on top of Paddy and they lay huddled together on the cold, concrete steps, engulfed by the smell of burning and thick clouds of black smoke.

Paddy started to howl as he struggled to get free from this nightmare. Hugging him closer, Josie could feel his heart pounding.

'Don't cry, Paddy, please don't cry.' She raised her head and looked up. Reflecting the inferno below, the sky glowed red. The planes, in stark silhouette, looked like enormous bats and seemed to fill the sky.

'Go away and leave us alone,' she screamed. 'I 'ate you Germans, I 'ate you!'

Paddy made one last desperate effort and broke free from Josie's grasp, running bewildered and frightened down the street. She ran after him, oblivious of the distant fires that blazed in the night sky, forming a complete circle around her. Just then a violent blast rocked the whole area, the force of it hurling her to the pavement. Dust and rubble fell like rain, then she felt a blow to her head and blood started to trickle down her face. For a few moments, she was stunned. Then she remembered Paddy; she had to find him. But where was he? She stumbled up the road. She could hardly see. Her eyes were sore from the hot dust that hung in the air, while in the distance she could hear the sound of fire engines and ambulances converging on the docks. Thick, acrid air filled her lungs, making it hard to breathe as she clambered over the debris that littered the road. Stumbling down Maze Hill, she stopped. Gasping in horror, she saw a brown, furry tail in a pool of blood and nearby lay Paddy's body partially covered with debris.

'Paddy! Paddy!' she screamed, 'Wot 'ave they gawn an done to you? Don't worry, you'll be alright, I'll 'elp you.'

Her hands tore at the debris that surrounded him; broken glass cut into her hands, smoke was burning her eyes, but she was oblivious to it all … she had to help him! He needed her!

Gently she gathered him in her arms as blood poured from a gaping hole in his chest. Paddy stirred briefly, his brown eyes opened, but then with a small pitiful whimper they closed again. A shudder went through his body … Paddy was dead!

Josie collapsed to the ground sobbing, still clutching him in her arms. She was oblivious of the planes, the bombs and the fire … She just wanted to die! She felt a hand on her shoulder, but for a moment she didn't move. In a daze, as if from a distance, she could hear someone calling her.

'Josie, Josie, you can't stay 'ere. C'mon let's go back to the flats.'

She raised a tear-stained face to find Arthur kneeling beside her. For a moment nothing registered, but then she realised that this was Arthur from upstairs, the one that was always trying to grab her and give her a kiss. She hated him. He was rough and swore a lot and, what was worse, mother would kill her if she found her talking to him, as she had always been warned not to have anything to do with the Dawson family.

He tugged at her arm impatiently and, instinctively, she rose to her feet, still clutching Paddy. A comforting arm was put around her shoulders and she turned, burying her face in the warmth of his old tweed jacket and sobbing as if her heart would break. Gently he led her back to the flats and they sat silently on the bottom step.

'Wot was you doin' out?' he asked after awhile. 'Why ain't you wiv yer mum?'

'She's gorn off, that's why. Gorn off to me auntie's.'

'Can't you get in then?'

She shook her head as he stared at her. Her small face was blackened by smoke, the rivers of tears creating white streaks like an Indian's war paint! For a moment he felt sorry for her – he wanted to protect her, but then the moment passed. Was he going soft? What would his gang say if they could see him now? Arthur Dawson, the toughest boy in the neighbourhood, feeling sorry for a stupid girl!

'Gimme yer dog 'ere,' he said gruffly, as he took Paddy's body from her grasp.

'Nuffink you can do for 'im now, 'e's gawn.'

Josie watched blankly as he laid Paddy down on the grass in front of the flats and covered him with his jacket. Silently she stared at the coat that covered him, her face etched with grief. Arthur sat down beside her, putting a protective arm around her shoulders.

'Tell you wot we'll do, we'll give 'im a proper burial as soon as it's light.'

She looked at him gratefully, her eyes full of tears.

'Can we do it proper, Arfur? Can we say prayers an all?'

'Course we can, if's that's wot you want.'

Dawn was breaking over a battle-scarred city as the 'All Clear' sounded. The noise stirred Josie from a fitful sleep in Arthur's arms. She rubbed her eyes and looked around at the clouds of thick smoke that still hung in the air – in the distance fires were still burning. Arthur stood up wearily, stretching his scrawny arms to the sky.

'Looks like they've 'it the docks – looks bad to me,' he remarked sleepily.

Panic swept over Josie. 'Me dad works at the docks! Wot about me dad, Arfur? D'yer think 'e's alright?' She paced up and down the concrete path agitatedly.

'I dunno, Josie. 'Ow the 'ell do I know? 'Ow can anyone be alive in those fires? If yer dad's dead – well, 'e's dead and there ain't nuffink you can do about it now. So come on, we've gotta to bury the dog before too many people are about.'

She stopped pacing and turned to face Arthur, her eyes like saucers in her blackened face. She drew herself up and confronted him.

'He's got to 'ave a box as well. 'E ain't gonna be buried wivout one; it ain't proper,' she shouted as Arthur turned and hurried off down the road. He turned and gave her a brief wave of his hand in acknowledgement and left her sitting dejectedly on the step, staring emptily into space.

Half an hour went by. From the street came signs of life as people emerged from a place of safety to make their way to work, while others congregated on street corners surveying the damage and talking in muted tones. In the distance she saw Arthur coming towards her carrying a shovel on his shoulder; he looked tired and pale. She waited until he reached the flats.

'Where did yer get that from?' she questioned, pointing to the shovel.

'Where d'yer think, Josie. I nicked it, of course.'

'Who did you nick it from? You wanna watch out the Old Bill don't get yer, doing fings like that.'

He scratched his head and laughed out loud. 'Course I won't get into trouble – it's the only way to get fings is to nick 'em. Cor blimey! You ain't 'arf stupid sometimes.'

'Where's the box, Arfur? Where's the box to bury Paddy in?' She sniffled as she tried to stop the tears that threatened to course down her face.

He turned towards her, anger showing in his tired face.

'I can't do bleedin' miracles for gawd's sake. I ain't seen a box for months – there is a bleedin' war on you know!' He paced in little circles; his nerves were at breaking point, but he couldn't show it – not him! Not Arthur Dawson – the boss of the Greenwich gang. He saw Josie staring at him, her teeth clamped down on her bottom lip as she tried to stop it from trembling … Bloody girls!

He held out a hand. 'C'mon now, let's go down by the railway; we can bury 'im on that little grassy bit near the station, but we'd better do it quick though, before too many people get about.'

But Josie's face was set resolutely.

''E ain't gonna be buried wivout a box. It ain't proper.'

52

'Oh my gawd! You're getting' on my bleedin' nerves about this bleedin' box. If you want one – then you get it!' He slumped back against the wall and closed his eyes.

'I will an' all, I will. You'll see!'

Josie stood up angrily and marched into the street just as the paper van pulled up outside the little shop on the corner and the driver started to unload the morning papers. She hurried towards it – that's where she might get a box, Mrs Price would give her one if she had any.

The driver gave her just a brief passing glance as she kicked away some pieces of rubble that lay in the entrance to the shop. All the windows were broken, and a part of the shop front wall had been blown away. She picked her way carefully over the broken glass.

'Mrs Price,' she called. 'Are you there?'

From the back room came the sound of footsteps and Mrs Price's ample body emerged through the door of her living room. She took one look at this blood-stained, dirty figure in front of her and threw up her hands in horror.

'My God, Josie! What 'as 'appened to you? Did you get 'urt in the raid last night? Where's yer mum and dad? They're alright, ain't they?'

Josie leaned back on the remains of the counter, suddenly feeling sick and faint. Mrs Price hurried round and, without a word, took her into the living room and sat her on a chair and knelt down in front of her.

'Now, child, tell me wot's wrong. Where are you hurt? Looks to me like you should go to the hospital.'

'I ain't 'urt, Mrs Price, it's me dog Paddy, they killed 'im,' she replied without emotion. The events of the past 24 hours had taken their toll. She had no more tears to shed, her heart felt like it was broken and life stretched before her like a grey, bleak tunnel.

''Ave you had any breakfast, Josie, anything at all?'

Josie shook her head. 'I ain't 'ad anyfink since yesterday, 'cause me mum ain't been 'ome, and I can't get in 'cause I don't 'ave a key.'

Mrs Price smiled sympathetically.

'Well, I guess she couldn't get back what with the raid being so bad. Don't worry, she'll be home soon – you mark my words. I can give you a bit of bread and a scraping of butter to be going on with, but I can't make you a cup of tea because we ain't got any electric. The raid blew it all out.'

She took some bread from the table and, barely touching it with butter, handed it to Josie who gulped it down hungrily. Then she remembered Arthur and the box.

''Ave you got a box, Mrs Price? I've got to 'ave a box for Paddy. Arfer's waiting for me at the flats and we're gonna bury 'im proper an all.'

Mrs Price put an arm around her shoulders.

'I'll 'ave a look for you love, but they're probably all in bits by now – just gimme a minute and I'll see.'

A few minutes later she returned with a large brown cardboard box and vigorously shaking the pieces of broken glass that had fallen into it onto the floor she handed it to Josie.

'Thanks, Mrs Price.'

'Bye, dearie … I hope your mum and dad are okay.'

Arthur was sitting on the steps with his head cupped in his hands when she got back.

''Ere you are, Arfur. Told you I'd get one, didn't I?'

'Been long enough, ain't yer,' he grumbled. He picked up the shovel then bent down to pick up Paddy.

She brushed him aside. ''E's my dog, I'll carry 'im.'

They walked in silence to the station, around the back of the booking hall and up a small leafy lane, which ran parallel to the railway. Patches of Michaelmas daisies and dandelions were swaying in the cool autumn breeze, their colourful heads bobbing up and down creating a riot of blues and yellows with the occasional flash of white.

'This'll do,' Arthur said, as he stopped nearby and started to dig a hole. Josie looked on, fighting back the tears as she tried to come to terms with the death of her Paddy. He worked in silence. The ground was hard and beads of perspiration showed on his forehead and trickled down his pale, thin face. Finally, the hole was big enough.

'Are you gonna put 'im in or shall I?' he asked, wiping his brow with the sleeve of his shirt.

'I'll do it – 'e's my dog.'

She knelt down and laid Paddy gently in the box. Then, slowly, she took off her coat and placed it over him, shivering as a blast of cold air brushed her bare shoulders.

'Shall we say prayers now, Arfur?'

'I dunno any bleedin' prayers. I ain't never been to church. 'Urry up if you're gonna do it. I want to go 'ome for me breakfast.'

He turned abruptly away from the scene in front of him, as he felt a tear trickle down his face, and quickly he rubbed it with his fist. What would the gang say if they saw him now? Arthur Dawson feeling sorry for a girl! He'd never be able to hold his head up again!

He looked at the blackened and burnt out streets in front of him, at the huge cranes, silhouetted against the glow of the fires, which were still burning in the distance … this was as close to hell as he could imagine. Then, through the silence he heard Josie's faltering voice.

'Please, God, look after Paddy for me. 'E didn't deserve to die. Those rotten Germans did it and I'll never forgive 'em. Amen.'

Arthur grabbed her by the hand and pulled her roughly to her feet.

'C'mon now, I gotta go 'ome.'

She turned and gave one last desperate look at the grave, then began to follow Arthur down the lane towards the flats. Just at that moment, her mother appeared from the opposite direction. She saw Josie and stopped abruptly.

'Josie!' she called, her voice raised in anger. 'Come here at once! Don't you ever do what you are told?'

'Wot's the matter wiv 'er?' muttered Arthur. 'She's in a funny mood, wotever it is.'

'She don't like me being wiv you, that's wot, so you'd better sling your hook, Arfur,' Josie replied as she ran towards her mother. Arthur quickly made himself scarce.

Josie looked intently into her mother's face, hoping to see some sign that she was pleased to see her, but mother's face remained angry.

'What are you doing with that boy?' she asked, grabbing Josie by the arm and shaking her violently. 'What have I told you, time and time again, don't mix with the likes of him. Just you wait until your father gets home.'

'But, Mum,' Josie blurted out, ''e's been …'

'That's enough of that my girl, I don't want your excuses. Now, where is that dog? Don't tell me you've left it indoors while you've been off with that Arthur. You've been up to no good I'll be bound. That animal will have wrecked the place. Really, Josie, you should know better.'

'Mum, 'e's dead,' Josie screamed. ''E's been killed, that's wot I tried to tell you – in the air-raid last night and you didn't even come 'ome did you?'

Mother stopped abruptly, her face turning pale. 'Did you say Paddy's dead?' she asked incredulously.

'Yes, Mum,' she replied sadly, as tears started to trickle down her face. 'I ain't got 'im anymore.'

'Josie, I know you're upset but I heard that we will probably be evacuated soon and you wouldn't have been able to take Paddy. It's all for the best.'

'D'yer think me dad is alright?' Josie asked nervously. 'He didn't come 'ome last night and there was fires all round where 'e works.'

'We'll just have to wait and see,' her mother replied, her voice trembling with anxiety. 'We'll just have to wait and see.'

The flat seemed empty and desolate as they opened the front door. Treading carefully over the broken glass that littered the hallway they made their way to the front room. All the windows had been blown out and the curtains hung in shreds. Pictures on the wall were hanging at crazy angles. Mother surveyed the damage silently, then turned and went into the kitchen and returned with a dustpan and brush.

'Here you are, Josie, get this mess cleaned up while I see to Molly.'

For almost an hour Josie worked in silence, ears strained

for the familiar sound of father's key in the lock, while gradually the flat took on some semblance of order. Paddy's bowl and blanket had been blown in a heap in the corner – she steeled herself to pick them up, and then hugging his blanket close to her chest, she went in search of her mother.

'Wot are we gonna do about Paddy's things. Can we keep 'em?'

Mother shook her head silently as she lifted Molly up in her arms.

'Put them in the bin over there, Josie, then go and sit down somewhere out of my way. I've got to get some tea on.'

Josie wandered into the front room and sat on the hard wooden chair next to the window, gazing forlornly out into a deserted street. The sky was overcast and a light drizzle began to fall; she sighed and rested her arms on the window sill. Suddenly, in the distance someone was coming towards the flats; she leaned further out of the window to get a better view. It was him! It was her dad and he was safe!

'Mum,' she screamed. 'Come quick, it's me dad. 'E's not been killed, 'e's come 'ome.'

For a moment there was a deathly silence, and then the air was filled with the protesting screams of Molly as she was scooped unceremoniously out of the bath. Mother rushed into the room and over to the window.

'So it is, Josie, so it is! Thank God he was spared. Now be quick and put the kettle on. He must be ready for a cup of tea and some food.'

'We ain't got any electric, Mum, the raid last night blew it out, so I can't make any tea.'

Mother turned. 'Well just cut up some bread and butter, that's all we've got.'

They sat around the table talking about the events of the night before. Her father recounting details of how he and his work-mates watched helplessly as wave upon wave of German planes dropped over 700 hundred incendiary bombs on the docks.

'We did everything we could to put out the fires,' he said wearily, brushing his forehead with his hand, 'but it was too much for us – we didn't stand a chance.'

Mother shook her head in sympathy. She could see that he was exhausted, and his clothing was scorched and sticking to his skin but, before she could help him, he needed to talk, he needed to release the horror that was locked in his mind.

'I lost seven of my mates in that raid,' he went on, almost as if he was talking to himself. 'Pity the poor devils' wives. That's if they didn't cop it. It's a right mess on the island. Whole streets just burned out. Little kids running scared with their clothes alight. God 'elp the poor little buggers.'

He lapsed into silence and buried his face in his hands.

'Josie was out all night in that raid,' mother said quietly. 'Got locked out of here. I was over at Gracie's and I couldn't get 'ome because of the raid.'

Father raised his head, his face was grey and drawn. His brown hair matted and dishevelled. He rubbed his eyes wearily.

'Wot d'yer mean by getting yourself locked out? A young girl like you roaming the streets all night! Anything could 'ave 'appened to you. Why did you go out at all?'

She looked across the table at him – she could see the anger rising in his face.

'Dad! It was those upstairs fighting again! I 'ate it I do, and I ran out so I wouldn't 'ear them. Then I couldn't get back in 'cause I don't 'ave a key.'

'She was with that Arthur Dawson,' Mother spat out. 'She needs a good hiding, that's what she needs.'

Father shook his head angrily. 'There's been enuf violence for one day Flo. Wot we need is to get away from these flats, especially them upstairs. It's about time we 'eard from the council about moving us to an 'ouse, now we've got the baby to think of. Go and see them tomorrow and see wot they say.' Mother nodded silently as he stood up and walked towards the bedroom.

'I'm gonna get out of these clothes and 'ave a wash – I gotta get back to work. God knows how many more bodies we will find!'

Chapter 4

Less than one month later, a letter arrived at No. 45 with the offer of a three-bedroomed house in Bellingham.

'Come now, Josie,' her mother said impatiently, 'let's go and look at the house straight away. You put Molly's coat on while I get the pram down the stairs.'

Josie gave a whoop of delight – they were going to look at a real house – they would even have a garden! Quickly she went over and lifted Molly from the cot and wrapped a shawl around her, then followed her mother down the stairs, barely able to conceal her excitement as they headed in the direction of their new home.

'Ain't it luverly, Mum?' Josie stood in awe at the modest end of terrace house. It stood in a street of about twenty identical houses surrounded by a large garden; two small fir trees stood like sentries, one each side of a pathway which led to the front door. A few neglected rose bushes struggled to survive under the front window and the long side garden was neglected and overgrown, but in Josie's eyes it was the most beautiful place she had ever seen.

Mother opened the door and stepped into a small, square hallway with two doors leading off, one to a large oblong front room and the other to a medium sized kitchen, while Josie ran up the stairs to look at the bedrooms.

'Mum, Mum, can I 'ave this little room? Please, please Mum.'

She had just opened the door to the third bedroom, a tiny oblong room with two narrow windows, giving a view of the side garden. Mother came into the room and gazed around in awe.

'No, Josie, you can't have your own room, whatever next! You will have to share the other bedroom with your sister. Even though she's away, it doesn't mean that the war is going to last forever and she'll want somewhere to sleep when she comes home. No, this room will do very nicely for your brother.' She turned to walk downstairs. 'We had better hurry up and get to the council office now and tell them we will take the house.'

The next few days were spent frantically preparing for the move. Josie's brother had returned to live at home, the firm he worked for having been demolished during the raid.

'Another pair of hands will come in very useful,' said mother, her eyes shining with pride as she looked at her son. Josie bit her lip. He was mother's favourite; she had always known that …

Finally the great day arrived. Peter Hill, who was a mate of father, had offered to help with the move.

'I've got a drop of petrol left over from that Woolwich trip,' he said. 'It'll be enough to take your little lot to your new 'ome, Charlie me ol' mate.'

With the contents of their home precariously perched on the lorry, they made their way through the desolate streets with Josie and her brother left to follow on foot. Finally they arrived at the house and with everyone helping, the furniture was soon unloaded and the house began to take shape.

It had been a busy day and father wandered into the garden for a breath of fresh air. He lit a cigarette and stood gazing into space, his mind going over the events of the day. Here they were in a proper house at last. Finally, after years of living in two rooms in someone else's house, then the council flat, the kids now had space and a garden to play in!

Josie wandered out into the garden and stood quietly by his side. Raising her arm, she tugged him by the sleeve until he turned to look down at his young daughter.

'Wot is it, Josie, wot do you want?'

She gazed at him proudly. 'Look, Dad, we've got our very own shelter now. We'll be safe in that won't we?'

He shrugged his shoulders and gave a wry smile. 'Let's 'ope we don't 'ave to use it too often. It's not very nice down there – just a big, black hole in the ground with those corrugated iron sheets over the top.'

He paused for a moment … what good would the shelter be if the bombing got really bad! He shook his head to dispel the troubling thoughts.

'I'll go to the shops now and see if I can get 'old of a torch and I'll try to do something to make it more comfortable for us, but it's awfully wet and damp in there.'

They turned and went back into the house where mother was busy checking all the windows to make sure that she had enough black-out curtains to go around. Shortly after 7 p.m. the all too familiar sound of the air-raid siren disturbed them as they sat around the fire. Father had managed to light it with some coal he had found in an old coal scuttle. Upstairs Molly was sleeping peacefully in her cot, unaware of the danger that surrounded her.

'I suppose we'd better get down the shelter,' said father reluctantly as he reached for his boots.

'Can't we stay 'ere, Dad,' wailed Josie, looking at him with pleading eyes. 'It's cold and dark down there. Please, Dad … I don't wanna go!'

'Now that's enough of that,' her mother replied. 'None of us wants to go down that shelter but we have to if we want to be safe.'

The heavy rumbling of approaching planes grew louder, intermingled with the muffled sound of explosions, and from the upstairs bedroom came the sound of Molly crying. Mother got up from her chair and went into the hall to get her coat, then wearily climbed the stairs.

'C'mon, get your coats on, it'll be cold in that shelter,' her father said, marshalling them in some sort of order. 'Wiv a bit of luck the raid won't last too long and the fire will still be in when we get back.'

Sadly they left the warmth and comfort of their new home and crawled into the deep, dark hole of the Anderson shelter. The night seemed endless – the incessant droning of planes and the rumble of explosions as bombs hit their targets made sleep impossible. Once or twice a bomb would be dropped dangerously close and the shelter would shake, with the vibration causing Josie to gasp with fear and bury her face in her hands.

'It's alright,' father said, trying to reassure her, 'we're safe enough down 'ere, as long as we don't get a direct 'it, that is.

Try to get some sleep, Josie. The time will pass quicker if you do.'

With the dawn came the All Clear – they had been down in the shelter for just over ten hours. Gratefully they hurried indoors, shivering in the cold, damp morning air.

'Best you go and get the kettle on, Josie, there's not much time before your father has to leave for work,' mother remarked, picking her way carefully through the debris that littered the floor. Josie nodded briefly as she made her way to the kitchen. All the hard work of the day before seemed to have been wasted. Everything was covered in dust; the kettle was lying on the floor in a corner. There was only one unbroken cup left … and there was no electric to make the tea.

London began to look battle-scarred and the nightly bombing raids were taking their toll. As each day dawned, people, thankfully hearing the All Clear, crawled out from the hundreds of hastily erected air-raid shelters, from the Underground stations, from any place that offered relative safety. Like an army of ants they banded together determined to see this thing through.

Father made his way wearily towards the docks. It had been an exceptionally bad night; heavy bombing of the capital had caused widespread destruction. For the moment there was no public transport and, like a person in deep shock, London was deathly silent. No sound, just the sight of scores of people picking their way through fallen masonry and rubble to get to work. He finally reached the Isle of Dogs and gasped in horror at the sight of utter devastation in front of him. As far as he could see, barely a house was left standing. Tears welled up in his eyes and he quickly rubbed them with his fists.

For a few moments he stood, silently cursing the war and a God who allowed this to happen. He remembered the little kids who, just a couple of weeks ago, had been running terrified through the streets with their clothes on fire. He shook his head. Poor little buggers! They went through all that ... and now they were probably dead!

Stumbling through the rubble, he could see in the distance the outline of a crane, standing like a giant albatross against the hazy skyline. Suddenly he remembered he needed some tobacco; he desperately wanted a smoke. He'd get it at old Joe's corner shop further along Manchester Road, but as he walked on he quickly realised that it wasn't there anymore! In its place a pile of rubble was smouldering, sending wispy clouds of grey smoke into the air and perched on top of it was Joe's old blue woollen hat, placed, as if by unseen hands, as a memorial to his seventy years of living on this very spot.

The constant nightly raids were taking their toll, not only on the surface but in the health of the people. The cold, dark dampness of the Anderson shelter was an ideal breeding ground for disease. Josie had always been delicate and had now developed a hacking cough which wracked her slight body, and father, in desperation, had brought home some raw linseed oil from work – he had been unloading it from a ship that had managed to reach England despite the vigilance of the German U-Boats out in the Atlantic. Every night before the raids started he would pour a large spoonful of the oil and tell Josie to take it. She hated the very smell and she wanted to be sick but there was no question or doubt about it – father made her take it.

The siren started wailing just as the oil was sliding down her throat one evening and like well-disciplined soldiers the family silently prepared to go to the shelter. Outside the moon shone from a bright starry sky, the air was bitterly cold; winter had arrived with a vengeance, making the time spent down the shelter very miserable indeed. They climbed down into the black hole and sat in silence while the familiar sound of gunfire echoed in the distance and the sound of approaching aircraft filled the air.

A dull thud, as bombs fell increasingly closer and closer, made Josie put her fingers in her ears and close her eyes. George, sensing her distress, poked her in the ribs.

'Coward, you're a coward, Josie. You're a yellow belly,' he laughed mockingly.

Furiously, she kicked out at him, catching him on the leg. He screamed out in pain, causing their father to turn around in anger.

'Don't you think there's enough trouble and fighting in the world wivout you two being at it as well. Stop it at once, yer 'ear me. Stop it!'

His last few words were all but obliterated by a sound like a hundred iron gates falling from the sky – it seemed to be coming straight for them. Josie screamed in terror and flung herself onto her father's lap. Quickly he wrapped his arms about her while George crouched in the corner, tears streaming down his face. Mother sat frozen in shock clutching Molly tightly in her arms.

'My God! Wot the 'ell is that?' father shouted, as a cloud

of thick, black dust filled the shelter, making it difficult to breath. In stunned silence they sat waiting – but for what?

The drone of the planes gradually faded into the distance as the full moon shone brightly, turning night into day. A few feet away, perilously close, lay a landmine – like a dark, evil demon, it sat silently waiting to devour them.

Several minutes passed before the sound of voices and the glimmer of a torch being shone into the shelter stirred then out of shock. A warden was peering into the inky blackness as he shone his torch around their startled faces.

'Quick! Get out of 'ere now,' he shouted. 'There's an unexploded landmine right next to you. God knows when it'll explode – I've got to evacuate this street, the whole area is to be cleared. Best you go to the orphanage in Overdown Street and wait until someone with a key turns up to let you in.'

There was a mad scramble out of the shelter and into the street. It was alive with people hurrying in the direction of the orphanage. Some had stopped to collect a few precious belongings. Old Mrs Wilson hobbled painfully along with her elderly, arthritic dog on a lead, muttering angrily to herself. Josie clutched her father's arm tightly as the family hurried through the night. The orphanage was over a mile away and in the distance they could hear a second wave of enemy aircraft descending on the capital.

Little by little a queue began to form as people reached their destination; gradually the line of people grew until it stretched down the road and around the corner. Silently and patiently they waited, after all, this was one lesson the war had taught them – to stay in line and not complain.

Father pulled out an old pocket watch from his jacket

and peered closely at the watch face – it showed ten minutes past two. He put it back in his pocket. How much longer would they have to stand there? It had already been just over two hours. Where was the person with the key? He rubbed his hands together; it was getting very cold! Molly was crying incessantly and her lips were beginning to turn blue. They huddled together to try and keep warm as the hours ticked by. The crowd started muttering angrily amongst themselves, unaware that just over a mile away a man's body lay, outstretched in the road; killed by falling masonry as he was hurrying towards the orphanage. From a cold winter's sky the moon shone, its silvery glow reflecting on the key that had fallen from his lifeless fingers!

The crowd shuffled nervously. They had stood outside the locked building for four hours now, while above their heads planes flew relentlessly and the sound of bombs exploding echoed through the night. A few people had decided to return to their homes regardless of the danger of the landmine. Old Mrs Wilson cursed the war, the air-raids and the world in general and trundled back home.

'I'm not going to die out on the street in a queue,' she said, angrily waving her fist at the sky. 'If I've gotta die, I'll die in my own 'ome, in my own bed and to hell with the Germans.'

Finally, dawn began to break over the city, bringing with it the relief of the All Clear and relative peace and quiet.

'Bloody fine thing, innit?' said Mr Jones, who along with the others had stood outside the orphanage all night. 'Tell us to bleedin' well come up 'ere and then leave us! Well, sod it, next time I'll stay put in me own 'ouse.'

The crowd nodded in agreement as one by one they dispersed and headed back to their homes. Josie and her family trudged along the road, exhausted by the lack of sleep.

Molly was inconsolable – she wanted her bottle and there was no pacifying her. They were just half a mile from home when they found the whole area cordoned off. An ARP man was standing guard and, as they approached, he stood in front of them, barring their way.

'Wot's this, then?' demanded father, indicating the erected barriers.

'No-one can go into this area until we've got the bomb disposal people out. There was a landmine dropped 'ere last night and you can't go into this area mate. You'll just 'ave to wait until I get the word that it's been made safe for you to go 'ome.'

'I know all that,' replied father crossly. 'The bloody thing nearly landed on top of us. Now 'urry up and get on with it then, me kids are starving and they need to get some sleep.'

It seemed as if their whole life revolved around orders; it had become a part of their life, without question. Silently and miserably, they stood cold and hungry waiting for the moment they could return to their new home.

Chapter 5

The agricultural college stood in majestic splendour among the green fields of Somerset. The late afternoon sun danced on its honey-coloured stone walls, while a soft wind gently teased the hosts of daffodils that surrounded the main gateway. Lucy looked in awe at this magnificent building that lay at the end of the drive.

'Cor! Ain't it luverly,' she gasped. 'Fancy me living 'ere just like a queen.'

Slowly, and a little nervously, she walked up the long, gravel drive to a large, ornate wooden door and rang the bell. A few minutes later it was opened by a well-built woman in her early forties. She was dressed in a green sweater and brown jodhpurs. Friendly brown eyes scrutinised Lucy, noting the slim, pale faced girl and her shabby clothes.

'You must be one of our new recruits,' she said with a warm smile as she held out her hand in greeting.

'Yes, Miss,' Lucy replied, staring down at the ground. She felt strangely awkward and ill at ease in this palatial place.

'What is your name, young lady?'

'It's Lucy, Lucy Brownley, Miss.'

'Alright, Lucy Brownley, follow me and we will get you settled in – by the way my name is Miss Ingram and I am the one who is here to help, should you have any problems. Of course, we hope there will not be any but – you never know!'

She followed Miss Ingram through the spacious hallway, marvelling at the beautiful wooden floors that gleamed in the reflection of the early summer sun shining through the mullion windows.

An ornate circular staircase led to the upper floors and she noticed a couple of girls about her own age laughing and chatting as they ran down the stairs together, then disappeared out of a side door. It made her feel good. After all, these girls seemed happy enough. She sighed happily and continued to follow Miss Ingram until they reached a small room, which served as her office.

'Lucy, you can leave your bags here and I will take you on a brief tour of the place. It's quite large so it may take a little time for you to find your way around. We have about a hundred or so girls at the moment and they share four large dormitories.' She paused for a moment, and then added with a slight grin. 'You see, Lucy, you will never be lonely here.'

Together they set off, looking first at a few outbuildings, which seemed to contain mostly farm implements, and then they made their way across a field to a small river where a plank of wood served as a small footbridge. In the distance cows and sheep could be seen grazing in the lush fields. Chickens roamed freely, scratching the ground as they searched for some choice titbit to eat, while an old farm dog raced around excitedly. Lucy was amazed to see girls no older than herself driving huge tractors, while others were stacking large bales of hay.

Miss Ingram smiled encouragingly as she noticed Lucy's look of concern at the hard, physical work the girls were doing.

'Don't worry, my dear,' she said soothingly, 'the girls were just like you in the beginning, but working here soon builds up muscle.'

Lucy smiled happily as she gazed around. She knew that she would love to spend the rest of the war here, even the rest of her life if need be. Finally, they made their way back to the house and Miss Ingram's office. The office was warm and inviting as they walked in. Miss Ingram made herself comfortable in a large, black leather armchair and with a wave of her hand she indicated that Lucy should take the seat opposite her. For a moment or two there was complete silence, except for the steady ticking of the grandfather clock which stood in the far corner. Miss Ingram studied Lucy critically for a few moments. She often wondered about some of the girls in her charge. What sort of homes had they come from? There was no doubt that they were a very 'mixed bag' and she had been quite shocked in the beginning at the sorry state of some of the girls who arrived at the college. Then there were others who obviously came from a totally different background; they were well dressed and well fed. Then there was Lucy! She sighed and straightened herself up in the chair, leaning towards Lucy with an intent look on her face.

'Now, my dear, the first and most important thing for you to decide is what area of farming you want to be in, because it makes a difference to the type of training we give you.'

Lucy looked at her with a puzzled frown as she nervously twisted a lock of her auburn hair. 'Wot d'yer mean, area of farming? Ain't it all the same then?'

'Of course not! You can either choose arable farming, dairy farming or there's poultry farming.' Miss Ingram paused for a moment, tilting her head to one side as she looked quizzically at Lucy. 'Which one do you feel would be more suitable for you?'

'I know already, Miss. I don't need to think about it. I want to work wiv animals, so I guess dairy farming is wot I should do.'

Miss Ingram nodded, then rose from her chair and beckoned Lucy to follow her.

'It's almost time for a milking session so I think it might be a good idea for you to see how the girls go about it,' she said as she walked quickly to the door. 'You can leave your bag on the floor, Lucy, it will be perfectly safe there.'

They took the same narrow path that led from the rear door into the fields until they came to a large shed which served as the milking parlour. Lucy watched fascinated at the sight of rows of girls sitting on low stools milking the cows. Some of them could be heard talking in low, soothing tones to the animals as they worked. Suddenly, impatient at the inexperienced handling of the milking session, one of the cows kicked out and knocked a pail of creamy milk all over the floor. Lucy giggled as a fat black and white cat jumped down from one of the rafters and started to happily lick it up. She felt a tap on the shoulder and turned to find Miss Ingram beckoning her.

'It is time for the evening meal shortly, Lucy, so I will

take you to your dormitory and then you can freshen up before supper.' They went back to the house and, after picking up Lucy's bag from the office, went up a flight of stairs, along a wide passageway to a door at the far end. Miss Ingram opened the door to a largish room and pointed to a narrow bed on the left.

'That will be your bed over there, Lucy, the one in the far corner.'

With a brief wave of her hand she disappeared down the stairs, leaving Lucy to face her new surroundings. Hesitantly, Lucy walked towards her bed, smiling a little nervously at a pretty, dark-haired girl who was sitting on the bed next to hers reading a letter.

'Can you tell me where I can wash myself?' she asked, as the girl put down her letter and stood up to greet her. A big grin crossed the girl's face as she took Lucy by the hand.

'Come with me, ducky. I'll show you. By the way my name is Margaret, but everyone calls me Marge for short. What's yours?'

'It's Lucy – Lucy Brownley,' she replied, happy in the knowledge that she seemed to have found herself a friend.

They went through the dormitory to a small door at the far end of the room. Marge flung the door open and stood back to let Lucy in. She gave a gasp of surprise at the sight of rows of pristine white sinks and bright, sparkling chrome taps set in the long, white tiled room, and at almost every sink there was a girl washing or cleaning her teeth. As she walked in, a few of the girls glanced briefly at her, the rest just carried on with what they were doing.

Lucy found a vacant sink and pulled out the piece of

cloth which her mother had given to her to use as a flannel, together with a bar of red, carbolic soap wrapped in a piece of paper. Lucy felt a wave of embarrassment sweep over her – she didn't have a towel to dry on and she had never owned a toothbrush! When she had finished washing she looked furtively around to see if anyone was watching her, then quickly patted her face dry on the hem of her dress. A few seconds later Marge appeared by her side.

'Come on, Lucy,' she said, pulling her by the arm. 'We'd better get to the dining room or else all the best food will have gone.'

They hurried down the staircase to the dining room and sat at a large, trestle table and waited in silence for the room to fill up.

'We have to wait,' whispered Marge. 'When everyone is here, Miss Ingram will take grace and then we will get served with our supper.'

Lucy nodded happily and gazed around the room – there was no doubt she was going to enjoy her stay at the college. All the girls looked so fit and happy and certainly the place was very beautiful. Thoughts of her own home took hold in her mind. Now she was embarking on a completely different way of life, one that was worlds away from her life in London. She wondered if her mother was missing her. Perhaps she should write her a letter. Maybe one day. Maybe tomorrow! She wished she could spend the rest of the war at the college but, of course, that was not possible. As Miss Ingram had said, when her training was completed, she would be transferred to a farm where Land Army girls were needed.

Precisely at 4.30 a.m. the next morning she was awakened by the sound of a gong echoing through the building. Lucy shot up in bed and rubbed her eyes.

'Wot the 'ell is that?' she gasped, as she looked around, unsure of her new surroundings. In the half-light she could see the dawn breaking through the open window, the glow of the sun on the horizon promising another beautiful day. One by one the sleeping girls began to stir. Marge turned over in bed and looked at Lucy sleepily, her big, brown eyes half closed as she struggled to stay awake.

'Don't panic,' she whispered, 'it's only the gong. That's to tell us to get up.'

'But, it's the middle of the night,' Lucy protested, and snuggled back into the warmth and comfort of her bed and closed her eyes. Marge swung a shapely leg over the side of her bed and stretched wearily.

'It is half past four, ducky, and you had better get used to it if you are going to work on a farm. It's not so bad; it's the first week that's the worst.'

Lucy groaned and threw the covers back, slipping her feet onto the bare, wooden floor just as the door of the dormitory opened and a short, sturdy woman with cropped blonde hair appeared in the doorway. She stood silently surveying the scene in front of her, her eyes glinting like polished steel.

'I want you out of here and downstairs in five minutes – now MOVE IT!'

With a final glance, she turned and marched resolutely down the hallway. Panic ensued as about twenty girls leapt out of bed.

'Where are my socks?' 'Where's my jumper?' 'Don't sit on my bed, I have just made it.' The noise was almost deafening, and filled Lucy with a sense of fear as she struggled to get into the clothes she had arrived in.

'Ain't you got your uniform yet?'

Marge stared in disbelief at the clothes Lucy was wearing to go to work in. Lucy looked around in dismay, all the others were dressed identically in brown dungarees, a matching jacket and wellington boots. She looked down at her long, shabby dress and worn shoes in dismay.

'No-one 'as said anything about a uniform to me,' she replied defensively. Marge smiled, sensing her embarrassment.

'Don't worry about it, ducky. We'll sort it out. Now let's go downstairs and get our mug of hot milk, and then I 'ave to go and check the animals before breakfast. When you've 'ad your milk, go and see Miss Wilson, she'll kit you out and tell you what your duties are.' She put a comforting arm around Lucy. 'By then we should be back for breakfast. If I get to the dining room first I'll save you a seat next to me.'

Lucy felt her stomach turn over with the excitement of her first day at the college. What would her friends think if they could see her now? What would her mother think?

Just as Marge had said, there were mugs full of steaming hot milk set on an old, but well scrubbed, wooden table, and gratefully picking up a mug she sipped the hot liquid, feeling its comforting warmth seep through her body. As soon as she had finished she made her way into the hallway to look for Miss Wilson's office. Eventually, she found it tucked away at the far end of the building. A large sign on the door commanded, 'Please knock and WAIT'. Lucy knocked nervously, then stepped back and dutifully waited. For a few minutes there was silence before a voice bade her to enter. Nervously she opened the door and peered inside. She could see an elderly lady sitting at a large, oak desk which stood imposingly in front of a large bay window with sweeping views of the farm.

The room was plain but elegant, beautiful green velvet curtains draped the window, hanging in soft folds to the floor. The walls were a delicate shade of cream and a glistening chandelier hung from the ornate ceiling. Lucy stood in awe at the sight in front of her. Never in her whole life had she imagined such splendour existed, except perhaps in the films she had seen on a Saturday morning, when, with Josie and her brother, they queued outside the local cinema for the 'tupenny' rush.

Only under fourteens were allowed in and, once inside, they were transported into a world of wonderment. They gazed enraptured at the stage as a brilliantly lit, multicoloured organ rose up from beneath the floor, filling the air with music, while heavy, red, velvet curtains slowly swept open to reveal a large screen and the movies started. The children would cheer the heroes and loudly boo the villains and, for an hour or so, they forgot about their own lives of struggle and poverty. For a moment she was lost in those magical moments of childhood … until a discreet cough brought her back to reality.

'Yes, young lady. Can I help you?'

Brown eyes peered over the top of horn-rimmed glasses;

frizzy grey hair circled her face like a halo as Miss Wilson waited for an answer.

'Please, Miss, I don't 'ave a uniform.'

Miss Wilson put down the pen she had been writing with and stood up.

'Well, we can't have that now, can we? Come now, let's see what we can find for you. I only hope that we have the right size because we haven't been able to get any uniforms for several weeks now – it's the war you know,' she remarked almost apologetically as she studied Lucy's figure.

'You seem to be one of the more popular sizes, so I am not sure if we will be lucky but let us have a look. Shall we my dear?'

She walked towards a side door which led into a small, square room filled with numerous boxes, all numbered and in order, then pulling several boxes from the shelves she started to open them, one by one. Finally, Lucy had her uniform. A pair of jodhpurs, brown dungarees, a shirt and a green jumper, and, lastly, a brown round hat that could be kept in place by two cords tied under the chin. A pair of sturdy brown brogues and a pair of wellingtons completed the ensemble. Miss Wilson nodded her head in the manner of one who was very pleased with the outcome and turned to Lucy.

'These should fit you alright, but if any are too big, except, of course, for the jumper, then we can get the tailoress to alter them for you. Now, off you go and get changed before breakfast – here is your list of duties. Find the group you will be working with and they will show you what to do. Good Luck!' And with a brief wave of her hand she was dismissed.

Returning to the dormitory, Lucy ran up the stairs two at a time, anxious to try on her new uniform – for the first time in her life she had a whole set of new clothes and she couldn't wait to see how she looked in them. Racing into the room she quickly undressed, throwing her old clothes in a heap on the floor and, almost reverently, one by one she put on her uniform. Her moment was shattered by the hollow sound of the gong summoning the girls to breakfast.

'I gotta see wot I look like first,' she muttered to herself as she rushed into the bathroom. She stared at her reflection in the mirror.

'Oh! My gawd!' she gasped. The transformation was amazing. The cream shirt complemented her fair skin perfectly while the green sweater enhanced her red hair. Lucy gave a yelp of joy and ran eagerly down the stairs. Now she belonged – she was just the same as all the others.

The sound of chatter and laughter filled the stately home as the girls returned from an early morning round and filtered into the dining room for a well-earned breakfast. A delicious smell of eggs and bacon filled the air and made her realise how hungry she was. Marge, true to her word, had saved her a seat and as they tucked into the delicious food Lucy felt strangely contented and at peace with the world for the first time in her life!

The next four weeks proved to be the hardest she had ever known. The working hours were from 5 a.m. until 5 p.m. every day. She was taught how to milk the cows, muck-out the pig sty and, most importantly, how to lift heavy sacks of grain without damaging her back. She learned how to plough a field and drive a tractor, and by the end of the day she sank exhausted on to her bed, back aching and with sore and blistered hands.

To Lucy, the milking sessions were the best. As she sat on the low stool she would talk to the animal in soft, soothing tones, sensing that it was a little nervous of her inexperience. Sometimes it would flick its tail vigorously and Lucy would feel a stinging slap around the face, but after a couple of weeks she had it down to a fine art!

Twenty-eight days had passed without a break and although she was exhausted Lucy felt fitter than she had for a very long time. The early morning fresh air, the exercise and good food put a sparkle in her green eyes and a glow on her cheeks. Sometimes she felt a little cut off from the world as there was no time to listen to the radio, and to find out how the war was going. Most evenings it was almost half past eight before they could relax in the large sitting room, where they would chat about their families, boyfriends – all the things they had left behind. Occasionally, someone would give a tune on an old piano which stood in a far corner and they would sing happily until 10 o'clock when they were sent to bed.

All too soon the training was over and the girls who had completed the course were summoned to appear in Miss Ingram's office. There was great excitement and speculation as to where they might be sent, and Marge and Lucy stood silently praying that they would be sent to the same farm. Miss Ingram stood and slowly looked around the room before she picked up a list from her desk and proceeded to inform the girls of their posting. One by one they were dismissed after being told where they were going; a rail pass was issued to them and, with a brief 'thank you for all your efforts', the fully-fledged Land Army girls were sent on their way. Several of the girls were in tears as they said goodbye to newly made friends, while Marge and Lucy stood biting their lips as they waited for their turn; they didn't want to be parted from each other. Suddenly, Lucy heard her name being called.

'Lucy Bownley, you will be going to a farm at Evercreech.'

Miss Ingram paused for a moment then looked straight at Marge. A slight smile flickered around her lips.

'As they need two girls to take the place of a couple of farm hands who have been called up, I have decided to send you as well. Now go and get packed, collect your passes and off you go. Good luck to you both.'

Outside the office Marge gave a scream of delight and grabbed Lucy around the waist and swung her around.

'Fancy the old girl letting us go to the same farm, ducky! She's not such a bad old stick after all … come on, Lucy, let's get our packing done and be on our way. There's not a lot of time before we have to catch our train to this place called Evercreech … wherever that is!'

Lucy shrugged her shoulders, she hadn't got a clue where it was either, but, at the same time, she didn't care. Working on a farm sounded like heaven and, if it was anything like the college, she would be so happy.

They linked arms and made their way to the dormitory for the very last time to pack a few belongings and say goodbye to the rest of the girls.

Outside, the old Land Rover stood waiting to take them

to the station and, as they climbed aboard, they could hear shouts and cheers from the girls who were left behind. They had mixed feelings, sad that they were leaving the college where they had been so happy and yet, at the same time, they were excited about this new venture. The Land Rover spluttered, and then belched a cloud of black smoke as the engine reluctantly burst into life. The girls knelt up on the back seat and watched the college gradually disappear from view as the Land Rover made its way down the sweeping, gravel path. In twenty minutes they were at the station, waiting excitedly for the train that would take them to Castle Cary Station where, so they had been told, a Mr and Mrs Westlake would meet them and take them to the farm, which was a few miles away.

'Wot d'yer think they'll be like?'

Lucy was staring into the distance deep in thought.

'I said wot d'yer think they will be like, Lucy? shouted Marge above the shrill whistle of the approaching train.

Lucy shrugged her shoulders. 'I dunno. S'ppose we'll just 'ave to wait and see.'

She looked down at her brown brogues and the jodhpurs she was wearing and felt a sense of pride – she felt very special in her uniform and for the first time in her life she felt as good as anyone else.

They jumped onto the train and into a carriage where they settled down happily as the train roared along the tracks. After a short while the train slowed down and came to rest at a small country station. Marge quickly jumped up and hung out of the window and saw a group of young soldiers waiting to board.

'Hi beautiful,' one of them called. 'Where are you off to then?'

'We've gotta get off this train at Castle Cary Station – is this it?'

'Shift out of the way, doll, and let us get in. Don't worry, we'll let you know when you get there.'

Marge giggled and slumped back in her seat while Lucy looked down at the floor as a sergeant jumped into the carriage followed by three privates.

The guard blew his whistle and the train started to pick up steam. Lucy raised her eyes and caught the eye of the sergeant, who was sitting on the seat opposite her. For a brief moment they just stared into each other's eyes, and then slowly he got up from his seat and sat down next to her. She blushed furiously and turned her head to escape his penetrating look. She felt a touch on her arm.

'Say, how long have you been in this mob then?'

Lucy turned shyly to face him. He was the most attractive man she had ever seen. Tall and blond, he reminded her of some of the movie stars she had seen on the screen. Her legs turned to jelly as she spoke.

'I've only been in it for a couple of months and that was for training.' Her voice trailed off as she desperately searched for something else to say. She was not very experienced with men, in fact she had never had a boy-friend thanks to her mother's strict rules. They were silent for a few moments. Marge could be heard giggling and whispering in the corner and Lucy wished desperately that she could be more like her.

The soldier leaned closer to her, looking deep into her eyes. She felt her face colour up.

'Why are you going to Castle Cary?'

'We're going to a farm somewhere near Castle Cary – wherever that is.'

He gave a long, low whistle. 'That's great. I'm stationed about ten miles from there, perhaps we could meet sometime. What about next week?'

Lucy looked at him hesitantly. 'I don't know.'

'You'd better hurry up,' he replied anxiously, 'your station is the next one.'

The train was already drawing into Castle Cary, causing Lucy to panic.

'I gotta go now, I'm sorry,' she said.

Among a flurry of goodbyes they jumped up from their seats just as the train pulled to a stop. Lucy opened the carriage door, feeling strangely sad that she had no time to fix a date with the soldier, and jumped down onto the platform, with Marge following close behind. A sudden shout made her turn around to see the soldier leaning from the open carriage window.

'Say, Ginger, what about our date? When and where can I see you again?'

'I don't know, I don't know,' she replied in a panic, as out of the corner of her eye she could see a middle-aged couple descending upon them, and she knew instinctively it was Mr and Mrs Westlake.

The train started to leave the station, slowly gathering speed as it pulled away. The soldier hung out of the window waving a piece of paper in his hand.

'Here, take this, write to me so we can arrange to see each other again.'

She ran forward eagerly, arms outstretched to take the paper, when a sudden gust of wind caught it and it fluttered, like an injured bird, from his grasp and disappeared between the train and the platform. Lucy stood sadly watching as the train disappeared from view, then turning around she came face to face with the disapproving stare of Mrs Westlake.

'You'll be they girls from the college, I be bound,' exclaimed the man, eyeing them up and down like prize fillies. He was a short, stocky man with black hair brushed back and a tanned, leathery complexion. He turned to his wife with a shrug of his shoulders. 'Don't look like they be much good to I – there be no meat on them-there bones. Can't see how they'll handle old Daisy. She'll give them a run for their money, oh ar!'

Mrs Westlake sniffed contemptuously, her thin, long nose flaring out at the nostrils. 'They won't be having any time for the likes of they soldiers. I'll make sure of that, Al. When they be finished outdoors there be plenty for they to do in the house.'

Lucy looked at Marge out of the corner of her eye. Marge grinned and raised her eyes to the sky in despair.

'Come along now, girls, we've no time to be wasting in idle chatter. Follow me!'

Mrs Westlake marched off the platform towards the exit like a sergeant major, while the two girls followed on, with Mr Westlake brings up the rear.

They reached the narrow road outside the station and climbed into a battered, old black Ford parked by the side of the road. Lucy and Marge sank into the back seat as Mr Westlake started the engine and slowly and carefully they made their way along the Somerset lanes. Dusk was falling and the lights from the car gave only a faint glimmer as they were shaded with black covers to comply with the black-out regulations. Lucy sat huddled up in the corner of the seat and stared out of the window, watching the fields and the hedgerows slip by. Occasionally she would see something move and a pair of bright, glowing eyes would watch as they drove by. No-one spoke, it was as if they were all engrossed in their own private thoughts. How was it all going to turn out? How long would they be forced to live with these people that they didn't know? And, already they didn't like!

After driving for about three-quarters of an hour, the shadowy outline of a large house came into view. It was set well back from the narrow lane that fronted it and tall oak trees stood like sentries at the entrance of the drive.

Marge nudged Lucy in the ribs. 'Say, Lucy, wot d'yer think of this then?' she whispered. 'D'yer fancy spending the rest of the war here?'

Before she could answer, the car slowed down and came to a halt at the front gate and Mr Westlake alighted. The car door was opened and they scrambled out, following Mrs Westlake through the gate and up the long, dirt path to the house where they waited impatiently as she fumbled in a large black bag to find the door key. Finally, after much muttering and grumbling, they were inside. Mr Westlake groped around in the dark, making sure that all the black-out curtains were securely in place before switching on the light and a snappy Jack Russell terrier ran around, excited at seeing some new faces and getting in everyone's way.

'This be it m'dears,' he said, as he switched on the light

to reveal a large gloomy hallway with an old grandfather clock standing at the far end, relentlessly and loudly ticking the hours away. A narrow strip of well-worn carpet covered part of the grey stone floor. Above their heads hung a single dim light covered with a shabby brown shade, while delicate, silvery cobwebs seemed to hang from every corner. Dust lay thickly on the few pieces of furniture like a grey cloak. Lucy shuddered as a spider ran from under a chair and scuttled across the hall in front of them.

'Now pick up your bags girls and come into the kitchen. When we've had a cup of tea I will show you to your bedroom.'

Marge gave a despairing sigh and picked up her suitcase. Obviously she was not impressed by what she had seen so far. Lucy followed on behind her and they entered a large, untidy kitchen. A black stove was almost hidden underneath a pile of dirty pots and pans, while a small red glow indicated that the fire was about to go out.

'Al, come in here at once, we need some more kindling for this fire,' Mrs Westlake shouted down the hall. Mr Westlake came shuffling along, grumbling under his breath as he picked up a large coal scuttle and disappeared out of a rear door. Mrs Westlake, with one sweep of her hand, pushed the dirty crockery that was still on the table to one end to make a small clear space. She turned to look at Marge, who was hovering in the doorway.

'Girl, get some cups and saucers from that dresser over there and set them on table while I make the tea, and be quick about it.'

Lucy smiled ruefully, it certainly was not the sort of place she had imagined – but they were here now and there was nothing else to do but to make the best of it until the war was over …

The sky was still dark over Sleepy Hollow Farm. In the hen house the cockerel stirred, opened sleepy eyes and looked around at the slumbering hens. He ruffled his feathers, stretched out his neck and crowed loudly and incessantly.

Mr Westlake stirred and shook his wife by the shoulder as they lay in bed.

'Let's be having you, Maude, it's time to get they girls up and working.'

Mrs Westlake pretended not to hear and her eyes remained firmly closed – she did not want to leave the comfort of her nice warm bed. Mr Westlake looked scornfully at his wife, then throwing the covers back and with a loud belch he clambered out of bed.

'Don't know why you married a farmer – you're bone idle, woman. Now, get out of that bed afore I push you out. Are you going to get they girls up or do I have to do it? Probably a better sight to look at in the mornings than you are anyway.'

His wife opened her eyes and gave a sniff of contempt at this remark. Swinging a pair of stick-like legs off the edge of the bed, she sat there for a few moments rubbing her eyes and yawning. Then, slowly, she got to her feet. Her once white nightdress hung from her body like a dirty grey cloud, while her black hair, lank and greasy, hung in strips around her face. She pulled on a large pair of knickers, which she had been wearing for the best part of a week. A vest and petticoat followed, topped by a shapeless brown jumper and baggy trousers.

Grumbling loudly, she shuffled out of the bedroom and down the hall to the far end where Marge and Lucy were lying awake wondering what the day would have in store for them. The loud banging on the bedroom door startled them for a moment.

'Get up at once you girls, it's time to be out on the farm. Can't have you lying in bed all day.' Mrs Westlake's voice echoed along the hallway.

'Coming,' shouted Lucy.

Mrs Westlake grunted in acknowledgement and shuffled back down the hall towards the kitchen.

Marge raised her head on one arm and gazed despondently around the bedroom. While the college had been immaculately clean and tidy, this place was the complete opposite. Everywhere you looked were layers and layers of dirt. The net curtains at the window had seen better days and hung there in tatters. The floor was bare except for a tiny bedside rug; an old washstand stood in one corner and a broken, green wicker chair in the other.

The large double bed was comfortable enough but it was debatable whether clean sheets had been put on for their arrival. She sat up in bed and shivered.

'God, it's cold in 'ere,' she said, quickly grabbing her jumper and putting it around her shoulders while Lucy went over to the washstand and poured the cold water from the jug into the basin. She turned to Marge with a grin.

'D'yer think Mrs Westlake will give us a kettle of hot water to wash with?'

Marge was sitting on the edge of her bed shivering in the cold morning air. She shrugged her shoulders. 'I dunno. Shall I go and ask her?'

'Might as well. She can't bite your 'ead off, can she?'

They both started giggling at this remark and Marge, her dressing gown flung around her shoulders, disappeared through the door in search of the kitchen and Mrs Westlake.

'Hot water! Whatever next! Bringing your fancy London ways down here, my girl. Cold water has been good enough for me and Mr Westlake all these years and it's good enough for the likes of you. Now be off and get back down here in five minutes, ready for work, or Mr Westlake will have something to say about that.'

She turned her back on Marge, who was standing just inside the doorway, and started to pour boiling water from a soot-blackened kettle into and old enamel teapot.

Marge shrugged her shoulders and put her tongue out in a defiant gesture, then turned and hurried back to their room.

'The old cow won't let us 'ave any 'ot water, Lucy, so we'll 'ave to freeze to death washing in that.'

Quickly splashing water over their faces, they got into their warm Land Army clothes and hurried down to the kitchen, where they found two mugs of tea set on the large wooden table and a couple of slices of toast.

'Get that down you quickly now, there's not much time afore Mr Westlake will be going out and he'll be showing you what to do.'

'Ar,' exclaimed Mr Westlake from the corner, where he sat on an old stool pulled up close to the fire.

They drank the tea gratefully, although it was only lukewarm, then hurriedly ate the toast and waited for a few moments while Mr Westlake pulled on a pair of green wellingtons which were caked with mud and straw.

'We'll be working the top field today,' he remarked as he stood up, struggling to get into his waterproof jacket. 'Now you girl there.' He pointed a grubby finger at Marge. 'You'll come with me. We'll go in the car round the road to it and t'other one can take Daisy over they fields and meet us there.'

With the girls following closely, he turned and marched out of the kitchen, through the back door, and down a rocky path towards a gate which bordered onto a neighbouring field. In the half-light, on the far side of the field, they could just make out the shape of a horse. Mr Westlake gave a low whistle and called.

'C'mon Daisy, c'mon girl.'

The horse looked up from its grazing and, with a slight whinny, galloped across the field towards them.

Lucy and Marge backed away in fright as it approached. Never in their lives had they seen such a large horse – although there were a couple of shire horses at the college, they were somehow not so intimidating. They backed away in fright as she got closer.

Mr Westlake turned towards Lucy. 'Get over to her and give her a pat on the nose. She's not a bad old girl – but you'll have to show her who's boss, or she'll lead you a merry dance, that she will.'

Lucy took a few trembling steps forward. Daisy towered over her as she hesitantly put out her hand to pat her. For a moment their eyes met and Lucy could have sworn that Daisy's possessed an evil glint!

'You can ride her over t' yonder field if you like, or you can walk over.'

'She can't ride no bloomin' 'orse,' Marge retorted angrily. ''Ow d'yer think she'd learn to ride 'orses in London?'

'Well, she's going to learn pretty quick. Old Daisy needs shoeing and she'll have to take her into the village tomorrow to the blacksmiths … she won't be walking that far I'll be bound.' He gave a loud rasping laugh. 'Now get hold of her bridle and take her up yonder hill.'

Nervously, Lucy took the bridle and started up the hill, while Marge and Mr Westlake jumped into the old Ford and disappeared along the winding road.

Daisy plodded purposefully across the field with Lucy running by her side. As they approached the far corner of the field there was a stream with a wooden bridge crossing it. Daisy stood and looked apprehensively at the bridge.

'Come on, Daisy, come on. We've got to go over there.' Lucy tugged sharply at the bridle but Daisy stood firm. Like a mountain, she would not budge.

'You stupid animal, get over that bridge; you'll get me in trouble if we're not over at the other field. You know they are waiting for us.'

Daisy stared blankly into the distance …

In frustration Lucy walked to the rear of the animal and

smacked it sharply on the bottom – that would work! Hadn't she seen it done many times in the movies!

Daisy gave a loud whinny as she reared up in anger, and then bolted over the bridge and across the fields with Lucy in hot pursuit. Finally they reached the top, where Daisy stood panting. She had proved her point … She was going to be the boss!

Lucy came to a breathless halt next to Daisy and gazed around in awe at the scene in front of her. A shaft of pale winter sun peeped through the drifting clouds, highlighting an old Norman church in the distance, while a flock of birds dipped and swayed at the sheer joy of being alive. Below, spread out as if by a master's hand, she could see sheep and cows contentedly grazing on the green fields, and for a brief moment the whole world seemed at peace!

'It's just like being in the movies,' she whispered to herself as she surveyed the scene with rapturous eyes. 'It's just like being in the movies.'

A sound made her turn around and she came face to face with Mr Westlake.

'We will be ploughing there today,' he said, waving an arm in the direction of the field to their right. 'I'll show you girls how to harness old Daisy and then you can get on with it. Now girls, I want it finished by tonight so don't go wasting any time.'

'Wot d'yer mean "we" can do the ploughing?' Lucy retorted. 'Where will you be?'

'I got other things to do. What do you think I got you Land Army girls for? You be here to help me and Mrs Westlake, so no more smart remarks. Now pay attention.'

Daisy was harnessed with very brief instructions from Mr Westlake and, once they had got the hang of it, he turned and smiled happily. 'I'll be off now you girls. Make sure you are back at the farmhouse at one o'clock sharp for lunch or if you be late Mrs Westlake will have cleared the table and you'll have to wait until tea-time.'

They stood silently as they watched his short, stocky figure heading towards his car.

'Say, Lucy,' Marge exclaimed excitedly, 'this is gonna be fun – whose driving the 'orse first?'

'Don't be daft, you don't "drive" an 'orse, you lead it. Didn't you take any notice of wot you were taught at the college?'

Marge giggled helplessly. 'I 'ad better things to think of – you know! Boys and things!'

'C'mon,' replied Lucy impatiently, 'you get 'old of Daisy's bridle and I'll guide the plough. We'd better get started or we'll never get this field finished today.'

They plodded up and down the field without too much trouble. Daisy had obviously done this many times and was happy to carry on without much supervision.

After a couple of hours Marge slumped down on the ground. 'I can't do anymore, I'm exhausted,' she gasped. 'We must 'ave walked bloomin' miles already today.'

Lucy looked at her watch, it was only 9.00 a.m. She grabbed Daisy's bridle. 'Whoa, Daisy, whoa,' she called. Her arms and legs felt like they were breaking, and she needed a rest, but Daisy plodded on oblivious to her calls.

'You stupid 'orse. Stop!' Daisy turned her head slightly to look at her with disdain, and then abruptly came to a halt, causing Lucy to fall heavily to the ground. She got up ruefully, rubbing her back, and hobbled over to where Marge was stretched out on the grass. Slowly and painfully she lowered herself to the ground and sat, deep in thought, sadly aware of the fact that life as a Land Army girl was going to be no picnic.

'We'd better get on with it,' Lucy said without much enthusiasm after half an hour had passed. 'I wish they'd given us a flask of tea or something and I couldn't 'arf do with something to eat. You know Lucy, we ain't had any breakfast either, only that little bit of toast she gave us.'

'I know,' Marge replied, reluctantly getting to her feet. 'I 'ope Mrs Westlake is a good cook. I really do fancy a nice hot dinner but, if 'er cooking is anything like 'er cleaning we ain't got much chance 'ave we?'

They worked silently for the next couple of hours. The sky had become overcast and a fine drizzle started to fall.

'Why didn't we bring our waterproofs?' Lucy said, feeling the soggy, dampness of the rain seeping through her jumper. 'We're gonna 'ave to remember to bring them every day while we are out in these fields, otherwise we'll catch our death.'

Marge nodded silently as the rain beat down even harder, while Daisy bent her head low against the driving wind.

Mr Westlake was already seated at the table when they walked in, but his wife was nowhere to be seen. Lucy wondered where their dinner was; there was no sign of cooking on the stove. The table, which was covered with grubby white cloth, held a large loaf, a reasonably sized piece of cheese and a few pickled onions in a jar and that was it!

'Sit down, m'dears, and tell I how much of the field you be gone and done since this morning. Pour y'selves a cup of tea from yonder and get one for I while you be at it.'

Marge slumped down in a chair next to him while Lucy picked up the teapot from the stove and poured three cups of tea.

'Is this our dinner?' Marge waved a delicate hand in the direction of the food on the table.

'Oh, ar!' Mr Westlake replied as he cut himself a large chunk of cheese and stuffed it into his mouth.

'When do we get proper dinner, like hot food, meat and vegetables,' Lucy retorted, feeling angry that, after working hard in the field all morning, in the cold and rain, bread and cheese was all they were offered. Even some hot soup would have been appreciated.

'Ah! We be getting dinner proper tonight. That's how Mrs Westlake likes it. You can't work on a full stomach. Now, tell I how much of they field be ploughed m'dears.'

He stretched his short, stumpy legs out towards the fire, slurping his tea as he waited for one of them to reply.

'About half I think,' Marge replied as she stretched across the table to retrieve the cheese that he had kept next to his plate. He grunted in acknowledgement, gave a great belch and then lapsed into silence.

Lucy looked around the kitchen as she started to eat a small portion of bread and cheese, but with no butter on the table it was difficult to work up an appetite for the uninteresting food in front of her. She thought longingly of the college, her mind taking her back to the happy times when they all gathered in the dining room to enjoy the lovely, piping hot food that was placed in front of them. Her thoughts turned to her mother and her family – there were constant reports on the radio about the heavy air-raids over London and the many, many casualties, and she wondered how they were coping. Perhaps she should swallow her pride and write to her mother … but, somehow, after her outburst about the baby, she felt reluctant to do so. Maybe one day!

'Now, let's be 'avin you, m'dears.' Mr Westlake's voice broke through her train of thought. 'Time you be going back to yonder field – there be only half an hour for lunch. Now, afore you go, pick up they buckets of swill from the back door and feed the pigs – now be off with you.'

Marge got slowly up from the table. The last thing she felt like doing was ploughing in the rain, she would much rather sit around the kitchen stove and chat. Reluctantly she followed Lucy out of the back door and then, picking up a bucket each, they went down the narrow path to the sty. The pigs snorted excitedly when they saw them with food. They were an awesome sight as they jostled each other to get to the front and in the best position for the food. The girls quickly emptied the buckets into the pigsty, and then made their way across to the field where Daisy had been left grazing while they had their lunch.

'C'mon girl.' Lucy tugged at Daisy's bridle. 'It's time to go to the top field and finish ploughing.'

Marge started giggling. 'You ain't 'arf funny, Lucy. Anyone would think that 'orse knew wot you were saying by the way you're talking to it.'

'And 'ow do you know it don't,' Lucy answered crossly. 'I gotta get it used to me. After all, I'm the one whose got to take it to the blacksmith's to be shoed tomorrow and I don't fancy that at all.'

Marge fell silent for a moment. ''Ow are you gonna ride it like Mr Westlake said? You ain't never been on an 'orse before.'

'I know that, I know that,' replied Lucy. 'I'll worry about it tomorrow. Now let's get on the ploughing or we'll be in trouble if we don't get it finished today.'

They turned and walked across the fields in silence. Lucy's thoughts turned towards the young soldier she had met on the train, wondering whether they would ever meet again. How far away did he say he was stationed? Ten miles or something like that! Maybe if there were any dances locally and she went, maybe, just maybe, he might be there looking for her.

As if reading her thoughts Marge suddenly broke the silence.'Say, Lucy, let's see if we can go out tonight. We could go into the village and see what's going on. Wot do yer think?'

Lucy nodded thoughtfully. 'We'll ask them when we've finished work. Yes, we will! We'll ask them tonight!'

Finally they reached the half-ploughed field and, after harnessing Daisy to the plough, continued working, battling against the wind and the rain. They were too miserable to talk; the bad weather conditions had got them down and all they wanted was to get back to the farmhouse and get out of their wet, soggy clothes.

Two hours passed. In the distance, the sound of aircraft

hummed monotonously, but Lucy was too engrossed in her own private thoughts to heed it. Suddenly a shrill whistle filled the air and a loud explosion rocked the ground as a bomb exploded nearby. Seconds later came the intermittent crack of machine-gun fire as the plane came swooping down towards them. Marge flung her arms around Lucy and together they fell as bullets strafed the ground, narrowly missing them. Daisy reared in terror and raced back to the safety of the farm dragging the plough behind her.

'Oh my gawd! They're Germans, Lucy – what'll we do? We've got nowhere to hide!'

They raised themselves up onto their knees, clinging to each other in the middle of the field, eyes wide with horror as they watched two Spitfires zoom in to attack the enemy. Trails of white misty smoke drifted through the sky as the planes ducked and weaved, while sharp, intermittent bursts of machine-gun fire filled the air. The battle raged for several minutes until the German plane, obviously sensing defeat, broke away and headed for home with the Spitfires in hot pursuit.

'Bloody good riddance,' shouted Marge as she jumped up and down with excitement. 'Come back 'ere and you'll get some more. You Germans won't beat us.'

In the distance a black cloud of smoke rose lazily in the air. Unknown to them, the solitary bomb that had fallen had ended seven lives: two of them being young sisters who had been evacuated from war-torn London to the 'safety' of the countryside.

'I think we'd better get back to the farm and find that

blooming 'orse,' Lucy remarked as she turned towards the path that led down the hill to the farm.

Marge nodded her head. Inside she was shaking with fear. How close they had been to being killed! How easily life can change in just an instance!

Silently they trudged down the long winding path until, finally, they could just make out the farm silhouetted in the mist of an autumn evening.

'Thank god for that. I wonder wot we've got for tea, I'm starving,' Marge said as she pushed open the gate to the farm.

'I'm looking forward to a nice, 'ot bath and an hour's rest on my bed, that's wot I want,' Lucy replied. 'It ain't really such a bad life is it?'

'I don't call this much of a life, working all day in a field till me back feels like it's breaking,' Marge said, stamping her foot on the ground. 'There ain't no young people that I can see – and where will we go on our nights out if there's nuffink in the village?'

'Perhaps Mr Westlake will give us a lift to that town we saw. Must be a bit of life there. Don't worry, Marge, we'll ask him as soon as we've eaten, okay?'

In the murky shadow of evening Lucy could just make out the outline of Daisy grazing in the adjoining field. A sensation of utter relief swept over her; at least she didn't have to worry anymore – Daisy knew her way home.

''Ere we are, Marge,' Lucy said, as she thankfully dropped down onto the stone step of the outhouse and started pulling off her wellington boots, which were caked with mud. She was longing to get out of her clothes, which the driving rain had made cling to her body like a second skin.

'I feel like a bloomin' navvy,' grumbled Marge, as she sat next to Lucy on the step. From inside the house they could hear Mrs Westlake calling.

'If that be you girls, you'd better hurry and get to the table. I haven't got time to spend in the kitchen all night. We have all but finished our meal, so you'll just have to make do with what's left.'

'Bloomin' cheek,' muttered Marge. 'Who does she think she is, talking to us like that?'

They hurried into the kitchen and sat down at the table. Mrs Westlake placed a plate in front of each of them and, with a wave of her hand, indicated that they should help themselves to whatever was left. Lucy looked around in dismay at the remains of what appeared to be a stew, a few boiled potatoes and a small amount of soggy cabbage that floated in a pale, watery liquid. She gave a deep sigh. Certainly, it was nothing like the food they had at the college, or, for that matter, nothing like her mother's cooking. A wave of homesickness came over her. I want to go home, she thought sadly. Perhaps I should get in touch with mother … perhaps I will! Yes, perhaps I will!

'Did you hear that there bomb that was dropped on Bridgwater?' Mr Westlake said, peering at them over the top of his glasses.

'Course we did. Frightened the bloomin' life out of us,' retorted Lucy.

'Aye so it did ol' Daisy, by the way she came hurtling home m'dears. You should have kept a better eye on her though. Ain't no good letting horses gallop free.'

Marge shrugged her shoulders and sank her teeth into a

piece of cake that was on the table. She chewed thoughtfully for a few minutes.

''Ow far away is this place Bridgwater then? Perhaps you could give us a lift tonight so we can see what's going on there.'

'Go to Bridgwater! Whatever next! This is a respectable house; there'll be no going out and picking up with soldiers and the like,' Mrs Westlake said crossly. 'Anyway, what time do you think you're going to have, there's the house to clean as soon as you have finished eating and you can start on this kitchen.'

Her husband nodded silently in agreement as he noisily slurped his tea. There was a stunned silence for a moment, then Lucy looked up, anger glinting in her green eyes.

'We've been working since 7 o'clock this morning in the field. We ain't supposed to work day and night you know. We 'ad our evenings off at the college.'

'Spoilt rotten there, by the sound of it. Time you girls realised there's a war on and I don't want anymore cheek from you or I'll report you to Mrs Williams.'

'And who the 'ell is Mrs Williams,' interrupted Marge, banging her fist down onto the table in anger.

'She's your area supervisor and she looks after the likes of you Land Army girls, sorts out problems and the like. She won't be too pleased to hear that you're already being difficult. Now, no more talking, get this table cleared and sort the kitchen out.'

'Can I 'ave a bath as soon as I've finished?' Lucy looked at Mrs Westlake apprehensively. Somehow it didn't seem a good time to ask her anything.

'We can't be wasting water now there's a war on,' Mrs Westlake said haughtily. 'Friday night is bath night and we will all have to share the same water.'

The following morning was bright and sunny but it didn't lift Lucy's spirits.

'You'll be going to the blacksmiths this morning,' Mr Westlake mumbled through a mouthful of toast, 'so hurry up with your breakfast. You need to be there afore he gets busy like. Ol' Daisy don't like hanging around m'dear.'

Lucy shuddered at the thought of taking that stroppy horse anywhere, but to have to ride her was ridiculous. She told him she had never been on a horse before! Why didn't he go himself?

Marge looked up from the paper she was reading, a grin stretched across her face. 'Rather you than me, ducky,' she said, raising her eyebrows.

Lucy got up abruptly from the table and went to stand by the side of Mr Westlake.

'Look, I'm ready now. I'll do it; you see if I don't, but you'll 'ave to put that thing on 'er … you know wot you sit on.'

In the farmyard, Daisy showed her annoyance by flicking her head back and forward. She could feel this 'slip of a girl' trying to mount her – but each time she slithered off the other side. She didn't need anyone to take her to the blacksmith; she had done it so many times over the years. Suddenly there was a thud on her back and a pair of arms flung themselves desperately around her neck … So she had managed it at last!

Daisy pricked up her ears as Lucy shouted 'Go Daisy.

Go!' For a moment Daisy didn't budge, then with a loud whinny she reared and started down the narrow dirt path at a brisk trot. Lucy shrieked in terror as she clung for dear life around Daisy's huge neck. She seemed to be so very high up from the ground. What if she were to fall off? Her arms were aching and she knew she couldn't hold on much longer when, finally, they came to a small village with tiny thatched cottages set on either side of the road. Daisy trotted briskly past the church and skilfully manoeuvred her way down a small narrow alleyway between two cottages which led to the village square.

A few of the locals were hanging about passing the time of day when Daisy careered around the corner and came to an abrupt halt outside the blacksmith's forge. Lucy shot off over Daisy's head and landed on the grass verge. For a moment she couldn't move – she couldn't even breathe! Then, gingerly, she started to rise to her feet, while Daisy stood proud and tall – she had proved she was still 'the boss'.

'Wot you be doin', lass? That's no way to get off a horse.'

Lucy looked up at the big, burly man leaning over her and shook her head ruefully.

'I don't know wot to do with that 'orse. It hates me, I know it does.' She rubbed her shoulder thoughtfully. ''Ow am I gonna get it back to the farm, that's wot I want to know.'

The blacksmith grinned, showing a perfect set of white, gleaming teeth.

'Go and sit down on that seat over yonder, lass, while I shoe ol' Daisy, then when I am finished I'll show you the proper way to ride. She'll be no trouble if you take heed of what I am telling you.'

Lucy hobbled off to the seat; slowly she lowered herself onto it and closed her eyes. Memories of home danced like a movie in front of her, and she thought about the young soldier on the train, the piece of paper as the wind took it far, far out of her reach.

She felt angry tears sting her eyes. Why was nothing working out like she had planned? There was only one way to ever hope that she might see him again and that was to go out in the evenings, maybe to a dance at the local village hall. If he really wanted to find her he would be doing the same thing and then, maybe, one day, they would meet again!

She must have drifted into sleep as it seemed no time at all that someone was shaking her by the shoulder. She looked up and saw the blacksmith grinning down at her, with Daisy in tow.

'Come on, lass, 'tis time for you to be on your way. Daisy will be getting impatient to get back to the farm for some food. Now, come here to me and I'll help you get on her proper like.'

He held out a huge hand to help Lucy to her feet. She grimaced with a pain that seemed to run straight down her shoulder to her arm, causing her to bite her lip. The blacksmith bent over, clasping his hands together as he stood next to Daisy.

'Get 'ere, lass, put one foot in my hands, grab her bridle and swing t'other leg over. Don't be afraid – if yer shows Daisy that you know what you be doing, she'll give you no more trouble.'

Tentatively, Lucy put her left foot into the palms of his hands and holding the bridle swung herself up and onto

Daisy's broad back. Daisy flicked her head around and stared at Lucy, then proceeded to sulkily lower her head and looked at the ground.

'Now, the first thing to remember, lass, is that 'orses have a bit of trouble with their new shoes, slipping and the like. Don't worry, though, she won't fall over, but she will take it a bit easier going home. Now take the reins and sit back and enjoy the ride, lass. Daisy knows better than anyone her way home.'

With a gentle pat, Daisy was off, slowly and carefully putting one leg in front of the other, and Lucy began to relax as her body responded to the gentle rhythm of the horse.

'Cor! Fancy me riding an 'orse, just like royalty,' she gasped. 'Wot on earth would mother think if she could see me now?'

Chapter 6

The letter that was to dramatically change their lives fell through the letter box three days after the land-mine had fallen nearby. Josie picked it up and stared at it, wondering who it was from. The buff-coloured envelope meant it was something official, that much she knew but, who was it from? It had her mother's name on it so, she had to give it to her, but somehow she had a sense of foreboding – a feeling that things were about to change.

'Mum,' she called, 'there's a letter 'ere for you.'

Mother's voice came back from the depths of the kitchen. 'I'm busy, Josie; just put it on the table in the front room. I'll get it when I have finished here.'

Josie put it down on the battered, old table and stood impatiently looking out of the window. What was in the letter? She knew it was an official letter and, deep down inside her, she felt uneasy.

When mother finally opened the letter, her fears proved well founded:

Mothers with young children are to be evacuated to a place of safety. Please assemble at Brookhowse Road Community Centre at 10 a.m. on the 16th November. You must bring the minimum of clothing with you and also any medications that you are presently taking as it may be several days before you will be able to get anymore.

Josie's mother stared hard at the words. So very impersonal, so matter of fact, her whole life was to be upended yet the letter came across as if it were no more important than a dental appointment. Slowly she walked into her bedroom and looked around. It wasn't much by some people's standards but it was her home! Her first proper house in twenty years of marriage! Now she had to leave it, maybe never to return. And what about Charlie? He was a good husband, how could she just leave him to face the dangers of working on the docks without the support of his family around him? She stared silently into space – two days! Just two days and they had to be ready to leave …

'Wot's the matter, Mum? Why are you standing there like that?'

She looked round to see her daughter standing by her side and for a brief moment she wished she could love Josie like she did her other children – but there was something there, something she could not explain. Maybe it was because of what happened years ago when Josie was a baby! It was her decision – not Charlie's. She had made her mind up and ruthlessly carried it out. Would she ever forgive herself? But you can't change the past and sometimes it comes back to haunt you. She gave a sigh and shrugged her shoulders.

'We have to be leaving here in a couple of days,' she replied quietly, her voice strangely subdued. 'The Government says it is better if we are moved to the country.

Start getting a few of your things together, we don't have much time.'

'Wot about me dad?' Josie asked as she peered anxiously into her mother's face.

'Your father will have to stay 'ere. He has important work to do, Josie, and George will also be staying here because he's just got himself a job at the docks.'

A pale winter sun peeped out from behind grey clouds, casting dancing figures across the green fields below, and puffs of billowy white steam belched from the train's engine as it travelled steadily along the track, leaving behind the grime and dust of London. It was packed with evacuees, children of all ages, ticketed like so many parcels. Despite the trauma that surrounded them they were excited and happy, filled with a sense of adventure. On the other hand their mothers sat quietly, hardly speaking as they watched fields flash by as quickly as their lives were changing.

Josie sat with her small sister on her lap. She had seen it all before – the trees, the fields and the animals – but for the rest of the children it was different. Most had never been outside London before and they sat happily gazing out of the window with pale, thin faces, their eyes filled with wonder at the magic of the countryside.

'Wot the 'ell are those?' shouted Tommy Blackmore as the train thundered past a herd of cows, causing them to run in blind panic to the far side of the field. Josie turned towards him with a superior look on her face.

'Cor, fancy you not knowing wot a cow is, you really are stupid Tommy Blackmore.'

He stuck out his tongue, then turned and continued to look out of the window. An hour slowly passed and Josie began to get restless.

'Where are we going, Mum?' she asked anxiously.

'I don't know, no-one has told us, but there is one thing I do know, we are not going Kent way, we are going in the opposite direction.'

Josie smiled happily. Well, at least she was not going back to Kent where her grandmother lived and back to that awful school! She really didn't care where she went. London was boring, there was no-one to play with and she was looking forward to this great, new adventure.

Her thoughts were interrupted by the slowing down of the train as it pulled into a station. No-one knew where they were as all the names of stations, towns and streets had been taken down for security reasons. Suddenly there was a squealing of brakes and a belching of steam as the train came to a shuddering halt. Nervously they alighted from the train and stood in uncertain groups until, finally, they were marshalled into some semblance of order by a group of women from the Women's Voluntary Service. Three large double-decker buses stood outside the station waiting to take them to their final destination. Several of the children started to cry – the novelty had worn off and they wanted to go home!

Through a small country town the buses followed in convoy, then out along a long country road with a few houses on either side. Josie watched fascinated; this was a totally new experience, for until now her life had consisted of London and her grandmother's cottage. She had never been to any other place. They journeyed for thirty minutes until finally the buses drew up at the entrance of a large country house. An impressive sweeping, circular drive leading to a magnificent old oak door made the mothers gasp at the splendour of their new home, but the house looked empty and forbidding, the windows bare and dirty, while the once carefully tended grounds now stood neglected and overgrown with weeds.

Clambering down from the bus they stood in small, uncertain groups – now the situation was brought home to them with stark clarity – they were stuck in this desolate place; this house that seemed to be in the middle of nowhere. No corner shop, no buses or trams! What would they do about shopping? Where would they be able to buy clothes when they had enough clothing coupons? The worst thing of all was the unbearable knowledge that they may be living here for several months or, even years!

Mrs Blackmore was the first to speak. 'C'mon it's no good standing 'ere just looking at the place, for gawd's sake.' She turned to grab Tommy by the arm and saw a rather large lady walking up the drive towards them. The woman was dressed expensively in tweeds, the outfit accentuated by a beautiful pearl necklace and earrings.

'Cor blimey, you ain't one of us are you dearie?'

The lady drew herself up and haughtily addressed the evacuees. 'Certainly not! My name is Mrs Pope and I live in the manor house at the other end of the village. I have the key to let you in and see that you get settled.'

'C'mon then, luv,' shouted a voice from the back. 'Let us in then, we're bleedin' starving and the kids are knackered.'

'Oh! Quite,' muttered Mrs Pope as she hastily took a key from a large black leather handbag and opened the door. The evacuees crowded in, excited and anxious to see their new home, but their first impression was one of great disappointment.

As the big oak door swung open, they were confronted by a large hallway which had obviously seen better days. There was no covering on the floor and no trace of any furniture. Silently they filed in, their shoes echoing in the emptiness like a thousand soldiers on the march. Once inside they stood, unsure of what to do next. Mrs Pope grandly flung open a door at the far end and beckoned them to enter.

'Come in and make yourselves at home, ladies. Now! Who is going to assume the role of cook? You will all have to decide what your duties are to be, but at the moment you need to elect a cook. Whoever it is to be can follow me and I will show her the kitchen.'

For a moment there was a deathly silence as the women all looked at one another.

'I'll do it. I like cooking.' A small voice rose from the crowd. It was Mrs Green, a slight dark-haired woman in her early thirties. Hanging onto her rather long, brown coat were her three small children, bewildered and looking anxiously at this strange lady who seemed to be taking control of their lives.

'Come along then, you can make a pot of tea for a start.'

Mrs Pope marched purposely forward like a sergeant major leading his troops into battle. Mrs Green and her children followed like new recruits.

Josie looked around the room that was to serve as their sitting room.

'Mum, it ain't as good as our 'ouse in London is it?'

Mother put a finger to her mouth. 'Ssh! Josie – not so loud.'

'Don't tell 'er to ssh! She's bleedin' right. Wot are we going to do 'ere?' came a voice from the doorway.

They stared in dismay at their surroundings. The only furniture in the room was a dozen or so hard wooden chairs placed around a bare wooden table. There were no curtains at the window and the floor was completely bare. In one corner stood a very old radio which looked almost too old to be in working order. Two battered, old armchairs stood, one on either side of an empty grate. A few of the mothers burst into tears while the rest tried to comfort and reassure them.

It was only a matter of about ten minutes when Mrs Pope returned, having left Mrs Green to her own devices in the basement kitchen.

'Come on, ladies, while the tea is being made I will show you the rest of the house.'

Silently and miserably they followed her. Adjacent to the sitting room was the dining room, at least five times larger than any they had ever seen before. Leading off from the left was a cloakroom with a toilet and a cracked white sink which looked as if it was about to fall down. The taps were slightly rusty and ancient wooden floorboards completed the picture. They trooped upstairs to view the bedrooms – six in all and each identically furnished with camp beds and a couple of small, wooden chairs.

'Ladies,' Mrs Pope said, looking around rather anxiously, 'you must obviously realise that you will have to share bedrooms – I think probably two families to each room. Perhaps you can hang a curtain or something from the ceiling to give yourselves a little more privacy. I will try and find something at the manor that you can use.' She paused for a moment to catch her breath. 'Oh! I must tell you that there is no gas or electricity laid on here but there is a good supply of candles downstairs in the kitchen cupboard and, of course, there is plenty of coal for the stove in the kitchen.'

Mrs Pope finished her speech looking rather flushed. 'Has anyone any questions before I leave?'

Josie's mother raised a nervous hand. 'What do we do about food? There doesn't seem to be any shops nearby.'

'There are two buses a day that will take you into Reading, which is a town a few miles away and you will find plenty of shops there. Also, the butcher calls once a week and the baker twice. Naturally the milkman calls every day so there should be no problems.' She turned and walked towards the door, then paused briefly to look at them.

'Goodbye ladies, I may be back later with some curtains.'

The following morning Josie was awakened by the sound of children's footsteps echoing through the house. She turned uncomfortably on the small camp bed. The rough army blanket that she had been given rubbed against her skin. She closed her eyes and desperately tried to sink back into the comforting sleep that she had been so rudely awakened from. Sleep, however was impossible. The children, refreshed from their night's rest, ran excitedly through the big house. Their screams of delight as they discovered secret hiding places made Josie decide – she might as well get up, there was no way she was going to get anymore sleep today! Lowering her feet onto the bare floor she stood up rubbing her eyes. Obviously mother had already gone downstairs and had taken Molly with her. Her bed, which was identical to Josie's, was empty, so was Molly's cot.

Their bedroom was a small portion of a larger room on the first floor overlooking the garden. Mrs Pope, true to her word, had returned from the manor late last night and deposited several very large green, velvet curtains with instructions that they were to be used to divide the bedrooms into smaller, family units. Josie felt a wave of homesickness sweep over her. 'It ain't as good as our 'ouse,' she muttered sadly, and for a brief moment thought longingly of London and their home. Then, with a brief shrug of her shoulders, she turned, grabbed her clothes from a nearby chair and went in search of a bathroom.

The sound of voices and the clatter of cutlery directed her to the basement and the kitchen, where she found a few of the mothers sitting around a large wooden table finishing their breakfast. Mrs Green looked up from the stove where she was busy stirring the remains of a large pan of porridge and smiled.

'Would you like some porridge for your breakfast, dearie?'

'Please,' replied Josie. She picked up a bowl from the side and went over to the stove where Mrs Green promptly dished up a large ladle of rather lumpy porridge.

Josie carried the bowl to a corner of the kitchen and sat at a table. Where was her mother, she wondered idly, as she looked around the kitchen sadly. There was no-one of her age group here at all, just mothers with young children – very young children!

The porridge wasn't very interesting so she pushed it aside and looked at the window, it had bars across it. For a brief moment she wondered why, then decided it was not important anyway. As her eyes took in the large garden and the field stretching beyond she felt a strange sensation in the pit of her stomach. She missed Paddy so much and she didn't understand what was she was going to do with herself while she was here. Please God, not another village school. The memory of the last one still lingered and haunted her. As she stared out of the window she allowed her mind to go forward – in six months time it would be her birthday. She would be fourteen and old enough to go to work. Her eyes shone with excitement. What would she do? Where would she work? But, most of all she would have her very own money … money to pay for her keep, to buy clothes or shoes when she had enough coupons. SHE WOULD BE A GROWN-UP!

When she had finished her breakfast, Josie wandered aimlessly out of the house and down the gravel path to the iron gates which fronted the road and stood gazing from left to right along a deserted road and the fields beyond. No shops – no fish and chip shop – NOTHING!

A solitary tear trickled down her face as the memory of Paddy returned to haunt her. How he would have loved to live here; there were plenty of fields to play in and rabbits to chase. Slowly she raised her eyes towards the sky, her voice trembling with emotion. 'You know what, God! I ain't gonna forgive those Germans for wot they done to my Paddy. I will 'ate them for the rest of my life.'

She leaned morosely against an old stone pillar at the side of the gate and lapsed deep in thought. The sound of a vehicle coming down the road made her look up to see an army lorry, packed with soldiers, just a few yards along the road, and she watched silently as it went by. From the back a few of the soldiers were looking out. They saw Josie and suddenly the quiet countryside erupted with the sound of whistling and shouting. 'Hello beautiful,' shouted one. 'I'll be back to take you to the pictures one day – wait for me.' The lorry and the voices faded into the distance and the countryside became silent once more.

Josie stared after it in amazement – they were talking about her! They said she was beautiful! She felt a rush of colour to her cheeks as she turned and ran into the house and up the stairs to the bathroom, where she stood, breathlessly, in front of an old cracked mirror which was propped up against the window.

He called me 'beautiful' she thought wonderingly. He thinks I'm beautiful. She stared at her reflection in the mirror – when did this transformation take place? The face that stared back at her was, if not beautiful, pretty and delicate. Blue-green eyes stared out from a small, perfectly proportioned face. Brown hair hung in loose curls on her shoulders. She felt a surge of pride as she noted her figure. Her breasts were developing and her body had begun to look soft and curved like a woman! Yes! Now she definitely was a grown-up…

Weeks turned into months. Life at the manor house took

on an air of boring monotony. Josie spent most of her time looking after her sister along with many of the other children. Occasionally, mother would announce that they were going to Reading, a small market town some seven miles away and Josie would get herself ready and they took the Thames Valley bus to town.

Josie was fascinated by Reading: it was crowded with soldiers and airmen. Most of them seemed to be British but sometimes she would see one that had a different country shown on a badge they wore. Exotic sounding places like the Bahamas, which, to Josie, seemed very glamorous and she prayed that the war would last, at least until she was old enough to join up.

It was just before Christmas 1942 and the war had been going on for three years when her mother received the devastating news that George had been 'called up' and was joining the Royal Air Force to be trained as an air gunner. She read the letter with trembling hands, her face pale with worry. Josie felt a surge of pity sweep over her as she watched.

'Don't worry, Mum, 'e'll be alright. Nuffink is gonna 'appen to 'im,' she said reassuringly.

Mother looked up, her eyes were full of tears. 'Thousands will die before this war is over,' she said, her voice breaking with emotion. 'It's in the lap of the Gods who will survive; we'll just have to make the best of it. Your father will miss him though; it means he will be on his own in London now.'

She lapsed into silence as Josie turned and picked up little Molly, who was crawling around on the floor, gurgling happily. She took her over to the window and stared at the garden beyond. First Lucy had joined up, now her brother – where would it all end? What would her mother say when she found out that she wanted to join the Air Force when she was old enough?

'Josie, it's time we sorted out a job for you,' her mother said as they were finishing breakfast one morning. Josie had celebrated her fourteenth birthday a few days before with just a few cards from some of the mothers and, of course, one from her own parents, but that was about it. Josie stirred her tea thoughtfully as her mother continued.

'I think you should go to the biscuit factory in Reading and see if they want anyone. There must be something you can do. After all, with so many in the forces they must be short of workers.' She hesitated for a moment and then continued.

'I'll give you the money for your bus fare, so you had better be off first thing tomorrow morning and see what you can do.'

Josie nodded her head as mother noisily pushed her chair back from the table, picked up Molly and turned to walk from the room. She hesitated as she reached the kitchen door and turned to look back at her.

'We have kept you for fourteen years now, my girl, and it's time you supported yourself – if you don't work, you don't eat. It's as simple as that.'

The Huntley & Palmers factory stood in the centre of Reading – it was a large, grey building that had stood on the same spot for over a hundred years. Josie looked at it with some misgivings. 'Looks like a bloomin' prison to me,' she muttered as she approached the big iron gates at the entrance. For a few moments she hesitated, this was her first interview and she didn't have a clue what to do. With a determined look on her face she walked up to an elderly man standing just inside the gates.

He smiled and said, 'Can I help you, luv?'

'I've got to come 'ere and get a job, me mum said so. Do you know if they want anyone?'

He stroked his chin thoughtfully. 'Don't know, luv. Go into that office over there.' He pointed a finger across the concrete yard towards a small wooden door. 'They will be able to tell you. Good luck anyway.'

She smiled gratefully and made her way to the office and pushed open the door. Once inside she found herself in a small, square room. A desk was placed in the centre, where a rather brash looking blonde sat filing her nails, a look of boredom on her painted face. She looked up as Josie entered and without a word indicated a nearby chair. Josie sat down and waited. Was she supposed to speak first? She had always been taught to only 'speak when spoken to', but perhaps it was different at an interview. The blonde stared at her thoughtfully for several minutes, still filing her nails.

'How old are you?' she asked.

'I am fourteen,' replied Josie, shuffling her feet nervously as the girl continued to look at her critically.

'You look older than that to me,' she declared. 'Are you exempt from war-work?'

Josie shrugged her shoulders. "Ow would I know? Me mum told me to come 'ere and see if I could get a job.'

The girl tossed her bright blonde hair from her face and pushed a form in front of Josie.

'Well, I need to see your identity card and you will have to fill in this form, then if everything is in order you can start in the packing department on Monday morning at 8 o'clock. You will be paid two pounds a week plus a bag of broken biscuits. Of course, you may well be drafted into war-work later on. That's what happens to a lot of our workers; they just get started then they are sent off somewhere else.'

Josie smiled happily. 'I don't really care where I work as long as I get some money.'

It was less than a week when she received a letter telling her that her interview had been successful and she was to report at 8 a.m. on the following Monday.

Every morning she caught the 7.30 a.m. bus to Reading and made her way to the Huntley & Palmers factory. Once there, she stood in line with about twenty other girls in front of a large conveyor belt which transported numerous large tins of biscuits. The supervisor showed her how to deftly pick up a few biscuits from each of the tins and pack them neatly into smaller ones. Music blared out from an old radio and the girls sang happily as they worked.

Finally, at the end of the week, Josie found herself on a crowded bus as it made its way slowly through the streets of Reading, heading out into the country and taking her to her new home. She was sitting on the top deck gazing out of the window, but every few minutes she fumbled in her handbag and took out the little brown envelope which contained her first week's wages. A surge of excitement swept through her body as she traced the outline of the coins with her fingers.

For the first time in her life she had some money – she had £1 10s! It seemed to be a fortune but she wouldn't be allowed to keep it because mother had insisted that she pay for her keep now she was working. Maybe she would let her have the 10s!

Suddenly, she had a feeling that someone was watching her and, as she turned around, her eyes met those of a young airman. Josie blushed furiously and turned away to look out of the window. He was very handsome, she thought. But why was he looking at her like that? She kept her eyes firmly fixed on the window until they came in sight of the manor house. Quickly she made her way down the stairs and stood on the platform until the bus drew up outside. Jumping off, she stood in the road, watching as the bus disappeared into the distance. The young airman gazed at Josie and prayed that somehow he would see her again.

Josie walked slowly up the long, gravel drive and entered the house. Her mother greeted her excitedly and she couldn't wait to tell her the news. Lucy was coming to live with them! Somehow she had left the Land Army and was being sent home to await instructions about war-work.

'But, Mum! How can she do that? How can she just leave the Land Army?'

Mother held out a letter. 'Here, read this. She doesn't say very much except that she will be coming back to live with us until she gets sent to do war-work.'

Josie read the letter intently. It was as brief as mother had said. Lucy gave no explanation, she just said that she would be arriving in a couple of weeks. Josie grinned happily. Perhaps her sister could get work in Reading, then they could go to work together and it would be great to have someone near her own age to talk to at home. It had been just over two years since the sisters had seen each other and she idly wondered what Lucy looked like now. Had she changed? Would she think she had changed? Mother's voice interrupted her thoughts.

'We will have to get hold of another camp bed and put it next to yours in our room. I know it will be a bit cramped but we will just have to make the best of it. After all there is a war on!'

Josie nodded in agreement, she didn't care. It would be so good to have her sister for company, maybe they would be able to go to the local dance hall that all the girls in the factory talked about. She would listen fascinated while they recounted their adventures at the Olympia the night before. It sounded so exciting, Josie couldn't wait to see if her sister would go with her – that was, of course, if mother would allow it.

The next week seemed to fly by and soon it was the day of Lucy's arrival. Josie sat on the bus that was taking her home, barely able to conceal her impatience to get there. She had noticed the young airman when she got on. He was sitting just a few seats in front of her. By some strange coincidence he had turned around to look at her as she got on the bus, and for a moment their eyes had met before she quickly looked away.

Lucy was sitting in the dining room talking to mother over a cup of tea when Josie arrived home. For a moment they just stared, taken aback by the enormous change in each other. Josie looked at her sister, noticing how much slimmer she had become; her face glowed with a healthy sheen from the long hours out in the fresh air and Josie thought how pretty she was and wished she had lovely red hair like her.

Lucy's first impression was one of utter amazement at the transformation in Josie. Two years had changed her out of all recognition. When Lucy had left London her sister had been a small waif-like figure whose only interest in life was her dog and playing in the back streets of London's docklands. Now, the person before her had blossomed into a very pretty young lady, barely recognisable from the one she remembered.

Josie joined them at the table and they sat recounting their adventures over the past two years. It felt so good to have Lucy back – someone to talk to and, most of all, someone to go out with, to go into town and go dancing like all the other girls at the factory. A feeling of excitement bubbled up inside her as she thought of all the wonderful times ahead, until her thoughts were interrupted by mother announcing that she was going to put Molly to bed. Josie looked up and nodded absentmindedly – she bent down and kissed Molly on the cheek as she was scooped up in her mother's arms and taken upstairs.

Josie turned to her sister. ''Ow did you manage to get out of the Land Army then?' She leaned forward and rested her chin on her hands and waited expectantly.

Lucy grinned and sank back in her chair, while her eyes took on a faraway look as she started to recount the events of the past few weeks.

'Well, it was like this,' she started. 'You know I was sent to this farm in Evercreech?'

'Yes, yes,' replied Josie impatiently.

'It was really an 'orrible place; we were not allowed out, even to the village shop. Anything I wanted I 'ad to tell Mrs Westlake and she would get it for me.'

Josie shook her head sympathetically. 'I wouldn't like that at all.'

'Neither did I,' Lucy sighed, as memories came tumbling back. 'We even 'ad to do all the cleaning of the 'ouse after we'd worked all day on the farm. Look,' she said, holding out her hands. They were covered in calluses and blisters.

'But 'ow did you get away?'

'Well, the final straw came when Mrs Westlake made us bathe in the same water as they 'ad. Week after week it was like that. Marge reckoned that Mr Westlake used to pee in the bath just to spite us. Anyway, in the end we 'ad a big row and they called in Mrs Williams.' She lapsed into silence for a few moments then continued. 'Anyway, Mrs Williams eventually came to sort things out.'

Another pause as Lucy stopped for a moment to sip her tea. Josie sat staring in admiration at her sister. Imagine standing up to all those older people and telling them you were not going to do everything they wanted – it was almost unheard of! Lucy put her cup down on the table and continued.

'Mrs Williams said she didn't 'ave another posting for us right away, so she would make arrangements to 'ave us sent 'ome. I gotta stay 'ere until I get sent on war-work.'

'Yes, yes,' interrupted Josie, 'but 'ow did you get 'ere? They think you live in London, don't they?'

Lucy grinned. 'It was funny really. Mrs Williams took us to the station and put us on the London train, because that's our proper 'ome address ain't it?' Josie nodded. 'Well, she didn't wait for the train to leave, so when she was out of sight

I told Marge that I was going to Reading 'cause I thought it was time to make my peace with mother.'

Josie nodded half-heartedly and waited anxiously for Lucy to continue.

'Marge wanted to go to London, 'cos she thought of all the good times she would 'ave there. Anyway, we exchanged addresses, said goodbye and I jumped out of the train, crossed over the line and waited for a train to take me to Reading and 'ere I am.'

'But 'ow could you get off a train in Reading when you've got a ticket for London?' Josie's face puckered up in a frown.

'It's easy, I just waited in the toilet for awhile and when the porter was busy wiv people who are boarding the train I just slipped out.'

They lapsed into silence, each deep in their own private thoughts. The first flush of excitement at seeing each other had passed and now they felt strangely distant. So much had happened in the two years they had been apart, there was so much to say ... yet there was nothing to say!

Lucy spoke first. 'Wot are you doing then? 'Ave you got a job yet?'

'Course I 'ave,' nodded Josie, her eyes shining with pride. 'I work at the biscuit factory in Reading. I get £1 10s a week and some broken biscuits to bring 'ome.' She hesitated for a brief moment, then, as an afterthought, said, 'Don't suppose you'd be able to work at the factory!'

Lucy shook her head, her auburn hair glistening in the pale shaft of sunlight that shone through the window behind her. 'No, of course I can't. I told you, Josie, I 'ave to wait until they write to me. I dunno wot they will say or where they will send me but I 'ave to do war-work and packing biscuits is hardly that, is it?'

Josie finished the last remaining dregs of her tea and stood up.

'Shall I show you the 'ouse now, Lucy?'

Lucy grabbed her bag from the floor and nodded. 'I can't wait to see this place; it looks huge from the outside. Let's go to the bedroom first then I can dump my bag on my bed. I don't fancy carrying it over the 'ouse wiv me.'

They climbed the stairs until they reached the bedroom which they shared with two other families. Lucy looked around in despair: the small section that had been allocated to them looked bleak and depressing. She noticed the bare wooden floor, the three camp beds and a cot pushed so close together that there was hardly any room to squeeze between them. One high-backed chair with well-worn green upholstery and that was all the furniture in 'their section'.

'It ain't very grand,' Lucy muttered, pulling a face, 'but still it's got to be 'ome to us ain't it? We've got no choice.'

Josie nodded. 'It's not so bad once you get used to it. The worse thing is these 'orrible army blankets, they are so rough they make my skin all red and itchy.'

Lucy threw her bag on the spare camp bed and took Josie by the arm. 'C'mon then, let's go and look around ...'

Several days went by and Lucy soon fell into the daily routine. She envied Josie, as at least she managed to get out of the house for several hours each day and mix with people of her own age. Lucy felt isolated – there was an uneasy peace with her mother – no word had been mentioned about that fateful day two years ago when Lucy had been so angry and disgusted and she had joined the Land Army to get away from it all. Yet, she knew in her heart that mother had not forgotten or, indeed, forgiven her for her outburst.

Exactly two weeks after her arrival, Lucy received a letter – which had been forwarded on to her by her father. It was from the Land Army head office, informing her that it had been decided to release her from her duties and that she was to report to the local Labour Exchange and register for war-work immediately. Slowly she folded the letter neatly and put it in her handbag while mother stood waiting expectantly for some indication as to the contents. They stared silently, uncomfortably, at each other until Lucy felt duty bound to volunteer the information.

'I've got to go and register for war-work straight away. They ain't got a place for me in the Land Army any more.'

Mother nodded briefly and turned as if to leave the room. As she reached the door she turned. 'I suppose you will need to stay here with us then!'

Lucy smiled. 'Well it ain't exactly the Ritz but it would be nice, perhaps I could go in with Josie tomorrow morning; she can show me where the Labour Exchange is. I 'ope I can get war-work around 'ere. I don't fancy travelling miles on my own.'

Early the next morning, Josie and Lucy were waiting for the bus to take them into Reading. The weather was just beginning to feel spring-like and the girls were happy to be together. They decided to meet at the People's Pantry at lunchtime. The food was cheap but very good and Lucy was looking forward to her day out in a new town.

The green double-decker bus laboriously trundled into view and pulled up, as if reluctant to go any further.

'I can only take one of you,' the conductor shouted as they ran towards it.

Josie looked at him appealingly. 'C'mon, let us both get on; she's my sister. We won't take up much room, please!'

The conductor laughed as he pulled them onto the bus and rang the bell. 'You know how to get round a man you do,' he said with a wicked grin on his face. They stood huddled up together on the crowded bus as it made its way slowly to town.

'You get off wiv me, Lucy, and I'll show you where you gotta go.' Josie shook her sister impatiently by the arm. 'Wot's the matter? You've been staring out of the window ever since we got on this bus.'

'I'm sorry, Josie, I was just thinking – you know, wondering how our lives would have been now if there had never been a war. What did you say?'

'I said get off wiv me and I'll show you where to go,' Josie said sharply. 'It's no good wondering about things like that – there is a war on and that's the end of it.'

Lucy turned her back and continued to stare out of the window.

Thirty minutes later the bus drew up at Reading Station and they made their way towards the factory. Once they reached the gates Josie pointed down the road.

'Go down there, Lucy, and left at the first turning. Go right down to the end and you'll see the Labour Exchange on the corner, but I don't suppose it'll be open yet, so get yourself a cup of tea at the station first.'

The factory hooter sounded, warning all employees that it was time to start work.

'I gotta go, Lucy – see you later.' Josie ran quickly into the grey, dark building and disappeared from sight. With a sigh Lucy turned towards the station, wondering what the future had in store for her. Everything was so unsettling! When would the war end so that they could get back to a normal life?

Josie tapped her foot impatiently on the floor as she waited at the restaurant for Lucy to appear. She had found a small table near to the window where she had a good view of the road, but where was Lucy?

Suddenly, in the distance she saw her heading toward the restaurant and as she drew nearer Josie beckoned, indicating the vacant seat next to her.

'Let me catch my breath,' gasped Lucy as she collapsed into the nearest chair.

'You're late,' Josie retorted petulantly. 'I've only got 'arf an 'our left, then I gotta be back in the factory.' She paused to look at the menu. 'I think there's still some shepherds pie left. D'yer fancy that?'

'I'll go and get it, Josie. You stay 'ere and mind our seats.'

Josie watched as her sister joined the small queue that had formed at the counter. She soon returned and placed a steaming plate of shepherds pie in front of her. 'Well! Wot's 'appened then? 'Ave they got any work for you ?' Josie asked impatiently.

Lucy nodded, her green eyes shining with delight. 'Guess what? I'm gonna be working not five minutes walk from 'ere. It's at Vickers, the aircraft factory on Station Road.'

Josie could hardly conceal her excitement. 'We'll be able to go to work together, Lucy, that'll be fun.'

There was a slight pause as Lucy reflected on that remark.

'I ain't gonna be able to go to work with you 'cause I'll be working nights to start with. It's only for a month then I'll do a month on days, then we can go to work together.'

They chatted, happily unaware of a young man watching them from a corner of the restaurant. He had seen Josie many times on the bus when he was returning to the Air Force base at Mortimer and she was coming home from work. As he stared, she suddenly turned and looked across the room – their eyes met. He smiled in recognition. Josie blushed and turned away ... then, out of the corner of her eye she caught sight of the clock on the wall.

'Lucy, I've gotta run, I've only got five minutes to get back to the factory and I'll get in trouble with the supervisor if I'm late. See you later on tonight.'

She pushed her chair back noisily from the table and hurried towards the door. In the far corner, the airman, seeing Josie was leaving, quickly paid his bill and followed her.

A chilly wind was blowing as she stepped out into the narrow street, making her shiver. Quickly she pulled her coat around her slim body then she felt a tap on her shoulder and, turning around, she came face to face with the young airman. For a few moments they just stared at each other, oblivious to the world and the people hurrying by.

'I hope you don't mind, but I wondered if you'd like to come out with me tomorrow night. That's if you're not doing anything else.' His dark blue eyes scanned her face as he waited for her answer.

Josie looked up at him. He was taller than her, extremely good-looking and, most of all, he really seemed to like her.

For a moment she didn't answer – visions of her mother invaded her mind – what would she say if she knew Josie was contemplating going out with an Air Force corporal! Certainly she would not approve of it but, perhaps, just this once, she could disobey her by pretending to go to her friend who lived in a small cottage near the big house. She took a deep breath and smiled.

'Course I will, if you want me to. Where will we go?'

The young man frowned and shuffled his feet nervously, looking down at the pavement.

Josie became impatient. 'Well 'urry up then. I gotta be in work in a minute and I'll be for it if I'm late.'

He raised troubled eyes to meet hers. 'I don't have much money at the moment and it's another week to payday. What about going for a walk?'

'Okay. I gotta go now.'

'I'll meet you at the gates to your house at half past seven,' he called after her as she ran down the road.

She disappeared into the factory where she found the supervisor waiting for her.

'You're almost five minutes late from lunch, Josie. You will be stopped a quarter of an hour's pay next week. Don't let it happen again, the whole line is thrown out if one of you girls is missing.' The supervisor stood tapping her fingers angrily on the board along the side of the conveyor belt. She was a tall, angular woman who struck fear in the hearts of all the young girls who worked there.

'Sorry,' replied Josie as she quickly took her place on the line.

Bright, loud, happy music came from over the radio and Josie sang at the top of her voice as she thought of the young airman. This would be her first date! What would they do? Where would they walk to? Would he kiss her? Would she let him?

'Hey, Josie,' called Kate from across the line. 'What's the matter with you? You've missed a couple of tins and, by the look on your face I'd say you were in love.'

'I've gotta date, that's wot,' Josie replied proudly, grinning from ear to ear.

'Josie's got a date! Josie's got a date!' several of the girls chorused. 'Watch out what you do when you're with this fella, or you might get yourself in trouble.'

'There'll be trouble for you girls if you don't get on with your work.' The supervisor strolled down the line as she spoke, fixing everyone with a steely stare. There was immediate silence except for the monotonous hum of the belt as it moved on and on.

Later, on the bus going home, a happy smile played on Josie's lips, while a bubbly sense of excitement surged through her body. She had a date! She just couldn't wait for the evening to come but as she walked through the door her mother was waiting.

'There's a letter for you, Josie. Who on earth could be

writing to you? It looks official to me. Now, hurry up and open it and tell me what it's all about.'

Josie picked up the small, brown envelope from the kitchen table, frowning slightly as she opened it, while a strange sense of doom swept over her as she started to read the contents.

'We write to inform you that you are required to register for war-work immediately. Please contact your local Labour Exchange and take this letter with you.'

Josie stared at the words in disbelief. Leave her job at the factory where she had so many friends and where for the first time in her life she was really happy! And, what about the airman? She might never see him again! As if from a distance she heard her mother's voice.

'Josie, what on earth is the matter? You look quite pale as if you've had a shock.'

Silently, Josie held out the letter, and then turned to stare blankly out of the window. Rain had just started to fall and the sky looked grey and depressing. She felt a stab of sadness in her heart. Suppose she did get sent away just as she had got herself a boy-friend. It was not fair! It just wasn't fair!

Her mother tapped her on the shoulder then held out the letter.

'I think you had better go first thing in the morning, Josie, but keep the letter so you can show it to your supervisor when you get back to the biscuit factory. You're bound to be late, that's for sure, and if you show them the letter maybe they won't dock you any pay.'

Josie pulled a face and dejectedly climbed the stairs to the bedroom and flung herself miserably onto her bed. Why did everything go wrong? She was settled and happy, her sister was living with her, and she even seemed to have a boy-friend! Now it might all be taken away from her. Tears stung her eyes as she tried desperately to stop herself from crying. She didn't hear the door of the bedroom open.

'Wot's the matter with you?' Lucy had come into the room and was looking at her with anxious eyes.

'I gotta go and register for war-work, that's wot's wrong – it's not fair.'

Josie's voice faltered away and she turned her back on her sister and stared out of the window.

Lucy gave a deep sigh. 'It's no good making a fuss, Josie. No matter wot you say or do, it won't make any difference. We've just gotta do wot we are told until the war is over.'

Lucy paused for a moment, then, as an afterthought, asked her about the airman she had seen Josie talking to outside the restaurant.

'It ain't gonna make any difference now. I will probably be sent miles and miles away and never see him again,' Josie replied sullenly.

'You mean that guy wanted to take you out? I hope you said no! You know how mother is about boy-friends. She won't let you go.'

'Well I'm going. I don't care – I'm gonna see 'im tomorrow night and don't you dare tell on me.'

Lucy shook her head in despair – Josie was so headstrong. 'It's your funeral if mother finds out,' she retorted as she swung on her heel and left the room.

The following morning found Josie outside the Labour Exchange, waiting patiently for it to open. The sign on the door said 9 a.m. but the big church clock down the road showed 9.15 a.m. She began to get fidgety – already she was an hour late for work. Why didn't someone come and open the door?

Almost ten minutes elapsed before it finally opened and an elderly man peered at her through thick horn-rimmed glasses as he held the door open for her to enter. Nervously, she sat on the edge of the chair he had indicated and waited while he seated himself comfortably on the opposite side of a large oak desk. Josie took the letter from her handbag and pushed it across the desk towards him. He adjusted his glasses, then with a brief glance at her he slowly read the letter.

'Where 'ave I got to go then?' she blurted out anxiously. The suspense was killing her. 'Are you gonna send me away?'

Brown eyes peered over heavy glasses. 'Just a moment young lady, just a moment. I have to see where you will be needed the most and, war or no war, these things can't be rushed.'

Josie slumped back in her chair and waited impatiently while he fumbled with a big wad of papers that he had taken from a steel cabinet in the corner of the office. Her heart was racing, he was going to send her miles away – she just knew it! Miles and miles away from everyone. She couldn't bear it! She felt tears welling up in her eyes and desperately tried to stop them trickling down her face. The old man looked up from the wad of papers – his face solemn and stern.

'We desperately need more workers at the aircraft factory,' he announced almost apologetically. 'I have to send you there – I have no choice young lady.' He wiped his brow, then shook his head sadly. 'We're in a desperate situation and we need you young ones to work hard and build us some more Spitfires or God help us!'

'Wot aircraft factory? Where is it?' Josie demanded, her heart thumping. Could it be the one where her sister was working? No, that would be too good to be true. Before she had the chance to say another word, the old man volunteered the information.

'Do you know Vickers the aircraft factory on Station Road?'

'Yes, my sister works there.' Josie's voice was almost a whisper filled with suspense.

'Well now, that's where you are needed and that's where you will go. Report to Mr Wicks the supervisor next Monday morning at 8 o'clock sharp and give him this.'

He handed Josie a form stating her name, date of birth, identity number and details of the factory. She grabbed it eagerly from his hand – her heart felt as if it would explode! She was not going to be sent away – she could stay in Reading! And she would still have a boy-friend.

'Thanks, Mister,' she shouted as she ran from his office. Her heart was bursting with happiness and the world was a happy place again. Flinging her arms in the air and giving little skips of joy she ran down the road – life was so good! The old man watched her from the office window, shaking his head in disbelief.

'What a strange girl! How can anyone be happy working eighty hours a week in that factory? Ah, the young of today! God help us – the young ones don't seem to be taking this war seriously at all.'

Still muttering to himself he turned and busied himself with the mound of paperwork on his desk.

Josie ran all the way back to the biscuit factory and thrust the letter from the Labour Exchange into the supervisor's hands.

'I'll be leaving, Miss. I'll be leaving on Friday 'cause I've gotta go and do war-work at the aircraft factory down by the station.' Josie stood proud and tall, she was going to do important war-work, just like her sister … she would be building Spitfires!

'You'll be working long hours there,' the supervisor said, shaking her head as she read the schedule attached to the letter. 'Have you seen the work rota on this form?'

Josie shook her head and shrugged her shoulders.

'It don't matter wot it is, I gotta do it, ain't I?'

'You'll be working from 8 a.m. until 8 p.m. all week. Then on Saturdays and Sundays you have to work from 8 a.m. until 5.30 p.m. It's an awful lot of hours, Josie. Not only that but how will you get home? Your last bus leaves at 6 o'clock.'

'Well, wot about me day off then?'

The supervisor shook her head slightly. 'You don't get a day off when you're doing war-work, Josie, and you can't take a day off unless you are sick. I mean really sick! You would have to have a doctor's note.'

Josie felt a pang of sadness sweep over her. She was going to miss the factory and all her friends … Even the supervisor!

Josie grimaced as memory of that conversation came flooding back. She wished the bus would get a move on –

she was meeting the airman at 7.30 p.m. and it was past 6 o'clock now! When she started work at the aircraft factory, how would she be able to go out? It would be 9 o'clock before she got home!

The bus pulled to a halt a few yards from the house. She jumped off and ran breathlessly down the road, up the gravel drive and straight into the kitchen where Mrs Green was busy washing-up. She turned as Josie came crashing through the door.

'You're in an 'urry, my girl, ain't yer? Where's the fire?' she remarked as she dried rough, red hands on a coarse towel.

'I'm gonna see my friend tonight. She lives down the road past the pub and I gotta be there by 'alf past seven, so is me dinner ready please?'

'Sit down, dearie, I'll get it out of the oven for you. Mind, it'll be hot though.'

Josie stared at the food in front of her. She wasn't a bit hungry; she was too excited and nervous to eat. She'd eat a little bit then run up to her room to get ready!

'Your mother has been waiting for you, Josie; she wants to see you as soon as you get in.' Mrs Green's voice broke through her train of thought, making Josie look up, wondering what mother wanted her for that was so urgent. She pushed her chair back and jumped up from the table.

'I'll go now, Mrs Green, I'll go straight upstairs.'

The bedroom door was open and she could see her mother sitting on her bed, holding Molly and staring out of the window to the vast countryside beyond.

'Wot d'yer want me for, Mum? I came up as soon as Mrs Green told me.'

She turned and a frown crossed her face. 'Well, Josie, I want to know how you got on today at the Labour Exchange! Are they going to send you away?'

Josie shook her head and grinned.

'I gotta go and work at the aircraft factory, you know the one Lucy works at! I start there next Monday.' She held out the piece of paper she had been given. Her mother read it intently then handed it back. For a moment or two she silently stared at her young daughter. Her Josie doing war-work! Making such important things as Spitfires, it didn't seem possible – she was only a child. A feeling of intense sadness swept over her – if only there was a way to erase the past! If only she could take Josie in her arms, tell her the truth and beg her forgiveness … she took a deep breath as if trying to dispel these troubling thoughts.

'I suppose that will be the end of our free biscuits, Josie, because if you don't work at the factory anymore they are not gonna give you any biscuits, are they?'

Josie shook her head sadly. 'I never really thought of that, Mum.'

'Oh well! I guess that's what war does, takes everything away from you. All I can say, Josie, is God help the Air Force if you are going to be involved in building the planes.' She stood up and turned to go downstairs.

'Mum, Mum,' Josie called in panic, 'can I go out tonight for awhile?'

Her mother turned swiftly and looked at Josie with suspicious eyes.

'Out! What do you mean? Where do you think you are going?'

Josie's face coloured up as her mother's eyes seem to pierce into her very soul!

'Well, that girl who lives round the corner said if I was fed up wiv being 'ere all the time I could go round there. Please let me go Mum!'

'Alright, my girl, but you be sure and behave yourself – no talking to any boys and you're to be home by 9.30 p.m. or there will be trouble.' She turned on her heel and walked out of the door.

Josie sat down on the edge of her bed and breathed a sigh of relief just as Lucy appeared in the doorway.

'Are you still going out wiv that Air Force fella, Josie? Are you really gonna do it?' Lucy looked worried as she stared at her sister.

Josie grinned, her eyes sparkling with excitement. 'Course I am. Mum thinks I'm going to Mary's 'ouse but I gotta be 'ome by 9.30 so I've only got two hours.'

Lucy shook her head in despair. Suppose Josie got into any sort of trouble – she would never forgive herself. She pushed the thought into the back of her mind. What was the use of worrying – Josie was strong-willed. She would have to learn about life the hard way. If she didn't listen to anyone else, then it was her own fault.

'I've just got a letter from Marge,' she said, desperately trying to change the subject.

'Whose Marge?' exclaimed Josie as she frantically searched through a cardboard box that contained her entire wardrobe.

'You know, my friend that I 'ad in the Land Army! She's in London now and she said it's really bad there, lots of damage from the bombing but she's 'aving a good time. She says she paints 'er legs brown to look like stockings, then draws a line up the back.'

Josie sat back on her heels and stopped rummaging through the box.

'Why would she do that? Seems daft to me.'

Lucy gave a sigh of resignation. ''Cause it's to make it look as if you've got stockings on, of course.'

'I ain't ever 'ad a pair of stockings,' Josie said almost to herself as she retrieved a crumpled blue dress from the box, looking at it critically as she shook it out. 'D'yer think this is alright to wear tonight, Lucy? D'yer think 'e will like it?'

Lucy smiled – she remembered that dress – mother had brought it home one day about four years ago. She had held it up proudly in front of Lucy and had said: 'Look what Mrs Spencer, the lady I do a bit of cleaning for, has given me. She said it would probably fit you a treat. Go on now, Lucy, put it on – put it on at once and let me see you in it.'

Lucy had tried it on excitedly: any new clothes, second-hand or otherwise were a rarity in the family and she was only too pleased to have it. The dress fitted perfectly, hanging in soft folds around her body, and Lucy had worn it and worn it, until it became too tight as she blossomed into a young lady. Now it was Josie's.

'I'd give it a bit of an iron if I were you; it's all screwed up, you can't wear it like that.'

'Oh gawd! Josie gasped. 'How am I gonna do that without mother asking me why I need to iron it tonight?' She paused for a moment staring at the crumpled dress. 'I ain't got anything else to wear,' she wailed miserably, looking at her sister who was lying on her bed watching her with an amused look on her face.

'C'mon, give it 'ere then.' Lucy stretched out her hand and took the dress.

'Go and get yourself ready and I'll iron it for you. God 'elp me if mother finds out though!'

Josie gave a yelp of joy and hurried into the bathroom; two seconds later she ran back into the bedroom. 'Could you lend me your lipstick, Lucy? I just want to use a little bit … please!'

Lucy shook her head in despair. Mother never approved of girls wearing make-up, especially at Josie's age! If she came upstairs and found Josie wearing lipstick and the blue dress she would go mad.

'You know wot mother is like, Josie, she'll kill you if she sees you wearing make-up. Not only that but I've only got a little left and it's so hard to get now.'

Josie stood her ground defiantly. 'Lend me some lipstick please,' she implored, stretching out her hands. Lucy hesitated for a moment, then shrugged her shoulders.

'Okay, it's your funeral if you get caught but whatever you do, Josie, please don't be late 'ome.'

Dusk was beginning to fall over the countryside as Josie crept out of the house and walked down the long drive to the gates, shivering in the blue dress. She should have worn a coat but the only one she possessed was shabby – another hand-me-down from her sister. Perhaps she should have worn it but she looked much prettier in just the dress and, with a little lipstick on, it made her feel very grown-up and important. She giggled as she thought how she had crept out of the house to avoid her mother.

The gates loomed up, barely visible through the gathering darkness, but there was no sign of him. Surely he hadn't let her down. If she went back indoors now she would likely be caught out by her mother and then life would not be worth living. She stood uncertainly by the gates, looking up and down the desolate road while the trees on the other side swayed and groaned in a fresh breeze that was beginning to pick up. Sudden panic swept over her and the countryside became a frightening place.

Josie leaned against a stone pillar as if to draw comfort from its cold, stone exterior. Then, from a distance came the sound of footsteps, so faint at first that she could barely hear them, then they became more distinct as they drew nearer and nearer. Her heart skipped a beat as she shrank back into the shadow of the stone pillar and waited half in excitement and half in terror as the footsteps stopped just a few feet away from her. Josie peered anxiously round the pillar. Was it him? Suddenly, the figure caught sight of her and let out a long, low whistle.

'Josie, is that you?' She nodded and smiled. 'You look so pretty in that dress. You look so different somehow tonight.' He gave a nervous laugh. 'I'm sorry, I didn't mean that you don't always look pretty but you just look special tonight.'

Josie was glad of the darkness, as she felt her face colour up in embarrassment.

Reaching out he took her hand and they walked towards the river, slowly, silently, neither quite knowing what to say. Suddenly Josie broke the silence.

'Wot's yer name then? You ain't told me much about yourself 'ave you?'

The airman let go of her hand and slipped an arm around her shoulder.

'My name is Michael – Michael Gardner. All my mates call me "Digger".'

Josie bent her head. Being on a date was very difficult; it was the first one she had ever had and she didn't know what say or what to do.

'Well, telling me your name ain't much is it,' she blurted out.

He laughed a soft, gentle laugh. 'Okay! Here goes, first I'll tell you my age … I am eighteen and my birthday is two days before Christmas. By the way, Josie, how old are you?'

She raised her eyes to meet his. The full moon glistened on her face, the light shining in her eyes creating an intangible aura. He caught his breath; she was so young, so desirable. There was something special about her! Something very special. They had reached the end of the field which led to the river. Michael stopped by the 5-bar gate and leaned against it, putting his arms around her slender body. He felt her tense, then gradually she began to relax and they stood gazing into the silent night.

'You still haven't told me how old you are, Josie.'

'I'm fifteen – I was fifteen last month.'

He smiled at her. 'I know you come from London, Josie, anyone could tell that just by your accent.'

Her face lit up with pride – she was happy with her background. Her dad had told her that cockneys were the best people in the world and he was always right.

'Where d'yer come from then?' she replied.

147

'Norfolk. I live with my mum and dad in a little village just outside Norwich.'

He reached into his breast pocket and pulled out a photo of an old, thatched cottage. Pictured on the path leading to the front door was a dark-haired lady cuddling a large black dog. 'That's my mum,' he said proudly, 'and that is my dog, Ben.'

Josie stared at the photo for a few moments before handing it back.

'D'yer miss 'er?' she asked. 'I don't think I'd miss my mum. Anyway, she's 'ere with me so it's not important is it?'

'I wish I was with my parents,' Michael replied sadly. 'I can't wait to go home. I don't want to fight in a war and be made to kill people I don't even know. I want to get back to my job and my friends.' He paused for a moment then added with a laugh, 'And Ben, of course.'

''Ave you got any bruvers or sisters?' Josie leaned closer to him as a feeling of sympathy swept over her.

He shook his head.

'Wot d'yer do in the Air Force then?'

'I'm training to be an air gunner,' he replied. 'Back in civvy street I was a mechanic but I guess they had enough mechanics so I have ended up being an air gunner.' He looked up towards the sky and pointed a finger at the full moon. 'See that, Josie? That's called a bomber's moon. When you are up there in a plane and it's a full moon, you can see most anything – like day it is.'

'I never want to go up in a plane,' retorted Josie almost defiantly. 'It ain't safe and, anyway, I 'ate 'em.'

For a fleeting moment, visions of Paddy lying in a pool

of blood appeared in front of her. Yes, she would always hate planes, no matter how long she lived.

Michael's voice brought her back to the present. 'Will you join up when you are old enough?'

'I don't know. Maybe, but I don't know. I gotta start doing war-work on Monday, making Spitfires. Wouldn't it be funny if you was up in one of the planes I 'elped to make.'

He tossed back his head and laughed loudly 'I can't imagine you making Spitfires – no way!'

Josie pulled away from him and stuck her hands on her hips defiantly. 'Well, my sister does, so why can't I?'

He grinned and squeezed her hand. 'I'm just teasing you, Josie – I'm sure you'll do just fine.'

They lapsed into silence, both staring at the moon as it cast its glow over the earth while a million stars dusted the deep velvety sky. The sound of the wind as it gently teased and danced through the branches of the willow trees was somehow comforting.

It was a magical moment and, all of a sudden, the whole world seemed at peace. Josie sighed as a feeling of contentment swept over her; she wanted to stay here forever and ever. She wanted Michael to be by her side forever and ever, but then in the distance the sound of approaching aircraft stirred her and brought her back to reality; to the horror of the war and the fear that never left her.

'Do you hear those planes? They are our boys off on a bombing raid over Germany,' Michael said, pointing excitedly to the sky.

In the distance silvery specks of light came towards them, glistening in the moonlight.

''Ow do yer know they are ours? 'Ow do yer know they are not Germans?'

Josie's heart was thumping, her legs felt weak as the memory of the London bombings swept over her. She looked around ... there was no place to hide! She was in that place of fear again, that place that invaded her dreams every night. As if from a distance she heard Michael's voice ...

'It's easy once you get used to it – our planes make a slightly different noise. I would know our boys anywhere; that's what comes of working on them every day.'

The noise grew louder – they were flying low, directly above them, their engines roaring in the silence of the night. Josie screamed and flung herself onto the damp ground in terror and put her fingers in her ears to stop the noise of the planes and the awful memories. Michael bent down towards her.

'Josie, what's the matter? Why are you so frightened? They are only our planes going over, they won't hurt you.' He pulled her to her feet.

'I know.' She was crying now. 'But I can't 'elp it, the only planes I know are the ones that bombed us in London and a lot of our 'ouses got blown up and a lot of people I knew got killed, so now, every time I 'ear a plane I panic.' Josie's voice trailed off miserably.

Michael put his arms around her trembling body and held her close. His heart reached out to her.

'It's okay, Josie – don't worry. I understand. It must have been awful for you in London. I haven't known any bombing yet and I don't want to.'

'They killed me dog Paddy,' she whispered, tears

streaming down her face. 'They killed 'im and I ain't ever gonna forgive 'em. 'E was my best friend and now I ain't got a best friend anymore.'

Michael hugged her closer. 'I'll be your best friend, Josie, if you'll let me.'

A sad smile crossed her face. 'Okay, you can be my best friend but I'd rather 'ave Paddy. Anyway 'e's gawn now and 'e ain't never coming back.'

The memory of Paddy's death made her shiver. Michael quickly took off his jacket and put it around her shoulders.

'Come on, Josie, let's walk, you are shivering, this will keep you warm.'

She pulled his jacket tighter around her body, feeling the warmth caress her like a soft summer sun as hand in hand they made their way along the riverbank, watching the dark blue water as it drifted gently downstream; the light from the moon bouncing off the little ripples creating an illusion of stars.

'Ain't it beautiful,' said Josie, as she bent down and trailed her hand slowly through the cold glistening water.

'Not as beautiful as you are, Josie,' he said softly.

She looked up at him and grinned broadly. 'I ain't beautiful, Michael, I'm just me!'

'Do you miss London very much, Josie?'

'Course I do. I want to go home and I want to see me dad and me bruvver. 'E's in the Air Force just like you and I ain't seem him for a long time.'

Michael suddenly looked down at his watch. 'Did you say that you've got to be in by 9.30, Josie?'

She nodded.

'Well, kid, we've only got ten minutes to get to your house.'

'Oh! My mum will kill me if I'm late, let's run quick.'

They arrived panting at the gates to the house and she quickly pushed them open.

'I gotta go now, bye,' she said as she ran towards the front door.

'Hey! Wait a minute – if I'm going to be your best friend I have to see you again. How about tomorrow night? I should be able to get off then.'

'Okay, okay, I gotta go now,' she gasped, breathing a sigh of relief to find that the door was still unlocked. In the distance she could hear Michael calling 'Same time, same place, Josie.'

Quietly she opened the door and crept inside. From the communal sitting room she could hear voices – one of them was undoubtedly her mother. Hardly daring to breathe she climbed the stairs and crept into the bedroom, picking her way carefully through the various sections where several small children were sleeping until she reached their part of the room. Pulling aside the velvet curtain dividing them from the others, she quickly undressed before her mother had a chance to see her in the blue dress.

Monday morning quickly came around – Josie was due at the aircraft factory at 8 a.m. She smiled as she sat on the bus taking her to Reading, remembering her last day at the biscuit factory – everyone seemed sorry to see her go, even the supervisor hugged her as she was about to leave. ''Bye, Josie, take care of yourself. It's important work you will be doing … Do it well Josie, do it well.'

The clock on the station wall showed 7.45 a.m. as she

hurried up Station Road towards the factory. Her heart was pounding with apprehension – how would she manage? Mother had told her that, according to the stories going around, Britain was desperately short of planes. 'We need hundreds more,' she had said. 'It's up to you young ones to work hard and make sure we get as many as is needed to win this war.' Michael had said how proud he was of her and Josie felt as if, single-handed, she alone was going to change the course of the war.

As she approached the building a uniformed guard stepped out in front of her.

'Halt, and state your business, Miss.'

'Well, I've come to work here, of course,' Josie replied, waving the letter she had been given at the Labour Exchange in front of his face.

After a quick look he pointed to a door on her left marked 'Office'. She took a deep breath, drew herself up tall and marched towards it, nervously pushing the door open. She peered inside, still clutching the letter in her hand. A slight dark-eyed man with a shock of curly black hair looked up from a rather cluttered desk, stared at her for a moment or two and then he beckoned her to come in.

'What can I do for you, young lady?'

'I've got this 'ere for you,' she said, thrusting the letter towards him. He took it from her outstretched hand then, with just the briefest glance at Josie he started to read it while she stood waiting and wondering what life would be like working in such an important place! It only took a moment or two before he placed the letter on his desk and held out his hand.

'Can I see your identity card, Miss?'

Searching inside her shabby black handbag she handed him the buff-coloured card.

After carefully scrutinising it he handed it back to her.

'Come with me and I will show you around, then I'll get you started,' he said, pushing his chair back noisily as he stood up and hurried towards the door.

Once out of the office they turned right and proceeded down a wide passageway and through another door. Josie gasped at the sight in front of her – there were four or five partly built Spitfires and crawling all over them like so many flies were young girls, while a few older men walked about shouting orders. The noise was deafening – music was blaring out from loudspeakers, intermingling with the sound of heavy machinery at full blast.

A light tap on her shoulder made her turn around.

'I'm sorry,' said the dark-haired man, 'I did not introduce myself. My name is Miller and I am your supervisor and this is where the assembly of the planes takes place.' He paused briefly to take further stock of her, then continued. 'This will not concern you – you will be upstairs where the small parts are made. Now, if you follow me, I will take you up there.'

He turned quickly and Josie followed him as he went up a steep flight of stairs, then through a dark brown wooden door which opened to reveal a very large square-shaped room in which there were rows of small machines pounding away, and at each machine a girl was busily working. Some were on a machine which drilled holes in metal, others were using a huge machine which cut metal into strips, and some girls were operating a machine which looked to Josie like a huge belt whizzing around. The deafening noise from the machinery made Josie wince and she quickly covered her ears with her hands as she followed Mr Miller as he walked across the room. He came to an abrupt stop at a large wooden bench where two young lads were busy sorting out metal pieces.

'This is where you will be working, Miss – alongside of these two lads.'

Josie smiled at them. One gave her a friendly wink while the other kept his eyes firmly on the bench and didn't respond. Mr Miller tugged her by the arm.

'Come with me for a moment and we will get you some overalls and, young lady, you'll have to wear a cap on your head for safety reasons and don't you let me ever catch you without it!'

When Josie saw the cap she made one resolution … she was not going to be seen dead in that thing! A few discreet whistles followed her as she made her way across the factory floor, kitted out with a pair of well-fitting dungarees and a cap perched precariously on top of her head, her thick, brown hair hanging loosely to her shoulders. At last she felt that she was important; she was about to build Spitfires and help win the war! The country needed her!

The bench was deserted when Josie reached it; the boys were nowhere to be seen. She bit her lip and looked around. What was she supposed to do now?

The sound of a male voice booming out from halfway across the room made her jump.

'Pick up those metal strips and bring them over here.'

She looked around to see Mr Miller across the factory floor waving his arms, beckoning her towards him. She nodded briefly and leaned over the bench. There were at least fifteen to twenty strips of metal, all about 7 ft in length. She put her arms around them and lifted but they were so heavy that she felt her legs begin to buckle under the weight. Dragging them from the bench she could feel them slipping from her grasp.

'Here, let me carry them for you, they're too heavy for you to lift.'

Josie turned to see one of the young men who had whistled at her, deep blue eyes looked saucily at her, while a big grin stretched from ear to ear.

They made their way across to where Mr Miller was standing. 'What the hell do you think you're doing lad?' he bellowed angrily.

'Well, I, er, well, I thought it was too heavy for her to carry them; she was nearly dropping them onto the floor,' the young man replied, his face colouring up.

Mr Miller grabbed him by the arm. 'Get back to your own job, lad,' he shouted. 'I'll be the one to decide what she can and cannot do.'

The young man scurried away with just the briefest, backward glance at Josie.

Mr Miller stared hard at her for a moment or two. 'So they were too heavy for you were they!' he remarked in a sarcastic tone. Josie nodded her head and remained silent. 'Well, young lady, let me tell you this – while you are here at the factory you are neither a boy or girl – I treat you all the same and everyone here does the same sort of work. I can't make an exception with you.' He paused for a moment and looked her up and down. 'Although you look as if a puff of wind would blow you away. What's the point of it all, if every time you can't do a job, one of the boys has to stop work to help you?'

Josie stared at the floor and shrugged her shoulders while Mr Miller gave a despairing sigh. 'Oh well! I suppose I have to put you somewhere doing something that you are capable of. Come with me.'

He strode across the factory floor to the far corner, stopping in front of a small machine. On the floor next to it was a large metal container holding hundreds of small, flat metal pieces about 4 inches in diameter. He pointed to the machine. 'You see this here? Well, this is used to smooth off the edges of those small pieces down there.' He pointed a finger at the box. Josie nodded. 'I'll switch it on and show you how to do it okay?'

Reaching around the back of the machine, he pushed a switch and the machine roared into life. The noise was deafening. Picking up one of the metal discs Mr Miller held it against the huge belt which was turning at an alarming speed. Millions of sparks flew into the air as the metal came in contact with the belt. Seconds later he threw the finished piece into an empty container and turned to face her.

'Do you think you can manage that?' he said, towering over her almost threateningly.

She raised her eyes from the floor and looked him squarely in the eye. 'Course I can do that – 'ow many do you want done then?'

'The whole box before you finish tonight … the whole box!'

He turned on his heel and walked away. Josie sighed and picked up a disc and started work. There were hundreds of small pieces; it was going to take forever! The heat from the metal hurt her hands and sparks flew into her face, but she soldiered on for about an hour. Then, switching off the machine she went looking for Mr Miller who was standing at the far side of the factory drinking a cup of tea. She marched up to him with a determined look in her eye.

'I need a pair of gloves and some goggles like the others on the machines. Me eyes are sore and my 'ands are getting burnt.'

Mr Miller slowly finished his tea before answering. 'So you want gloves and goggles do you?' She nodded. 'Well then I suggest you go down to the store room and ask for some.'

Josie went in search of the store room. Somehow, she had a feeling that she wasn't going to be very happy making Spitfires.

Back at the manor house, Josie's mother was standing silently looking out onto the garden. Winter was setting in. She missed her home in London desperately. She missed Charlie and their new house, the corner shops and her friends. It didn't seem fair – they had just got their new house and then, three weeks later she had to leave. A sad smile crossed her face as she thought of her only son, now serving with the Royal Air Force. Only two more weeks and then his training would be over and he would be going on raids over Germany. A sudden shiver ran down her spine. Supposing something happened to him! Supposing he got killed! She shook her head ... there were hundreds of boys out there fighting for their country – why should it be her son that was killed, anymore than anyone else. No! He'd be fine and soon the war would be over and they would be together again in their own home. After all, didn't Winston Churchill say as much during his speech to the nation a few days ago – if anyone knew how the war was going it would be him.

She turned away from the window and went down the stairs to the sitting room; she needed to find some company to help her get rid of this feeling of gloom. As she opened the sitting room door she could see a few mothers were sitting in a small circle, surrounding Mrs Blackmore who was sobbing inconsolably.

'What's the matter?' mother whispered to Mrs Green, who was sitting nearby with a troubled look on her face. Mrs Green turned, tears glistened in her eyes.

'It's 'er 'usband,' she whispered. 'It's a telegram from the War Office an' it says he is missing believed killed.'

'Oh my God!' mother cried, as the stark reality of the war hit home – so this is how quickly your life can change. One minute you are happily married then the next minute you are on your own. Who will be the next one to get a telegram? It could be any one of them!

'Mum, Mum,' cried little Tommy. He tugged at his mother's arm. 'Wot's wrong, Mum?' There was no answer, she just reached out her arms and cradled him close, burying her face in his shock of curly black hair, while silently and sadly the mothers left the room, each one acutely aware that tomorrow it could be one of them!

The next few months went by quite uneventfully. Josie

got used to the work at the factory and Lucy had been promoted to an inspector. Working together gave them both the support they needed, especially as the last bus to Burghfield left the station before they finished work at 8 o'clock. For the first few days Josie grumbled incessantly about the walk home.

'It ain't fair,' she protested, as they wearily made their way along the dark country roads. 'Why should we 'ave to work twelve hours in that place and then 'ave to walk five miles 'ome. This ain't no life! By the time we get 'ome it's bedtime, then we 'ave to get up and start all over again.'

'You'd feel worse if you were one of our soldiers, they don't even get home … and wot about yer brother? 'E don't get 'ome at all,' Lucy retorted, but Josie would have none of it!

'I still think it's unfair,' she replied defiantly.

Lucy turned on her sister. She was tired and she was stressed and since they had been working at the aircraft factory both of them were totally exhausted. The war had been going on for nearly three years now – Lucy was fed up and the last thing she wanted to deal with was a stroppy sister! Angrily she grabbed Josie by the shoulders and spun her around.

'When I was reading the paper the other day, Josie, it said that 'itler said that when they win the war, they are going to take young English girls and put them in big houses where they will have to mate wiv his best soldiers 'cause, 'itler said that all the babies born to them would grow up to be a super race – the best in the world.'

Josie looked at her with wide, astonished eyes. 'I never knew that – 'ow do you know these things Lucy?'

''Cause I read the papers, Josie, and you don't.'

'Well I ain't gonna mate wiv any German. I 'ate them I do. They can't make me!'

Lucy shook her head. 'You wouldn't 'ave any choice, Josie, they would just come and take you away and no-one would know where you were. So shut up, Josie, things could be worse.'

Silently and thoughtfully they continued along the road …

Several months passed. Molly started walking, the trees came into blossom … and Josie was in love. Michael had been promoted since qualifying as an air gunner and was taking part in many raids. They could only meet on a Sunday evening because of Josie's work schedule, and when they had a date and he didn't turn up she would wait by the gate, looking anxiously up and down the road for what seemed to be an eternity until she heard the unmistakable sound of a squadron taking off from the nearby base. She knew then that he would not be with her that evening. Miserably she would turn away and slowly walk down the path to the house, hating the war and the planes that took him away from her.

One day, at work, rumours were circulating in the factory that the airbase at Mortimer had sustained heavy losses in a raid the previous night night – half the squadron had been wiped out. Josie was working on the cutting machine. Her cap was, as usual, perched on top of her head, but inside she felt shaky and sick – the news had upset her and there was no way of finding out if Michael was safe! She would have to wait until tonight. Absentmindedly she

161

leaned across the machine and as she did so a lock of her hair got caught in the machine, pulling her head relentlessly toward the sharp jagged metal edge. Josie fought to reach the switch at the back of the machine – blood started to trickle down her face just as her fingers closed around it, but she managed to throw the switch and the machine fell silent. Desperately she pulled at her hair tearing some of it out by the roots, then, terrified, she ran towards the Inspector's office, where she knew she would find Lucy.

'My God, Josie, whatever 'ave you done?'

Lucy looked up in shock at the sight of her sister standing in the doorway, blood pouring from her head. Quickly she jumped up and took Josie by the arm.

'Come on, I'm gonna take you to the first aid – 'ow on earth did you do it?'

'My hair got caught in the machine and it's cut me 'ead,' Josie blurted out between sobs.

Lucy looked at her in dismay as they hurried towards the first aid office. Would she never learn? How many times had she been told to cover her hair – that was the whole idea of the cap? Well, perhaps now she would listen, but, somehow, she didn't think so.

The man looked at the cut closely. 'You'll live don't worry,' he said reassuringly, as he dabbed iodine on her head. Josie winced with pain.

'I don't think you should work the rest of the day though. I'll have to speak to Mr Miller about it.'

He turned to Lucy. 'Take your sister into my office for a moment while I sort this out.' Then, as he made for the door, he patted Josie on the shoulder. 'Worse things happen at sea my girl, worse things happen at sea.'

Josie burst into floods of tears. The strain of wondering each time she saw Michael whether or not she would ever see him again was getting too much for her. So many times the plane he was in just managed to limp back to base. Now there was news that some of the planes didn't make it back to base last night. When would it all end?

Lucy put a reassuring arm around her. 'Don't cry,' she said. 'You ain't hurt yourself too bad and your hair will soon grow back again.'

Josie sniffed and wiped her eyes. 'I just want to go 'ome, Lucy, back to London and our 'ouse. I want to see me dad and, oh, I wish I still 'ad Paddy. Why did he 'ave to die, Lucy? Why?'

Before Lucy could answer, the door of the office was flung open and the first aid man hurried inside. 'Okay, young lady, Mr Miller said you can have the rest of the day off and we'll see you in the morning at 8 a.m. sharp. You'll have to stay away from those machines for awhile, though, till you are properly healed. Now off you go and take my advice – go straight to bed when you get in.'

He patted her again on the shoulder then opened the door for them to leave.

The bus trundled laboriously along the road as it made its way to Mortimer. It was barely 11 o'clock and Josie sat looking out of the window, her mind in a turmoil. Would Michael be at the gates at 7 o'clock as arranged or was he in one of the planes that didn't make it back? It would be another eight hours before she knew, another heartbreaking eight hours …

The footsteps were soft in the distance as Josie leaned against the stone pillar, her ears straining to pick up any sound, anything that would tell her Michael was okay. The footsteps came closer and closer, almost in rhythm with her heart as it beat faster and faster. Then he was there, standing in front of her with his arms outstretched. She flung herself forward and his arms wrapped tightly around her, holding her as if he never wanted to let go. Silently they clung together. Michael felt tears sting his eyes and fought to keep his emotions under control as reality struck him and he realised the fragility of their relationship. In his mind's eye he relived the carnage of last night – a plane burning fiercely as it plummeted to earth – the pilot struggling to free himself from this inferno; his navigator slumped across the plotting table with a bullet through his head. Against all odds they had made it home … but how long would their luck hold out?

The next few weeks were unbearable – every time Josie went to the factory she had a panic attack. The sight of the machinery and the memory of her accident haunted her so much that her hands shook and she was unable hold the metal pieces. Finally, she was sent for by Mr Miller.

'Josie,' he said quietly, 'I'm going to send you in front of the doctor. You are no good to us the way you are. Maybe he can sort you out, I'm sure I can't.'

'Wot d'yer mean, send me in front of the doctor. I ain't got nuffink wrong wiv me,' she replied crossly.

'Well, you are going anyway – tomorrow morning at 9 a.m. sharp. Report here.' He thrust a piece of paper in her hand and walked out of the room.

Josie studied it for a moment and, recognising the name

of the doctor, she gave a wry smile. He was a crotchety old devil and would probably send her back to work, saying that she was wasting his time. Well! Mr Miller can take the blame for that. Didn't she just tell him that there was nothing wrong with her?

It came as a surprise when the doctor recommended that she should be released from war-work. After spending almost half an hour in the surgery he had come to the conclusion that she was suffering from severe mental stress. 'In fact,' he added kindly, 'if you stay where you are you will most likely have a nervous breakdown and you won't be any good to anyone then.'

Josie walked back to the factory in deep thought – where would she go now?

She hated the factory, the long hours and then the long, tiring walk home, but now she had to find another job … but where?

'I have to leave 'ere – the doctor said so,' Josie informed Mr Miller as soon as she got back to his office. She held out the doctor's report and waited.

A frown crossed his face as he read it and then he shook his head sadly.

'I suppose you'd better go straight away, no point in hanging around,' he remarked. 'Go to the office and hand in your dungarees, then go to the wages office – they will let you know what money you have to come.'

'Thanks, Mr Miller,' she replied brightly, happy in the knowledge that she would never have to work in the factory again. She didn't like it. The work was far too heavy for her and the hours so long that she had no life at all, but things would be different now – she would be able to see Michael more often ... she couldn't wait until tonight to tell him the good news!

They were standing by the gate. Few words had passed between them and Josie was worried. All evening Michael had been quiet and withdrawn and now he was just staring into space. She put a tentative arm around his waist.

'Wot's the matter with you,' she said, as a feeling of unease swept over her. 'You ain't 'ardly spoken to me since we've been out.'

There was a strained silence for a few moments as he turned to face her.

'Well! Wot is it then?' Josie's eyes glistened with fear – didn't he love her anymore? What would she do without him? The thought was unbearable ... of course he loved her, hadn't he told her so many, many times?

He took her in his arm and held her close; she would never know how much it hurt him to tell her!

'I'm being posted to another squadron. I can't tell you where and I don't know when. All I know it is soon and I don't even know if I will ever see you again.' He buried his face in her hair. 'Oh, Josie, I'm so miserable. Sometimes I hate this war. I don't want to kill people that I don't even know, but then I think that if it wasn't for the war I would never have met you.'

She pressed her face into the tunic of his uniform; the rough cloth rubbed her skin as tears streamed from her eyes making dark, soggy patches. For several minutes she could not speak – the pain was too great.

'Why can't we get married before you go?' Josie's voice seemed to come from a long way off, as if someone else was speaking. She gave a start of surprise – was that really her asking him to marry her?

Gently he tilted her chin as he looked into her eyes.

'Josie, don't you think I have thought about it many times, but you are only fifteen. We couldn't anyway, and even if you were older it wouldn't be fair.' He paused for a moment. 'Do you know how many of my mates have been killed?' he said almost angrily. She shook her head. 'I couldn't place a burden like that on you, Josie, you have to be free; you're like a little butterfly, you have to spread your wings.'

She bowed her head, her heart was breaking. She couldn't look at him.

He held her at arm's length, staring at her as if he wanted to imprint the memory of her forever in his mind. She could hear the trickle of the river as it made its way downstream; she saw the dark, velvety blue of the night sky above her and, in that instance, somehow she knew that their lives would never be the same again.

Michael was still holding her at arm's length. She looked up at him with tear-drenched eyes. His voice was faltering as he spoke.

'I will write to you as soon as I can, Josie, and I promise that I'll always love you no matter what happens.'

She made no reply but only a small motion with her head. He pulled her close again, tilted her face and kissed her gently on the lips.

'Say, kid! If we are lucky enough to survive this war let's

get married, then we can get a little cottage somewhere in Norfolk near my work. You'd meet my parents and all my friends – everyone will love you, Josie, just like I do.'

A grin spread across her face and she nodded eagerly as he took her by the arm. They walked in silence back to house. The sound of a squadron of planes flying low overhead filled the night air.

When they reached the iron gates he kissed her lightly on the forehead. 'I have to go now, Josie.' His voice was breaking with emotion. 'Think of me, think of me often … I love you so much.'

He turned quickly and walked away, his footsteps echoing along the road until they faded in the distance …

Chapter 7

It was early spring 1942. Rumours were flying around the town … the Americans were coming! Some said that many of them were to be based just some ten miles from Reading. The news was greeted with mixed feelings.

Most of the young girls could hardly conceal their excitement. The only knowledge they had of Americans was from the movies, so in their minds they would all be handsome and very rich! They might even marry one of them and then be whisked away, away from the drabness of England, away from the rationing and a life of constantly doing without. They may even be lucky enough to get a pair of nylon stockings.

The older women, on the other hand, heralded the news with foreboding. The Americans would only bring trouble to the town. Hadn't they seen the movies from America? Drinking, gambling and womanising. Oh dear, it might even result in a few illegitimate babies!

Old Mrs Birchell stood on the corner of Piggots Row discussing their arrival with Mrs Riley and Mrs Cowan. 'You mark my words,' she said with a voice of impending doom, 'they'll come over here with their fancy ways, getting up to no good. I'd like to know what they're doing over here – took them long enough didn't it.'

'What took them "long enough"?' queried Mrs Riley, peering over the rim of her thick bottle glasses. She was never very quick on the uptake.

'Well, Edna, you know, getting into the war. They waited until the worst was over. Did they help us when those poor people in London and Coventry got blown up night after night? No! They just want the glory that's all.'

Mrs Cowan gave that irritating giggle that always made Mrs Birchall angry. Sometimes she wondered why she ever bothered to talk to the woman. She was so common! She felt Mrs Cowan poking her in the ribs.

'It might bring a bit of excitement into our lives. I wouldn't mind going out with one,' she said coyly, fluttering her eyelashes.

'You silly old boot,' Mrs Birchell exploded. 'Why would they want to even look at you – plenty of the young ones around for them to choose from?'

The two women glared at each other for a minute, then Mrs Cowan with a toss of her blonde hair disappeared up the road.

'I don't know, Edna – that woman drives me crazy. She's nearly sixty and yet she tries to act like a teenager. Really! It's ridiculous.' Mrs Birchell gave a deep sigh then continued. 'How are things going at the manor these days, Edna? I heard that the colonel got recalled a few weeks ago.'

Edna nodded her head. 'I was a bit worried at the time because the colonel insisted that Mrs Benson got rid of some of the staff and, well, to tell you the truth, I am the oldest one there so I thought I would be the first to go.'

'Don't be silly, Edna,' Mrs Birchell interrupted. 'You've

been working at the manor for at least twenty years or so, ever since your poor Bert got killed in that accident at his job. Why would they want to get rid of you?'

'It's my legs, Lil, they are not as good as they used to be. Sometimes I've got a job to get around and I'm sure they must have noticed it.'

Mrs Birchell took her by the arm, she could see tears beginning to form.

'Tell you what, Edna, come on indoors and I'll make us both a nice cup of tea and you can tell me all about it. You've got time before you go back to the manor haven't you?'

In the centre of the town, Josie was busy at her new job. No sooner had she left the factory than her mother had sent her to the Labour Exchange, her mother's favourite expression ringing in her ears: 'If you don't work, Josie, you don't eat. It's as simple as that.'

With her evidence of exemption from war-work she was given a choice of several jobs, but the one that appealed to her was as a waitress in Wellstead's, a large department store in the centre of the town. The money was not good but, as the old man at the Labour Exchange had said encouragingly, 'You might pick up a few tips if you are lucky.'

Armed with an introduction, she hurried towards the store full of excitement about the new adventure in front of her. When she reached the entrance to the restaurant she stood in awe at the grandeur of it. About a dozen girls, all dressed identically in plain black dresses, white frilly caps and tiny frilly aprons, darted about carrying trays of food and drink. A lush, deep red carpet covered the floor, while in the far corner a three-piece band was playing, the pianist almost

171

obliterated by a huge palm which stood in isolated splendour. Two sparkling chandeliers hung from the ornate ceiling.

'Oh! How beautiful!' Josie gasped as she looked, open mouthed, around the room.

'Can I help you, Miss?'

Startled, she turned to find a dark haired lady smiling at her.

'I've come for a job. 'Ere is the letter they gave me at the Labour Exchange,' Josie replied, wondering if she would be considered good enough to work in such an up-market place. The lady read quickly through the letter, then extended her hand in greeting.

'Let me introduce myself, I am Miss Jackson, the manageress. I can't tell you how happy I am to see you. We are so desperately short of waitresses.' She shook her head. 'The trouble is that young girls like you soon get called up to do war-work. Oh, I do hope that doesn't happen to you.'

Josie smiled. 'It's okay, Miss, I've already done my war-work and they won't 'ave me back because I got injured at work.'

'Do you think you could help us out today? I could really do with someone to clear the tables.' Miss Jackson asked anxiously.

Josie quickly nodded her head.

'Well, go over to Peggy, the girl at that station over there.' She pointed to the far corner, near to where the band was playing. 'Peggy will help if you have any problems.'

For a moment she hesitated as she looked Josie up and down. 'I think we must try to find you a uniform before you start work. Come with me to the stock room. I'm sure we have something in your size.'

After being suitably kitted up, Josie crossed the restaurant to where Peggy was just leaving a table after picking up an order from two rather fearsome looking dowagers. She gave Josie a quizzical look.

'I guess you must be starting work here – well I suppose it's obvious isn't it from the way you're dressed?'

Josie nodded, feeling a little apprehensive; she had never met anyone quite like Peggy before. She was tall and slim with bright blonde hair which cascaded down onto her shoulders, and she had heavily made-up green eyes. Josie stared at her fascinated – she looked like a movie star she thought admiringly.

Peggy looked at her with a slight smile on her face. 'Don't look so scared. I'm not going to eat you, you're only a kid – don't worry I'll see that you're alright here.' She pointed to a table laden with dirty dishes. 'Can you clear those and take them through to the kitchen over there?' She indicated a door at the far left. 'And you can get a tray over there by my station.'

'Okay,' replied Josie. She had taken to Peggy immediately.

The next few hours passed happily. She loved the calm, classy atmosphere of the restaurant – most of all she liked working with Peggy, who always had a smile and a cheerful word for everyone.

All too soon it was 5.30 p.m. and the restaurant became deserted. She was just taking off her uniform in the staff room when Peggy walked in and immediately went to the mirror and started to put even more make-up on her face.

'How did you like your first day kid?'

'It's really great, I think I'm gonna always work 'ere, that is until I get married.'

Peggy swung round in amazement. 'Married! she said incredulously. 'Do you mean you have a boyfriend that you are going to marry? But you can't, you're too young.'

Josie looked at her with an air of defiance. 'Course I've got a boyfriend. Wot's more 'e's in the Air Force as an air gunner.'

Peggy shook her head in amazement. 'You look such a kid, I would never have imagined you'd be courting. Where is he now?'

For a brief moment Josie didn't answer, as a feeling of sadness descended upon her like a big, black cloud. 'I dunno where he is – 'e was sent away and I ain't 'eard from 'im since.'

Peggy felt a pang of sympathy. 'You poor kid. How long has it been then?'

'It's been nearly seven weeks.'

Peggy smiled, showing a film-star set of teeth. 'I expect he's fine; they don't get much time to write in the forces, you know, and he could be anywhere, even overseas.'

''Ave you got a boy-friend?' Josie asked curiously.

'A boy-friend? No! I have got a husband and a little boy, he's two years old and his name is Andy,' she said proudly. 'My husband is in the Air Force, just like your boy-friend, except he's not an air gunner, he's ground crew.'

Josie nodded briefly – she had just noticed the clock on the wall and it was almost 6 o'clock. Her bus would be leaving soon.

'I gotta go now, Peggy,' she replied with an apologetic grin. 'My bus leaves in fifteen minutes, and if I miss it I've gotta walk 'ome.'

'Where do you live then?' Peggy asked, patting her blonde hair in place as they walked together out of the restaurant.

'Burghfield. Do you know it?'

Peggy screwed up her nose as she gave it some thought. 'Isn't it a little village on the way to Mortimer?'

'Yes, and it's a long way to walk if I miss the bus. I know because I walked it every night when I worked at the aircraft factory.'

Peggy thought about Josie as she made her way through the town and over the bridge to her home in Caversham. She seemed so young and yet her eyes held a sadness, as if she had all the problems of the universe on her shoulders. Yet she had spirit; she was a fighter.

Reaching the end of the bridge, she turned right along the riverbank until she came to 17 Piggots Road, a little two up, two down terraced house. A warm feeling swept over her body. She loved her little home, she reflected; her life would be perfect if only Tom were here instead of being 'somewhere in the world' fighting in a war. She put her key in the lock and almost immediately she heard Andy's excited screams of delight … his mother was home!

As soon as the door was opened he ran towards her, arms outstretched, brown eyes aglow with happiness. Peggy picked him up and swung him around.

'How has he been today, Meg?' Peggy asked her sister as they went into the sitting room and sat down.

'He's a little angel, Peggy, I've never known such a good

175

kid,' Meg replied, fondly patting her nephew on the head. 'By the way, there's a letter for you on the table – looks to me like it's from Tom.'

She put Andy into her sister's arms then ran to the table and picked up the letter, anxiously scanning the envelope. There was no way she could tell where it had been posted; any sort of information had been obliterated. She sat down on the nearest chair and clasped the unopened letter close to her heart. After all these weeks without news of him ... now there was a letter! She savoured the moment as she thought of the time when Tom had been drafted. Andy was just three months old, that's all! Now he was two. Tom was missing so much of Andy's growing up – surely the war wouldn't last much longer.

Peggy was halfway through reading the letter when she was interrupted by Meg.

'I have to go now,' she said, pulling on her coat. 'See you tomorrow.'

Peggy nodded absentmindedly as she continued reading. Tom sounded lonely and homesick. He said how much he missed her – how he loved his little family. The squadron was being moved again, but he could not tell her where or when or even why! She shuddered at the thought; so many men were getting killed. What would life be without Tom? A strange sense of impending disaster swept over her – she bent down and picking Andy up from the floor hugged his tiny body as if she never wanted to let go.

Josie clambered breathlessly onto the bus just as it was preparing to leave the bus station. She climbed to the top deck and gratefully sank into a vacant seat. Glancing around her she saw the bus was full, as usual, mainly with Air Force personnel from the nearby base at Mortimer. She thought sadly of Michael and of the first time she had seen him; just like this on the bus going home! Where was he now? Why had he not written to her? Would she ever see him again?

As the bus made its way along the country roads, Josie stared blankly out of the window into the still darkness of the night. Since leaving the aircraft factory she had not seen much of Lucy because she was on night work a lot of the time now. Michael had gone, her brother was away in the Air Force, father was still working in London on the docks and mother didn't seem to have much time for her! She gave a deep sigh as tears threatened to well up in her eyes; a feeling of intense loneliness swept over her – she missed London. She missed their new home and the comforting banter of cockney life, but what bothered her most of all was the fact that nothing ever seemed to last. Life was so uncertain!

The bus pulled to a stop near the manor house, and as she hurriedly ran down the stairs she wondered whether there would be a letter from Michael. She ran down the gravel pathway towards the door, her heart pounding in anticipation. Mother was in the kitchen talking to Mrs Green as Josie opened the door.

'How are things going at the restaurant, Josie?' she asked, turning to face her daughter.

Josie pulled out a chair from under the table and sat down. 'Its luverly, really posh and I got a shilling in tips today.'

Mother raised her forefinger and wagged it in front of

177

Josie's face. 'You put everything you get in tips into a savings account, Josie. Always remember this – your bank book is your best friend.'

Josie raised her eyes to the ceiling – she had been planning to buy a lipstick, if there were such a thing to be found in any of the shops, but now that was out of the question. Mother would insist on seeing evidence that the shilling had, indeed, been put into the bank.

'Mum, are there any letters for me?' Josie's heart was racing as she waited impatiently for her to answer. It had been months since she had heard from Michael and she was getting very worried. Maybe he had been killed in a raid! How would she ever know? The authorities would inform his parents as next of kin – not her. Mother shook her head and resumed her conversation with Mrs Green while Josie walked sadly from the room and went upstairs to fling herself morosely on her bed.

4th August 1942

It was a bright, sunny Wednesday afternoon and the air hung heavy with anticipation as crowds lined Broad Street. News had reached the town that the Yanks were on their way and they would be marching through the main street sometime during the afternoon. Most of the townspeople had never seen an American before – except in the movies, of course – and they were a little uneasy at the prospect of having an American airbase not ten miles away.

Mrs Cowan was standing eagerly on the corner by

Wellstead's department store, hoping to catch the eye of some Yank. She didn't feel uneasy; here was an opportunity to get a man at last! Wherever there were pubs, there were soldiers – wherever there was a pub you would find Mrs Cowan! She couldn't lose. She patted her blonde hair and wiggled her way forward to get a better view.

Josie and Peggy had just finished work. Wednesday was their half-day, so they made their way along the main street and stood on the steps of St Mary's church and waited. Little did they know that this day was a day that would change their lives forever! An hour passed and there was still no sign of the Americans and Peggy was getting fidgety.

'Josie, I'm not standing here much longer because I have to get home to Andy. My sister wants to go over to see her friend this afternoon and she won't be very happy with me if I'm not home soon.'

Josie yawned and stretched her arms in the air, she was feeling bored with all this waiting about – perhaps they had better go home. She was just about to suggest this to Peggy when from a distance came the unmistakeable sound of marching feet. The sound grew louder and louder until a column of American soldiers marching four abreast came into view. Josie stared at them as they passed by. A heavy silence hung in the air as the people watched them with suspicious eyes. She turned to Peggy. ''Ave you ever seen such a scruffy looking lot of soldiers, Peggy? I wouldn't go out wiv any of them, would you?'

Peggy raised her thin pencilled eyebrows. 'You would look scruffy, Josie, if you had travelled halfway around the world on a ship, all crammed up like a lot of cattle.' Out of the corner of her eye she caught sight of Mrs Cowan across the road, boldly waving a bright red scarf at the troops. 'At least, Josie,' she giggled, 'there's someone who's going to make them very welcome; so they won't care whether you go out with them or not.'

Josie shrugged her shoulders. 'Well, I've got my own boy-friend, even if 'e's not here at the moment. I'm gonna wait for him, don't matter 'ow many Yanks ask me out.'

The Americans marched down the street looking very subdued as they passed the silent, waiting crowd. No-one, with the exception of Mrs Cowan, cheered or waved flags … after all, it had taken America a long time to decide to come into the war. For months Britain had had its back to the wall, now they were here like conquering heroes. Well, it was just a bit too late for their liking!

Chapter 8

Several weeks went by and the small market town was bursting at the seams with military personnel. The Americans flooded the town during the evenings, outshining the British troops with their far superior uniforms, which fitted perfectly and looked as if it had been tailor-made for each and every one of them. Full of confidence and with pockets full of money, chocolate and nylon stockings, they soon dazzled the young girls. Mrs Cowan could be found most nights proudly hanging on the arm of an American staff sergeant, with an 'I told you so' look on her face as they toured the pubs and got steadily drunk together. British soldiers and airmen, seeing the Americans take over their town and their girlfriends, could be seen standing in small, forlorn groups on street corners looking like the poor relations in their rough, ill-fitting uniforms. As far as they were concerned, the problem with these guys was that they were 'oversexed, overpaid and over here!' The sooner they got drafted into combat the better!

The restaurant became very busy. The elderly, staid ladies taking afternoon tea looked with disproving eyes at the strangers in their midst. They didn't quite know how to take these American servicemen who were so brash and forward.

At a corner table, near the band, sat Daphne Benson, surveying the scene in front of her, a half smile crossed her face. In her hand she held a long, cigarette holder. She was an elegant, classy lady, in her mid-thirties, the wife of Colonel Benson, who was 'somewhere in England' serving his country – and Daphne was bored! The manor house was a lonely place since her husband had been posted, leaving her with just two servants, Edna and Mary, to attend to her needs. She sighed as she picked up her cup of tea. When on earth was this damn war going to end? Was life ever going to get back to normal? A feeling that someone was watching her made her turn around. She caught the eye of a young American serviceman … and for a moment their eyes remained locked in a steady gaze. Daphne felt a tingle of excitement run down her spine as he smiled and nodded. She turned away and elegantly poured herself more tea from the delicate china tea-pot. From the corner of lowered eyes she watched as the American sat drumming his fingers on the table as if trying to make up his mind about something. He pursed his lips, then, as if a decision had been made, stood up and started to walk towards her. Daphne felt that familiar tingle of excitement as she watched the lithe movement of his muscular body.

'Excuse me, ma'm,' he said, leaning over the table, while dark, sexy eyes appraised her body, 'but it doesn't seem quite right to me that we should both be "taking tea", as you Brits call it, on our own. May I join you?'

Daphne raised her eyes and leaned forward, raising her skirt slightly as she did so. A slight smile crossed her face as she indicated the chair opposite her.

'Be my guest,' she replied huskily.

'Josie,' Peggy said breathlessly, just as they were getting ready to close the restaurant, 'these Yanks want to know if we will go dancing with them Friday night at the Olympia. What do you say?'

Josie shook her head. 'No, I don't think so, Peggy, because there is no way I can get 'ome afterwards.'

The blond haired American sitting on the far side of the table looked Josie up and down appreciatively.

'Say, honey, live a little,' he drawled as he leant back in his chair puffing on a small cigar. 'We'll see you get home alright babe.'

Peggy grabbed her by the arm. 'You can stay with me, Josie, if you like. It's not far to the Olympia from where I live. Come on, Josie, be a sport, come with us, we can't just work all the time you know.'

Josie looked at Peggy, whose eyes were imploring her to go. What the hell! Hadn't she always wanted to go to the Olympia! Now was her chance! What did that Yank say? Live a little – and he was right. She had never known much music or laughter in her life – she would live a little and it was about time too.

'Okay, but I 'ave to ask me mum first.'

Hurriedly they made arrangements to meet outside the Olympia on Friday evening and, as the soldier left, Josie turned to Peggy, her face flushed with excitement.

'I can't wait to go dancing at the Olympia, Peggy. When I was working at the biscuit factory, all the girls there used to go every night, but I couldn't get back 'ome, unless, of course, I walked. But me mum would never allow it.'

Peggy gave her a sympathetic grin and put her arm around her shoulder. 'Don't worry, you'll be able to go tomorrow night I'm sure and we are going to have such fun together. You'll see!'

Josie nodded and grabbed her coat as she made for the door.

'I've got to go now, Peggy, or I'll miss me bus. Bye now.'

It was just after 6.30 p.m. when Josie arrived home. Mother was obviously anxious to talk to her because as soon as she entered the front door she was waiting.

'Come upstairs a minute, Josie, I have something to tell you and we might as well get it over before you have your dinner.'

Josie frowned; her eyes held a puzzled expression as she followed her mother up the stairs to their bedroom. Her mother seemed a little ill at ease and Josie felt a strange sinking sensation in the pit of her stomach – something was wrong, seriously wrong!

Several minutes passed before mother finally spoke.

'I have to tell you, Josie, that I have found myself a nice little job in Reading, as a cook in a private school.'

Josie took a sharp intake of breath and stared at her mother in disbelief.

'I know it has come as a shock to you but at least I will have some money of my own coming in and we will surely need money when we finally go back to London. God knows what state the house will be in – and the furniture! Well, heaven knows if there will be anything at all left.'

'But, Mum, wot is going to 'appen to me? Can I come wiv you?'

Mother shook her head. 'No, I'm sorry, Josie, but there's only room for Molly – I can't take you as well. The best thing you can do is to look for some lodgings in Reading and until you find something you can stay here – it's no problem.'

'Wot about Lucy, Mum? Wot is she gonna do?'

'Don't you worry yourself about Lucy,' she replied, wagging her finger as if to emphasis her words. 'Lucy has been told that she is being transferred to an aircraft factory down in Somerset and she is leaving this week-end.'

Josie jumped up angrily and turned on her.

'Why didn't Lucy tell me that she was leaving – it's not fair – everyone's leaving me behind. Wot am I supposed to do?'

'How can Lucy tell you, when you never see each other nowadays? What with you on days and she works nights. I only knew yesterday that she had been told about the transfer to another factory.' Mother shook her head in despair and walked towards the window and stared into the gathering dusk. Josie seemed to be so insecure at times! The look on her face when she told her that she was taking a job in Reading reminded her of that day many years ago … Josie was just three years old and she had the same look on her face then. Was she destined to be haunted forever by the memory of that one mistake she had made?

'I don't know wot to do,' Josie said miserably, as she sat in the staff room talking to Peggy the following morning. 'I didn't 'ave time to tell her I wanted to go dancing at the Olympia because she was so busy telling me that she has got a job in Reading.'

185

'What do you mean? Got a job in Reading? What can your mum do when she's got your little sister to look after?'

'She's got a job in a school as a cook and she can take Molly wiv 'er, but I can't go because there ain't no room.' Josie stared moodily into space trying to deal with this new blow that life had dealt her.

Peggy sat deep in thought for a moment or two, then suddenly jumped up and took Josie by the hands. 'Tell you what, Josie, how about it if you came and lived with me at my house. I've got a spare bedroom and if you move in straight away you don't even have to ask your mum if you can go to the Olympia this week, 'cause she wouldn't know.'

Josie looked at Peggy, her eyes shining with excitement.

'Do your really mean it, Peggy – I mean really mean it?'

'Of course I do, it'll be like having a sister. Now, come on we've got to get on the floor and start work or we'll be in trouble. See what your mum says about you moving in with me tomorrow – there's no point in waiting about is there?'

Mother was busy in the bedroom when Josie arrived home that evening. Josie studied her face anxiously. What would she say about moving in with Peggy? Would she let her?

'What are you hovering around here for, Josie? Don't you think you should go down to the kitchen and have your dinner? Mrs Green will be waiting to clear up you know.'

Josie took a deep breath. 'Mum I wanted to tell you that I've found somewhere to live in Reading like you told me.'

Mother sat down on the bed, arms folded and stared at Josie. 'Well, come on Josie, tell me where are you going to live and who is it with?'

'Well, Mum,' she began, her voice faltering as she tried to get the words out, 'you know I told you about this girl I work with.'

Mother interrupted. 'You mean that one who has dyed hair and is married?'

'Yes,' Josie replied, hesitating for a moment. 'She is really nice and I would be near to where I work.'

Mother was silent for a few moments, while Josie shuffled her feet nervously as she waited for her decision. Finally, she spoke.

'It doesn't seem the best of places for you but I can't worry about it. Just mark my words, Josie, if you get into any trouble, don't come to me to sort it out.'

Thursday found Josie, with her meagre belongings in a small bag, boarding the bus to Reading for the last time. She had packed the blue dress; after all it was about the only thing she had to wear when she went dancing.

That evening the two girls were talking excitedly about their night out with the Americans.

'What are you going to wear, Josie?' Peggy asked as she struggled into a very tight, green silk dress and critically studied herself in a long mirror propped up against the wall.

Josie hesitated for a moment. 'Well I 'ave my blue dress that I wear on special occasions. Do you think it will do?'

'How can I tell?' Peggy replied laughing. 'I have never seen it! Go on, Josie. Go and put it on then come down and show me.'

Josie hurried up the stairs to the bedroom that was hers. She passed little Andy's room and glanced through the open door where she saw Andy happily playing with his toes in his cot. Suddenly a feeling of sadness swept over her as she thought of Molly. She missed her funny little ways – she was walking now and getting up to all sorts of tricks. I wonder how she will get on at that school with all those posh kids, she thought. Grabbing the blue dress from the suitcase, she quickly put it on and ran down the stairs.

Peggy frowned as Josie stood silently in front of her. She didn't feel comfortable in the blue dress anymore. Somehow it didn't seem to fit, especially across her bust … she must have grown – she certainly did not remember it being so short!

'You can't wear that dress to the Olympia,' Peggy said, shaking her head. 'It's much too small for you.'

Josie looked at her in dismay. 'I ain't got anything else to wear.' Her voice rose almost to a wail as she slumped miserably into the nearest chair.

'Tell you what, let's see what I can find for you in my wardrobe. We are about the same size and I know there will be something that will look good on you.'

They raced each other up the stairs to Peggy's bedroom, giggling like two little kids as they fought to be the first one in the room. Peggy flung open the door of an old oak wardrobe and Josie anxiously peered inside. There were only a few clothes hanging up: three years of war and the fact that they could only buy clothes when they had enough clothing coupons had taken its toll and clothes that had worn out were difficult to replace.

Peggy reached across in front of Josie and grabbed a skirt off the rail. It was a bright red cotton, circular skirt and Josie looked at it apprehensively. She had never, ever seen anything quite like it! Peggy thrust it into her hands, then reached into the wardrobe and pulled out a skimpy black top.

'Go on Josie – go and try them on. You'll look great I'm sure.'

Josie went back to her bedroom and sat on the bed for a few moments. What would her mother say if she saw her dressed like this! But then she wouldn't see her, would she? After all, she was only going to wear these clothes for one night and mother would certainly not be at the Olympia. Hurriedly she got into the skirt, then pulled on the black top and turned to face the mirror. She gave a gasp of pleasure – it was perfect in every way. The skimpy black top accentuated her blossoming figure and the skirt was tight at the waist but then flared out, falling in soft folds to her calf.

Peggy gasped in amazement as she walked in through the door to stand proudly in front of her.

'My God! Josie you look just like a film star, a real film star!' She paused for a moment then, turning to her dressing table, she selected a wide, shiny black belt. 'Put this on now,' she said, as she handed it to her. 'It's the finishing touch.'

Josie took the belt and fastened it around her slim waist.

''Ow do I look now, Peggy?' she asked excitedly as she twirled around.

Peggy smiled and nodded approvingly. 'You'll be the belle of the ball.'

It was Friday night … the night that they had arranged to meet the Americans outside the Olympia at 7.30 p.m. As they hurried through the darkened streets, Josie could hardly bear the excitement she felt. It swept over her body like a huge wave; it was the first time she had ever been out at night and not have to face her mother's disapproval when she arrived home.

The Americans were already waiting for them; in their hands each clutched a little parcel which contained a pair of nylons stockings and a bar of Hershey chocolate.

'Gee, honey, you sure do look swell,' said the blond-haired sergeant as he took Josie by the arm and guided her through the door, while Peggy followed with the other one in tow. Loud, happy music engulfed them as they made their way down a plush red entrance hall leading to the dancehall. Josie gasped in amazement at the scene in front of her. The dancehall was huge and down each side were elegant arches which separated the dancehall from a cosy, red seating area. Sparkling crystal chandeliers hung from a white ornate ceiling and in the centre a silver ball twisted gently, sending cascades of gleaming dots of light dancing over the crowded floor.

Like a kid in a candy store she stared around her ... it was mainly occupied by American servicemen and most of them had very attractive girls hanging on their arms, while a few British airmen stood in small groups looking decidedly dejected. The American took her by the hand and led her onto the dance floor. She hesitated for a moment, then pulled her hand free from his.

'Say, honey, what's the matter?' he asked anxiously.

'I ... er I can't dance. I 'ave never been dancing before in my life.'

She felt her face colour up as she spoke. All the other girls seemed to be doing it okay. Why couldn't she?

'You're kidding me, honey, come on let's dance … just follow me and you'll be fine.'

He pulled her onto the floor and started swaying to the music while Josie watched for a moment or two. Suddenly she felt herself in tune with the rhythm as her body surrendered to the beat and she was lost … lost in another world! A world of glamour and excitement; of opulence and danger! There was no war, no hardships, and no hunger! The night was magical and, as she danced the night away, she knew that there was only one thing in life she wanted, apart from being Michael's wife, and that was to be a dancer.

The evening passed too quickly and soon they were playing the last waltz. The American suddenly burst out laughing and Josie looked at him with a frown on her face.

'Wot are you laughing at? I ain't done anything wrong, 'ave I?'

'No, honey, but the thing is we don't even know each other's name. I've had such a great time that I forgot to ask you.'

Josie smiled as he took her in his arms. 'My name is Josie, wot's yours?'

'Hank,' he replied, holding her close. 'Hank Williams.'

As they danced the last waltz she was oblivious of the other dancers. The feel of his arms around her reminded her of Michael and how much she missed him. Where was he? Why didn't he write? She melted in the strength of Hank's arms and closed her eyes. She couldn't bear this torture of not knowing what had happened to Michael but, somehow, it was easier when she was with Hank.

The music faded and the dance was over, but Hank was still holding her.

'Can I take you home, Josie?' he asked, as he took her hand and led her from the dance floor.

Josie shook her head. 'No, I gotta go home wiv me friend because we live together.' She pulled her hand away and started to walk towards Peggy who was in deep conversation with his friend.

Hank hurried after her. 'Can I see you again, then? I'll be off duty on Wednesday. How about it?'

Josie gazed up at him, her eyes gleamed with mischief. 'Okay! But, only if you'll take me dancing again.'

'Anything you want, baby, anything you want. I'll meet you outside at 7.30 p.m. ... and don't forget.'

Peggy had finished her conversation and was calling her to hurry up – she was anxious to get home. Her sister was baby sitting and didn't like to be kept too late at the house. Together they linked arms and stepped out into the enveloping darkness of the night.

Peggy had a torch which shone just a pin-prick of light to comply with the blackout regulations, but Josie was afraid of the dark. Yet, when she was with Michael, it was different. In the inky blackness the sound of other footsteps echoed in the night, sometimes receding into the distance, but others seemed to be coming straight at them. Peggy sensed Josie's fear and put her arm around her.

'You're afraid of the dark aren't you?'

Josie shuddered. 'I don't know why, but I always feel that

I'm shut in a dark room and I can't get out. Ever since I can remember I've been afraid of that room.'

'Tell you what we'll do, Josie, let's sing. That will take your mind off the walk home.'

'Wot shall we sing then, Peggy? I only know a few songs.'

'Let's sing "There'll Always Be an England" to start off with – everyone knows that song, even you Josie.'

'D'yer think there will always be an England, Peggy?' Josie's voice faltered as the memory of the London bombings flashed before her. And her sister's warning that if Hitler won the war he was going to force young, fair-haired girls to mate with his crack SS troops and, as he said, create a super-race scared her half to death.

'Josie!' She heard Peggy's voice and it startled her out of her memories. 'Josie, don't you ever think like that, we won't lose this war. We've got to win, we've just got to.' Then at the top of her voice she started singing and, as Josie joined in, their voices echoed through the dark, silent night. In the far distance a man's voice took up the song, then another and another, all singing in unison, until some gradually faded away into the distance while others became louder and stronger.

They crossed the bridge and made their way down to the towpath, still singing loudly. Behind them, someone clapped their hands, but it was so dark they couldn't see who it was, but Josie felt comforted in the knowledge that in the darkness of the night there were always people around – even if you couldn't see them, they were there – and they were friends.

The following day, after work, Peggy and Josie walked back to the little house in Caversham, chatting about the previous evening. After a short while Peggy noticed that Josie had become very quiet and subdued.

'What's wrong with you, then?' she enquired. 'You've become very quiet.'

Josie stopped and swung round to face Peggy.

'Well, don't you fink it's wrong to go out with Joe when you're married?'

She couldn't help sounding a little cross; it had been bothering her since the previous night.

Peggy looked at her with a hurt expression in her eyes. 'Do you really think I would do anything to hurt my husband, Josie? Well, let me tell you this. When he was called up, we knew we could be apart for a long, long time, maybe even years! So we talked about it and decided that we should be able to go out and have friends of the opposite sex. Josie, no-one knows what's going to happen, these are hard times for all of us – look how many soldiers and civilians are being killed every day – people just like you and me Josie – we have to have a bit of fun don't we? After all, we might not be here tomorrow.'

Peggy's eyes looked at Josie imploringly. 'Don't you understand? I still love my husband to bits but sometimes I think that I might never see him again and going dancing makes me forget for a little while. It's the only way I can cope with this war, Josie, the only way!'

Josie shrugged her shoulders, feeling embarrassed. She had no idea that this was an arrangement that Peggy had with her husband and she wished she had kept quiet and not said a word about it.

'I'm sorry, Peggy, it's none of my business wot you do. I

just think of Michael and I know that when I get married I'll never go out wiv anyone else.'

Peggy smiled a little sadly. 'You're only a kid, Josie, you know nothing about the world. Things change when you get a little older, you'll see!'

The next few weeks passed happily for Josie. Her job was going well, and she went dancing several nights a week. Sometimes, when he could get leave, Hank would meet her at the dancehall, and for once in her life she began to feel more settled. But still she fretted about Michael; it was six months ago that they had last seen each other and it was four months since she had had a letter from him.

On a couple of occasions she went to see her mother and Molly at the school, but, as usual, there was always this distance between them and she was glad to leave and get back 'home' to Peggy's, where she now felt like one of the family.

Chapter 9

Daphne was lounging luxuriously on the red divan as she waited for Joe to arrive. As usual she had given the servants the night off and now the coast was clear for an evening of passion. She reflected on that day two months ago when she first met him in the restaurant at Wellstead's. In her mind's eye she could still see him, striding towards her, with his lean, lithe body and those dark, sexy eyes contemplating his conquest. At first she was a little put off by the fact that he was a half-caste, but when he told her that his mother was part-Indian, it stirred something in her ... two months, she thought dreamily ... two months she had been seeing him in the sanctuary of the manor.

There was no way she could be seen in the town with another man; her husband would be sure to find out and that would be the end of their marriage and her position in society. No! It was best to keep the affair under cover – no-one would ever suspect – she was careful, so very careful!

Edna, who was her live-in housekeeper, had been with her for over twenty years now and, luckily, she was a creature of habit. Sunday was her day off and, as regular as clockwork, she would go and visit her mother who lived less than a mile away. Then, in the evenings, at 7 o'clock, she would retire to her own quarters in the west wing. As for Jenny, well, she was just a simple girl who did the rough work around the house and she was only about a few hours in the mornings … No! she was safe enough – her secret would never be discovered.

Daphne picked up an opened letter from the silver salver lying on the small occasional table next to her and read it through it one more time. It was from her husband stationed 'somewhere in England'. It read:

Dearest Daphne,

I hope this letter finds you well. As you know I cannot tell you very much about my own position due to security but [the next few words had been obliterated by the censor] I think I will be getting a few days leave before then … I'll let you know … and look forward to seeing you. Until then, take care of yourself old girl.

Your loving husband
Charles xxxxx

Tossing the letter back onto the table, she stretched her slim arms into the air, and then ruffled her long, dark hair. In fifteen minutes Joe would be here. A satisfied smile crossed her lips. Oh! What bliss to have found such a lover as Joe – so different from her husband who was so boring in bed but at least he did have money and position. What did Joe have to offer? Just great looks, a great body, and great stamina.

As she glanced across the room at the table, which had been set by Edna before she retired for the evening, a feeling of pleasure swept over her. Champagne stood chilling in a silver ice bucket, while cold cuts of meat and a plate of sandwiches vied for attention as an ornate centrepiece. Silver cutlery gleamed in the seductive glow of light from the crystal chandelier hanging low from the ceiling. As always, the scene was set to perfection. They were the privileged upper class and the effects of the war had not reached them yet!

Daphne smiled … she was ready to receive her guest.

Snow fell silently from a dark winter's sky. It was almost Christmas Eve and the war had been going on for three long years. Josie and Peggy were on their way to the Olympia ballroom. Tonight was going to be special! A Christmas Ball! For this special occasion, Peggy had made Josie a long skirt out of a pair of black-out curtains and, after rummaging through her wardrobe, had found a long dress that she had bought for her own honeymoon. She had also persuaded Josie to let her bleach her hair. At first Josie was terrified of what her mother would say when she saw her, but then the thought that she might look as glamorous as Peggy made her change her mind, and now she was a blonde!

The Olympia was bursting at the seams, everyone determined to have a good time this Christmas Eve and to hell with tomorrow!

Hank was pacing up and down by the entrance as they arrived, looking a little sheepish and ill at ease. But Joe was nowhere in sight.

'Where's Joe?' Peggy asked immediately 'Why isn't he here?'

Hank crossed his fingers behind his back and took a deep breath.

'Sorry, Peggy, but Joe couldn't make it tonight, he had to be on guard duty.'

Peggy stamped her foot angrily. 'Well, that's nice isn't it? Couldn't he have let me know – rather than standing me up at the door?'

Hank felt his face colour up – he knew where Joe was and he was not happy about the situation. Why did he have to pick married women to go out with – especially such a high profile one as that Daphne. God help him if he ever got caught!

'He didn't have a chance, Peggy; he had to take the place of a guy who got sick.'

Hank felt the words stick in his throat; he hated to lie to her but he couldn't let his buddy down either. When he got back to the base he would have a word with Joe, after all there were loads of pretty girls in the town without making a play for a society dame!

He felt Josie pulling him by the arm. 'C'mon, Hank, let's go in, it's freezing standing here.' She grabbed Peggy with her other hand. 'You'll 'ave a good time, Peggy, don't you worry. Lots of fellers will be glad to have a dance with you, especially the way you're looking.'

Peggy gave her a forced smile as they made their way into the dancehall, where she promptly saw someone she knew and disappeared into the milling throng.

'Say, honey, let's go and get a beer at the bar, I really could use a drink,' Hank said as he spotted two vacant chairs in the far corner. 'You sit there and I'll be back as soon as I can but there is one hell of a crowd waiting to be served.'

Josie nodded, and then watched him as he made his way

through the crowd. She leant back in her chair and scanned the room. Most of the people were now familiar figures to her, especially the girls. It was the same ones every time she came – but it was different with the servicemen, they were there for a short while and then were never seen again and a fresh lot of faces would appear. Her gaze settled on a young British airman who was sitting across the room from her and for several moments they were held in a locked gaze until Josie turned away to look for Hank. The airman had made her feel uncomfortable; there was something about him that reminded her of Michael. She turned to look at him again and saw that he had left his seat and was walking towards her – she watched mesmerised until he was at her side.

'Excuse me, but is your name Josie?' he asked hesitatingly.

'Yes,' she replied, 'but 'ow do you know my name?'

'My mate Michael showed me a picture of you. He met you when we were stationed at Mortimer didn't he?'

Josie's heart gave a leap. 'You know Michael? You know Michael?'

He nodded his head sadly. 'He was one of my best mates. One of the best!'

A stab of pain seared through her heart.

'Wot d'yer mean "was" your best mate? Tell me he was moved to another base, tell me he ain't ...' Her voice was shaking as tears filled her eyes.

The young airman's face turned pale. 'Don't you know what happened? Surely you know. Oh God! What have I done?'

Josie jumped up from her seat and grabbed him by the

arms, shaking him violently. 'Tell me for God's sake – tell me 'e's alright.'

'He's dead, Josie, he's dead! Four months ago – we had just been transferred and we were waiting to go overseas.' He paused for a moment, as if unable to go on, but then he regained his composure. 'Michael went on a night raid over Germany. The plane got a lot of damage but they managed to make it back to base. The landing wheels were jammed and they crash-landed. Michael was lucky because he got thrown clear, but when he saw that his mate was trapped, he crawled back to help him … and they nearly made it, but then the plane exploded.' He turned his head, desperately trying to stem the tears that were threatening.

Josie stood frozen to the spot, holding her hands to her mouth to stop herself from screaming. Screaming out to the whole world.

'NO! This isn't true! It's a mistake! Oh God No! Not my Michael!' She felt the world spinning as a comforting darkness slowly surrounded her, and she slumped to the floor just as Hank appeared, hurrying across from the bar with two drinks in his hands. He had noticed this 'limey' talking to his girl – he would sort him out! But when he reached them and he saw the tears in the airman's eyes and Josie on the floor, he realised that something serious had happened – it was not just a question of a guy trying to chat up his girl.

Quickly he put the drinks on the table and knelt down and lifted her head from the floor. The young man knelt beside him. 'She didn't know … she didn't know,' he kept repeating over and over again.

'What didn't she know, pal? What have you told her that she didn't know?' Hank demanded impatiently.

Josie stirred and opened her eyes. For a few moments she remained silent, but then tears coursed uncontrollably down her ashen face. Hank helped her to her feet while a crowd of people milled around to see what was going on. Peggy suddenly appeared pushing her way through the crowd.

'Josie,' she cried in alarm. 'What's happened to you?'

Hank looked at Peggy bewildered. 'It's something about her boy-friend … This guy says he's been killed!'

'Oh my God!' Peggy put her arms around Josie and held her close.

'I want to go 'ome,' Josie whimpered, 'I just want to go 'ome.'

Hank nodded to Peggy, 'I'll take her. Perhaps the walk home in the fresh air will help.'

As they made their way along the riverbank the snow began to fall more heavily, shrouding the trees in gowns of white, while the reflection of stars shone on the slowly moving water. Josie remained silent, and neither of them spoke; it was as if no words were good enough – nothing could take the pain away. She stopped on the riverbank and bent down, trailing her hand through the water as memories of those nights, such a long, long time ago, filled her mind.

'Oh, Michael!' She sobbed as her tears fell to join the ripples in the water. ''Ow am I ever gonna live without you?'

They reached Piggots Row. It was strangely quiet for a Christmas Eve and the house looked cold and dark when they arrived. Little Andy was spending the night with his aunt in another part of the town. Josie could barely open the door. Her hands were shaking and tears blinded her eyes as she walked almost mechanically up the stairs to her bedroom and flung herself onto the bed, leaving Hank standing in the doorway, unsure of what to do.

He couldn't leave her like this, she might do something silly! Quietly he closed the door and went inside, following the sound of her crying. He reached the bedroom door. Josie was lying on the bed sobbing uncontrollably. For a moment Hank just stood there and then slowly lowered himself onto the bed and took her in his arms. She turned and clung to him desperately, trying to find solace in his arms. His grip tightened around her …

Goddam it! He was only human after all; he needed her and she needed him! Slowly and gently his hands started to explore her body. He felt her whole body tense, but then Josie gave a brief sigh as she surrendered to his love-making, while a little voice in her head kept repeating … It doesn't matter anymore! Nothing lasts forever … Tomorrow you could be dead!

It was early spring and the grounds of the manor house were ablaze with a riot of colours, as if they had been painted by an artist's hand, while a watery sun peeped out from behind the clouds creating an ever-changing scene.

Daphne was seated at her bedroom window, but she did not see any of the beauty. Her mind was too busy contemplating, scheming – but would Joe be a willing party? She shrugged her shoulders and stood up. The best thing to do was to have a walk down to the lake now, before Joe arrived. If she took the path from the back door no-one would see her – it was very secluded. Smiling, she turned and made her way to the door.

The sun was warm on her back as she negotiated the narrow, winding path. It was the perfect day – but she still wondered whether Joe would agree. He was almost neurotic about being seen with her; it would be a disaster if they were caught together and the only place they could be together was at the manor house when the servants were not around.

She reached the summerhouse and stood watching the ducks as they proudly led their brood of little ducklings around the lake. Her mind was still on Joe – because of his coffee-coloured skin and Indian blood, he was classed as a black man according to the laws governing American troops overseas and, as such, he was committing a crime by having an affair with a white woman. That alone was serious enough – but she also had to be careful, after all if Charles ever found out she could lose everything and no man was worth that!

Back at the base, Hank was lying on his bunk watching Joe as he carefully checked the pockets of his uniform, making sure that he had everything he needed. Joe smiled to himself, it wouldn't do to get Daphne pregnant, but it was okay, as the guys in his unit would say, he was well equipped! The packet of condoms was safely tucked into his breast pocket and now he could be on his way. He had the whole day off and he was going to make the best of it! Rumour had it that they would soon be shipped overseas and there would be no time for women and sex; they would be in the fighting line.

'Say, Joe…'

He turned around quickly and saw Hank sitting on his bunk staring at him.

'I wish you wouldn't go and see that dame today, she's bad news for you and it will only lead to trouble.'

'I know what I'm doing, buddy, don't worry about it – I'm not a kid, you know.' Joe's voice was a little sharp and impatient.

'But, man, you could have any woman. Why choose her for god's sake?'

Joe grinned and shrugged his shoulders. 'She's one hell of a hot babe, Hank – it's a shame to let her go to waste.'

He turned and picked up the keys to the Jeep with a flourish, then walked smartly out of the barracks.

The mid-morning sun was shining on the manor house as Joe drove up and parked the Jeep round the back of the gatehouse, well away from prying eyes. He jumped out and started to walk down the long, circular driveway until the house came into sight, then he stopped for a few minutes, as he always did when he visited Daphne – the view always managed to take his breath away. His eyes took in the golden hue of the Hamstone building, mellowed over the years but still amazingly beautiful. The mullion windows sparkled in the rays of the sun and the ornate brass fittings on the heavy oak door gleamed as if to welcome any visitors. Lush green lawns swept down to meet up with well-tended flowerbeds and to his right, in the distance, he could see the glittering blue water of the lake.

What would his family back home think if they could see him now! It was so different from his life in Alabama, especially the poorer area where he lived with his parents. It was just an old shack with no running water! That was home to him, but he still couldn't wait until this goddam war was over and he could go back home, to his girlfriend Louella and the wedding they planned to have as soon as he returned.

He had almost reached the steps leading to the front door when he saw Daphne beckoning him from the half-opened door. She was wearing a very scanty, short dress and from the look on her face she was ready for him. He ran up the steps and, as he reached the door, an arm came out and pulled him bodily into the house, where they both collapsed, laughing, on the plush green carpet covering the floor …

Daphne looked across the table at Joe as he sat smoking a cigar after a light lunch where the champagne and food had flowed freely. Joe caught her eye and winked at her. She smiled – now was a good time to ask him, but would he risk it? There was only one way to find out and that was to just ask him outright.

Getting up from the table she walked round to Joe, who was watching her with half-closed eyes as he puffed on his cigar. She put her hands on his knees and ran them slowly up and down his thighs. He threw his cigar onto the ashtray and grabbed her by the arms and held her tight.

'Come on, honey, let's go into the bedroom,' he said huskily.

'No, Joe, not the bedroom – it's such a lovely day, let's go down to the lake and make love. Just imagine it, the warmth of the sun on your back – or mine!' She giggled. 'Think how exciting it would be.'

'But, honey,' Joe protested, 'what if someone sees us?'

She placed a finger over his lips and kissed him on the nose.

'No-one is going to see us, Joe – it's Sunday, the staff have the day off and there is no reason for anyone to come here, and, anyway, they wouldn't see us if they did.'

She ran her hands over his body as she spoke; he would not be able to resist her much longer. He gave a soft groan and grabbing her by the hands, pulled her towards the back door …

Colonel Benson was furious as he drove his Bentley towards the entrance to the manor house. Where was that damn woman? He had tried ringing her before he left the base but there was no answer. Well, it was her own fault that she didn't know about the unexpected leave he had been given – he'd picked the phone up as soon as he knew. What more could a man do? As he drove through the gates something caught his eye, something that glistened in the sunlight, just behind the gatehouse. He stopped the car and walked slowly and silently to the rear of it. His face turned red with anger. It was a damn Yankee Jeep! What the hell was a Jeep doing on his land? He ran down the drive half in anger and half in fear. What was Daphne doing allowing a Yank to park his Jeep by the gatehouse? Perhaps she was not aware of him being on the premises! He ran into the house calling her name but there was no sign of her, then he noticed the back door was open. How many times had he told Daphne to be careful, to close the back door? Someone could easily get in and steal the family possessions and she wouldn't even know about it. He would have words with her when he found her! But, where the hell was she? The winding path to the lake seemed longer than he could ever remember as he hurried down it and, as he drew nearer, he could see there was someone on the grass by the lake. He started to run, calling out for Daphne, his breath coming in short, painful gasps.

The sound of her name being called startled Daphne. It had been an exquisite experience, as she knew it would be. As soon as they had got to the lake she had seductively slipped out of her scanty dress and knickers and Joe had taken her straight away. Now they were laying in each other's arms. She was still naked, but what did it matter, no-one could see them! Now she could hear someone calling her name! Startled she peered over Joe's shoulder and gave a gasp of horror at the sight of her husband running towards them. She had to think quickly, she wasn't going to lose everything because of a damn Yankee soldier. She started to struggle ... she had to make this look good!

'Help,' she screamed at the top of her voice. 'Help me, Charles, I'm being raped.'

Colonel Benson drew his pistol and pointed it straight at Joe's head.

'Get away from my wife, you bastard, and put your hands on your head or I'll blow your bloody head off.'

Joe looked desperately at Daphne. Their eyes met. Then she jumped up and ran to her husband, sobbing hysterically as she told him how she had been attacked by this Yank when she was taking a stroll in the grounds.

With his gun still pointed at Joe, the colonel, with one arm protectively around his wife, took the soldier back to the manor house and called the military police. Within fifteen minutes they had arrived and had taken Joe to the local jail.

Daphne spent the evening being pampered by her husband … after all, his poor wife had had the most dreadful experience.

The news spread like wildfire, first through the camp, and then filtered out into the town: 'Yank accused of raping the wife of Colonel Benson', screamed the headlines of the local paper.

Mrs Birchell crossed her arms over her ample bosom as if to emphasise her words. 'I told you when they first arrived in the town that they would be trouble,' she said, glaring at Mrs Cowan as they stood on the street corner. 'Now, look what we've got – some Yank raping the wife of the colonel. I mean … what is this world coming to!' She shrugged her shoulders as if at a loss what to say.

Mrs Cowan shrugged her shoulders. 'I think the colonel's wife is bit of a flighty one, if you ask me. I never did like her.'

'No-one is asking you, Beth! All I'm saying is that it's not safe for any woman these days with those Yanks about, even in your own home, like the poor colonel's wife was when this dreadful thing happened to her. Anyway, I haven't got time to be gossiping with you all day, I've got to get into the town and get something for my old man's dinner.'

'I'll come with you, I could do with a walk.'

Mrs Birchell raised her eyes to the sky then marched purposely down the road with Mrs Cowan almost running behind her.

'What does Edna think about it all?' Mrs Cowan gasped.

'I haven't seen her since this terrible thing happened,' Mrs Birchell replied shortly, then deliberately quickened her pace. In the town, Josie was trying to console Peggy as the news reached them that Joe had been arrested on a charge of rape.

'I can't believe Joe raped that woman – he's not that sort of guy, Josie. I've known him for a long time now and he really is sweet – he couldn't do it! He just couldn't do it!'

Josie didn't know what to say. Hank had told her a couple of months ago that Joe was having an affair with Colonel Benson's wife but he had made her promise not to say anything to Peggy. Now she was torn between Peggy and Hank, but she couldn't take sides … they were both her friends.

She put her arms around Peggy. 'It's alright, Peggy,' she said soothingly, 'I know Joe wouldn't do anything like that – don't worry 'e'll be alright, they'll let 'im off, you just wait and see.'

It had been two weeks since Joe was arrested and the town was beginning to settle down and find other things to talk about. But it was different for Josie and Peggy. He was a close friend and there was nothing they could do to help him. Since Joe had been arrested there had not been much news as to what was going on. All they knew was that he was being held in jail until the time of his trial and no matter how much they tried to obtain more information, or even be given permission to see him, they were met with steely stares and a hostile reaction. As far as the authorities were

210

concerned they were dealing with a black man who had raped a white woman – there was nothing more to discuss – he deserved what was coming to him.

10th February 1943

When there was a lull in the restaurant, Peggy called Josie over to her station.

'Wot is it, Peggy? I gotta 'urry up 'cause two old ladies 'ave just sat down on one of my tables and you know 'ow 'ateful they can be sometimes.'

'I just wanted to tell you that it's my sister's birthday today and she is coming to town this afternoon and bringing Andy with her. As it's our half-day today we've arranged to meet for lunch in the People's Pantry – you know, Josie, that cheap government restaurant down near the station.'

Josie nodded her head impatiently.

'Well,' Peggy continued with a sigh, 'all I wanted to tell you is that, if you like, you can come as well. It'll make a nice change to have lunch out.'

Josie nodded. 'Okay, I'll come wiv you when we finish work. Now I've gotta run. Those old ladies are looking around like they wanna kill somebody.'

The restaurant clock showed 12.45 p.m. and they had just fifteen minutes before the store and the restaurant closed. After a frantic dash to get all the tables cleared and set up for the next day, Josie and Peggy were in the staff room getting changed. Everyone else had left, but Josie couldn't find her purse and Peggy was getting agitated.

'Look, Josie, I am supposed to meet my sister at one o'clock and it's that time now. Do hurry up and find the damn thing.'

'You just go on and meet her, Peggy, and I'll stay 'ere till I find it. It's got to be somewhere 'cause I 'ad it when I came to work.'

'Okay, kid, but hurry up … meet us in the restaurant; we'll save you a seat don't worry.'

Peggy turned and ran from the room as Josie started searching the rest room more thoroughly. A few minutes later she found the purse on the floor, partially hidden by a long curtain hanging from the window. Grabbing it quickly in her hands she ran down the stairs, where she met the night watchman who had just come on duty.

'Hello, young lady, you're a little late leaving today ain't you?'

'I lost me purse, Mr Evans, but I've found it now. I'm gonna have lunch at the People's Pantry,' she said excitedly.

'Then you have a nice time, Miss, and take care.'

'You, too, Mr Evans,' she replied, smiling happily as she stepped out into the street.

In the distance she could hear the familiar drone of approaching aircraft. She quickened her pace – planes terrified her now – she had to get to the restaurant quickly.

The aircraft sounded low, far too low! Panic-stricken, she looked up just in time to see a plane swooping towards her, while the sharp rat-a-tat sound of machine-gun fire filled the now empty street. Josie ran blindly along the road. Suddenly she felt a pair of arms dragging her forcefully into a doorway as bullets strafed the whole street. Seconds later came the sound of a shrill whistle, and then a loud explosion. And then a second bomb exploded, sending a huge cloud of grey dust into the air, turning daylight into semi-darkness. She screamed and looked around, dazed from shock. Then her eyes began to focus on the man who had grabbed her. He was watching her closely, while somewhere in the distance came the familiar sound of fire engines racing to what was now a scene of utter devastation.

She turned to the man. 'It's just like when I was in the Blitz in London,' she said shakily. 'I dunno wot I would 'ave done if you weren't 'ere, mister … you've saved my life!'

The man was silent, his face shocked and pale. Silently he took Josie by the arm and they stepped out of the doorway and into the road. Josie gave a gasp of horror as she saw that the restaurant where she had worked, and which she had just left some five minutes ago, was now a shell. She ran up the road towards it – what about the night watchman! Where was he? Was he dead? She reached the pile of rubble and started pulling at it frantically, calling out his name, 'Mr Evans, Mr Evans, where are you?'

But there was no answer – no sign of life. Then she remembered Peggy – she would know what to do. They were so lucky it was their half-day, as otherwise they would have both been killed – just like Mr Evans had been.

She turned and ran down the road in the direction of the People's Pantry, but, as she turned the corner, a stab of fear went through her heart. In front of her a cloud of thick grey smoke was rising lazily from the scene of utter devastation … the People's Pantry had taken a direct hit from the second bomb. She ran, stumbling over debris that was strewn all over the road.

'Please, God,' she prayed, 'let them be alright. Please, God, they 'ave to be alright. Don't take them away from me!'

She reached the remains of the restaurant and started pulling desperately at the heavy bricks.

'Peggy, Peggy, where are you? Answer me, Peggy, please,' she cried, as tears streamed down her face.

An ARP man ran towards her. 'Miss, come away, there's nothing you can do – it took a direct hit – no-one survived.'

She turned on him angrily. 'My friend and her little boy are in there. I've got to find them … they're not dead … do you 'ear me … they're not dead!' she screamed.

The man shook his head sadly and walked away. Gradually more people arrived on the scene to help retrieve the bodies that were buried there.

Josie worked for over two hours; her hands became burnt and bleeding as she wrestled with large pieces of smouldering wood and concrete, but, somehow, she didn't feel the pain. Then as she lifted one large piece of wood she saw something yellow amongst the dust and debris. She tore at the debris frantically until she pulled it free – it was a yellow, furry duck just like the one Andy had and which he carried with him wherever he went.

'Oh, my God! Andy, Andy where are you?'

Desperately, she pulled at a smouldering plank of wood and a little arm came into view, then bit by bit she dragged more pieces away until she saw Andy's body laying on its side, his fair hair encrusted with dirt and fine pieces of stone. His little face was beginning to turn blue.

Josie picked him up and felt for his heart – but there was no beat. Andy was dead. She cradled him in her arms, sitting on the pile of rubble, rocking back and forth as if in some small way she could comfort him. How long she sat there she would never know – all that she could recall was someone bending over her and gently taking him away. She couldn't even move – it was as if she was rooted to the spot, and she knew, deep down inside her, that Peggy was somewhere in that rubble – and that Peggy was dead too. But she didn't want to leave them; they were her family and now they had been taken from her, just like Michael.

She raised her eyes to the sky. If there was a God up there, why was he letting this happen? Why did he take people from her that she loved? Had she been so bad in her life that he was punishing her? The sound of someone stumbling over the rubble startled her and she turned to find Hank by her side.

He fell to his knees and clasped her in his arms. 'Thank God, Josie, you're okay. Gee baby, when I heard the news about the bombing I went crazy wondering if you were okay. I managed to get a few hours off and I went straight to the restaurant where you work, but, honey, it just isn't there anymore. Then someone said they needed help round here – there are a lot of people trapped. They say that over a hundred people were in the restaurant when it got a direct hit.'

Hank paused for a moment, as if hardly able to comprehend what had happened. 'I couldn't believe my eyes when I saw you, Josie – why are you just sitting here?'

Josie rubbed her face with her hands in despair. 'It's Peggy and Andy! Oh, Hank, they're dead. They were 'ere. I

215

was supposed to be 'ere but I lost my purse and I was late. I should 'ave been 'ere … I would 'ave been dead too.'

Hank stared at her. In his mind he kept thinking of his own country – they had no idea what it was like to have bombs fall on their towns, or to see family or friends lying dead in the road. Yet the Brits took it all in their stride, and you had to admire them – they were a tough race.

Josie was staring into the distance, her face blackened with dirt and grime, her eyes empty with despair.

'Come on, Josie, you can't stay here. Let me take you home.'

'I can't go home – I don't 'ave an 'ome now Peggy's gone – I don't know wot to do.' Her voice trailed off and she lapsed into silence.

Gently he took her by the hand and led her from the ruins of the restaurant to the river, where they sat on its grassy bank silently staring into the water.

'What are you going to do, honey? What are you going to do about tonight?'

He hesitated for a moment as he realised that she hadn't even thought about the trauma of going back to the house she had shared with Peggy.

'I can't go back to the house tonight,' she cried. 'I don't ever want to go back.'

Hank put an arm around her and pulled her close to him.

'It's okay, babe, don't worry – I have to be back at the base by midnight, but we will find somewhere before I have to leave.'

He pulled her to her feet. 'Let's go back into town. I know of a bed and breakfast place that a lot of our guys stay at when they are on leave. I'm sure it will be okay for you, Josie.'

Silently they walked along the tow-path and then over the bridge towards the town, both of them deep in their own private thoughts.

Hollybrooke House was situated on the outskirts of the town – an old Victorian house, it stood tall and proud in its own grounds. Josie looked at it suspiciously.

'I dunno if I can afford to stay in a place like this, Hank,' she said as they approached the main door.

'Don't worry, I've got plenty of money.'

The woman looked at the tall, good-looking American and then her gaze took in the bedraggled, blood-stained girl by his side.

'Do you have a room for tonight?' Hank asked.

'A double room I presume,' she replied with a slight smile on her face.

Hank shrugged his shoulders. 'Don't mind which, ma'am, it's only for the young lady here. She has been bombed out from her home and needs a bed for the night.'

'Poor little love,' the woman replied. Then, hurrying round from the desk, she put an arm around Josie's shoulders and led her to a room just down the corridor.

'You just make yourself at home, my dear, and if you don't feel like getting up for breakfast in the morning, I'll bring it to you.'

Josie nodded briefly and walked aimlessly into the room. Hank followed her.

'Why don't you take a bath, honey? You'll feel much

217

better when you're all cleaned up. I've got a few hours before I am due back at camp so I'll just sit here and wait for you – just take your time.'

She sank into the bathtub and washed the grime and the blood from her body.

Her mind was a blank – somehow she seemed to have died inside and life seemed to stretch like an endless, winding road in front of her and there was nothing left. She didn't want to see or talk to anyone at the moment – not even Hank! Why had she been spared? What was the point of it all? Then her thoughts turned to Lucy and she sighed heavily. It seemed an eternity since she had seen her sister, although in truth it was only about eight months, but she missed her; she needed her so much.

The landlady smiled as she saw Josie coming down the stairs the next morning.

'Are you coming in for breakfast, dearie?' she asked.

Josie shook her head. She couldn't face food – she didn't even want to face people – she just wanted to go and look for Peggy.

'Your young man, the one who brought you here last night, has left a message for you, dearie. He said for you to wait for him, he's got a couple of days leave and he's on his way. Shouldn't be too long now. Come and have a cup of tea. You surely look like you could do with one.'

Josie followed her into the dining room and sat in the corner waiting for Hank. There were only a few people having breakfast and, as they ate, they talked in muted tones about the bombing of the night before. Josie thought of Peggy. Had they found her yet? Where could she go to find out if she was really dead? But, of course, she must be dead, no-one could have survived that blast.

She was turning these thoughts over in her mind when the door opened and Hank came into the room and sat down beside her.

'Are you okay, honey?' he asked, but in his heart he knew she wasn't – but what else could he say to her. Nothing could take away the pain and misery she was going through.

Blankly she stared at him, and then slowly nodded; her eyes were dark and haunted.

'I want to go and find out about Peggy, Hank; I gotta know wot has 'appened to 'er.' She looked at him in desperation.

He nodded his head and got up from his chair. 'Come on, Josie, we will find out somehow. It's best to get it over with as soon as possible.'

He put a comforting arm around her shoulders as they made their way to the site of the bombing. There they found several soldiers clearing up the area. Hank walked up to one of them.

'Say, buddy, we're looking for a friend of ours who was here yesterday when it got hit. How can we find out where she is?'

The young soldier wiped his brow and shook his head. 'All the bodies have been taken to St Mary's Church for identification. Sorry, mate, but there were no survivors. It was a direct hit – the poor buggers didn't stand a chance.'

Hank patted him on the shoulder and walked back to where Josie stood.

'They have taken everyone to the church for identification, Josie. I'm so sorry, honey, but no-one survived.'

He put his arms around her and she clung to him silently and desperately for a few moments before pulling herself away.

'I am going to the church,' she said quietly. 'I'm gonna say goodbye to Peggy.'

The old church hall was silent except for the sound of footsteps as people quietly filed up and down the long rows of the dead – occasionally grief would overcome someone and the sound of uncontrollable sobbing filled the air. Hank stared at the victims as he followed Josie along the long rows. There were young and old, women and men, teenagers and young babies lying on trestle tables, their lives cut abruptly short. He wondered how any of it made sense! How many more were to die before this damn war was over? These were innocent people going about their everyday business; people who didn't want this war – why should they have to die for it? He thought of his own country – they didn't know how lucky they were!

At the far end of the hall a small portion was designated for babies and young children who were as yet unclaimed. There they found the body of little Andy ... he looked like a little cherub with his curly blond hair and milky white skin. Josie bent over and picked him up, cradling him in her arms as if trying to comfort him in some way.

'Honey, what are you going to do with him – shouldn't you leave him where we found him?'

She turned to face him, with Andy still clutched in her arms. 'Peggy is somewhere 'ere in this room and I'm gonna find 'er. Andy belongs with his mum, even if 'e's dead!' she replied defiantly.

They soon found Peggy, lying on a table, half-covered

with a sheet; her blonde hair framing her face like a halo. There were no visible signs of injury, just a small bruise on the side of her cheek. She looked so peaceful and beautiful it didn't seem possible that she was dead. Josie gasped and pulled Andy's body closer to her, then, fighting back the tears, she carefully laid Andy next to his mother and kissed them both. Slowly, Hank pulled the sheet over their bodies and then, taking Josie by the hand, turned and walked out of the church. Suddenly he stopped on the church path and turned to face Josie.

'Honey, don't you think you should see your mother and tell her what has happened? She will be worried about you, Josie. Everyone knows about the bombing and the death toll, which is, so they say, now over one hundred people.'

Josie nodded her head. She knew that was all she could do right now. Go and see her mother and see what she had to say. Perhaps for a few days she could stay with her at the school.

'I'll come with you, Josie, if you like.'

She shook her head in desperation. 'No! No! You can't come – she don't like Americans and she won't 'ave anything to do wiv me if she sees you.'

Hank smiled. It was a little reassuring smile. He had realised in the past few days that he loved her so much. He thought about the letter he had written just two days ago to his fiancée, telling her about Josie and his feelings for her. He wanted to break their engagement so he could ask Josie to marry him. But what were her feelings for him? After all, she had never said she cared for him, and ever since that night when they had made love she had kept him at arm's length. She still seemed to be in love with the English guy who got killed. Maybe she needed a little more time, but one day he would ask her.

Josie left Hank at the end of Westcott Road and made her way to No. 7, where her mother worked as a cook. It was a large, detached house in a road of equally large, imposing properties. At one time No. 7 had been a large private home but now it was a private school for the children of wealthy people. She walked slowly up the driveway and rang the bell, feeling acutely aware of her dirty clothing – she had been in them for two days, and they were stained with dirt and blood. What would she say about her appearance and, more to the point, would she find the courage to tell her she was pregnant?

The big, oak door swung open and she was confronted by a tall, grey-haired lady, beautifully dressed in a tweed suit. She eyed Josie up and down with some suspicion.

'What do you want?' the lady asked finally. 'I am sure you have come to the wrong address.'

'I've come to see me mum,' Josie replied. 'She works 'ere as a cook.'

The lady thought for a moment. 'Are you her daughter?' she asked incredulously.

Josie nodded her head.

'Have you been in an accident? Your clothes are very dirty and I must say you really look quite ill.'

Josie ignored her question.

'Could you just tell my mum I'm 'ere.' She didn't want to talk to strangers, she just wanted her mum to tell her that everything was going to be alright.

'You should have gone to the back door, my dear – that's the servants' entrance down that path there.'

The lady pointed in the direction of a small gravel path leading to the rear of the building. She gave Josie a brief smile, then stepped back inside and closed the door.

Josie followed the path until she was at the rear of the house, where, through a window, she could see her mother busy at a sink. Her heart sank at the thought of confronting her. With trembling fingers she pressed the bell and the nausea that she had been experiencing lately began to overwhelm her. The door suddenly opened and her mother stood there, her eyes confirming the shock she felt at the sight of her daughter's appearance.

Josie felt tears well up – she wanted her mother to put her arms around her and say everything was going to be fine, but her mother was remembering that time, so many years ago, when Josie had had the same desperate look on her face when she had picked her up from that children's home in the north. Two and a half years Josie had been there until the scandal broke and it was closed down … now the memory came back to haunt her!

'Josie, what on earth are you doing here in that filthy state? I knew it was wrong for you to share a house with that Peggy – now look at the state of you! What your father would say if he could see you now, God only knows!'

'Please, Mum, can I come in?' Josie was feeling on the point of collapse and was grateful when her mother stood aside and indicated to her that she should go into the kitchen. She pulled out a chair from under the kitchen table and told Josie to sit down.

Josie sat nervously on the edge of the chair, not sure how

to begin – so much had happened in the past few weeks. Dare she tell her mother that she thought she was pregnant? Mother's voice interrupted Josie's train of thought.

'I'll make you a cup of tea, but by the look of you, Josie, you need a good bath and some clean clothes. This is what comes of living with people like that Peggy – and just look at your hair! I'll bet she was the one who dyed it for you.'

Josie took a deep breath. 'Peggy's dead, Mum,' she said, her voice barely audible.

Her mother swung around from the sink. 'What on earth are you talking about? Dead? How can she be … she's only a young woman?'

'In the bombing yesterday; she was at the People's Pantry when it got blown up and 'er little boy was with 'er.'

Mother's face turned visibly pale as she stared in disbelief at her young daughter. She felt uncomfortable – past memories were fighting with the present – her mind flashed back to the time, many years ago, when Charlie collapsed at work with a burst ulcer and was hospitalised for weeks. Without his wages coming in they were starving, until that day when Mr Manelli who owned the grocer's shop made a proposition. Sex for food! She had become pregnant and when Josie was born it was obvious that she was his child. She was so different from her other two, who were blonde and fair-skinned. Over the years the guilt had never left her and she had taken her frustrations out on Josie. Now, seeing her sitting in front of her with her face buried in her hands, she felt remorse. It was time to break down the barriers she had put between them – but how could she do that without revealing her secret?

A heavy silence hung in the room while Josie debated whether or not to ask her mother if she could stay with her, but she had no choice because she had nowhere else to go.

'Mum, can I come 'ere and stay for awhile. I ain't gonna go back to Peggy's 'ouse, and I don't know wot is gonna 'appen, but I just can't stay there.'

Her mother turned to face her. 'I will have to ask Miss Rope, but if you do stay here, Josie, there are certain rules that you will have to abide by. You can't be out every night. That will have to stop. Now, stay here while I go and find Miss Rope and ask her.'

She disappeared out of the kitchen door and Josie heard her footsteps echoing along the long passageway. Josie sat deep in thought. She had to tell her mother about her pregnancy, but obviously now was not a good time. She had to tell Hank! It was his baby and he had a right to know, but why was she finding it so difficult to talk about it?

Her mother soon returned. 'You can stay here for a while Josie. Miss Rope says she doesn't mind, but you will have to share my bedroom.'

'Thanks, Mum,' Josie replied, feeling like a great weight had been lifted from her shoulders. 'I'll go and get my things from Peggy's 'ouse now – I should be back in a couple of hours.'

Hank was still waiting patiently on the corner of the street. She smiled when she saw him. He was always so reliable. Life would not be the same without him, but the Yanks were pulling out soon … it could even be tomorrow!

'What did your ma say, Josie? Can you stay at the school with her?'

Hank was anxious; their time together was running out and he would feel much better if he knew she was back safely home with her family.

'It's okay, me mum said I could stay for awhile but I gotta get my things from Peggy's and I've only got two hours, so can you come wiv me Hank?'

'Sure, honey, but it won't be easy.' He felt a lump form in his throat and hastily swallowed as they turned and made their way towards the towpath – both acutely aware that the last time Josie was at the house it had been a home full of love and laughter – now it would be just a shell.

The young airman sat in shocked silence, unable to comprehend what had happened. His eyes took in the few toys scattered around the floor where his son had been playing less than 48 hours ago. His wife's slippers were thrown casually in the middle of the room. How many times had he told her about leaving them lying around for someone to fall over? Now she would never walk through that door again. He picked up Andy's pyjamas from the armchair and clutched them close to his heart, trying to imprint the smell of his warm little body forever in his mind.

He had always thought that if anyone in his family got killed in this war it would be him! Not his family. Not his wife and little boy. He buried his face in his hands as the reality of it all swept over him and raw sobs shook his body. He was not aware of the front door being opened or of Josie as she walked into the kitchen.

She knew instinctively that it was Peggy's husband, although they had never met. She also knew that it was not the time for conversation – he needed to be alone! Hank stood uncertainly in the doorway, sensing the man's despair. He didn't know what to do. Nothing could take the man's pain away. Nothing could bring back what he wanted most in this world. He was best left alone to grieve.

Josie crept stealthily up the stairs to her bedroom and started to pack her meagre belongings – she picked up the skirt that Peggy had made her for the Christmas Ball at the Olympia and cuddled it close to her body for a moment, then quickly pushed her clothes into a bag and tip-toed downstairs to where Hank was still waiting by the front door. Josie turned and looked sadly at the house that had been her home for such a short but happy time and then, gently, she closed the front door. That chapter in her life was closed and finished forever.

'Shall we have a seat here for awhile, honey?' Hank pointed to a wooden bench on the riverbank.

Josie nodded silently.

They had hardly spoken since they had left Piggots Road for the last time – there was an air of uncertainty between them. Hank felt uneasy – he knew they would be pulling out soon, he could see the activity around the base, something big was going on, but they wouldn't be told anything until the last minute. He was in love with Josie and he needed to know how she felt about him – he wanted to tell her about the letter he had sent just two days ago, telling his girl-friend in the States that he had met someone else and that he wanted to break off the engagement, but so much had happened in the past few days, it just didn't seem the right time.

Josie was a strange girl, she never gave any indication of how she felt about him. He glanced at her out of the corner of his eye and sighed. She was just sitting on the bench staring across the river, probably thinking of that guy in the Air Force, but that was long ago and it was time to get on with life!

'Some day, kid, if we survive this war, let's get married.'

It was almost as if Josie could hear Michael's voice as she stared into space. The river was, after all, a very special place – a place that would forever belong to her and Michael – nothing could ever change that. She knew, in her heart, that Hank loved her and she sensed that he was about to ask her to marry him, but she belonged here, by the river where she first found love and where precious memories were made.

Chapter 10

In the town, Mrs Birchell was busy with her washing; steam from the boiler wafted across the little scullery at the back of the house. She hated washing day but it had to be done, and once it was over she could settle down with a nice cup of tea and put her feet up. She had managed to get hold of a couple of old magazines and she was looking forward to a couple of hours of peace and quiet. A timid knock on the back door broke through her train of thought. Who on earth could that be at this time of the day, and especially on her washing day? If it was that annoying Mrs Cowan she would give her a piece of her mind – she knew that she didn't like visitors, especially on a day like today. With a deep sigh she opened the door and came face to face with Mrs Riley!

'Hello, Edna, what a surprise to see you during the week. Usually you are busy at the manor. Is there something wrong?'

Edna nodded her head. She looked pale and unhappy.

'Come on in, then, and I'll make us a nice cup of tea and you can tell me all about it. Go on, straight through to the living room and sit yourself on the sofa. I won't be long making the tea.'

As she stood waiting for the kettle to boil she couldn't help wondering what had brought Edna to her door. They had always been good friends but these days they did not see much of each other, especially as Edna was having a bit of trouble with her legs and liked to stay at the manor house when she was off duty so she could rest them a bit more. She placed the two cups of tea onto a tray and carried it into the living room.

'Now, Edna,' she said, settling herself comfortably on a chair opposite, 'is there some trouble at the manor then?'

Mrs Riley shook her head slightly. 'It's not really trouble – it's to do with that American soldier who is in prison.' She paused for a moment while Mrs Birchell sat with bated breath. How could Edna be connected with something to do with that American soldier? She could contain herself no longer.

'Well, out with it, Edna! What is going on? And why have you come to me about it?'

Edna shook her head sadly. 'To tell you the truth, I didn't know who to turn to and I really need some advice. Then I thought of you.'

Mrs Birchell nodded her head impatiently and waited for her to continue.

'You know they have charged that American with raping Mrs Benson – well, he didn't rape her – it was all her fault.'

'But, how can you say that – he was caught in the act by Colonel Benson.'

'I know, but you see, on the day it happened … well, it was my day off and I had told Mrs Benson that I was going to visit my mother, as I usually do on a Sunday. Anyway, I was getting ready and my legs started to really play me up and I knew I couldn't walk that distance, so I decided to stay at the manor and just take it easy. Anyway, I pulled my armchair up to the window and sat looking out. I have such a lovely view from that window, Lil. I can see right down to the lake.' She stopped for a moment and took a sip of her tea.

'Did you see Mrs Benson with that American then, Edna?'

'Yes, I saw them walking down the path together. She was dressed in such a revealing dress that I was quite shocked, to tell you the truth. She was all over the American, pulling him along by the hand, though I think he was enjoying it as well, Lil. Anyway, I watched as they went down to the lake and then …' She gave a short gasp and put her hand to her mouth. '…you won't believe what happened next!'

'Well, tell me for goodness sake, Edna. Hurry up and spit it out.'

'Mrs Benson stripped off all her clothes and flung herself on the grass. Then she grabbed the soldier by the hand and pulled him on top of her. He didn't rape her … more like she raped him!'

Mrs Birchell sat in shocked silence for several minutes, mulling over everything that Edna had told her. It was an incredible story, but if Edna told it, then it must be true! She was a very honest woman. Abruptly she got to her feet and started to pace the floor, stopping every now and then to put her hand over her mouth, and looking very pensive as Edna watched her anxiously. Suddenly, Mrs Birchell stopped pacing and turned to face her.

'Why haven't you told the police this? For goodness sake, Edna! What are you waiting for? Think of what it must be like for that poor young lad, so far from his family and friends and to know that he's being accused of a crime that he didn't commit.'

Edna bowed her head and covered her face with her hands, then she spoke in a voice that was barely audible.

'I'm afraid of losing my job and I know it is wrong of me but I think they will let him off. If I went to the police it would cause such a scandal in the village that I would have to leave and I don't know where I would go. It would be difficult to go to mother's house because she's only got one bedroom, so that wouldn't work.'

They sat in silence for several moments, then Mrs Birchell spoke.

'You came for my advice, Edna, and I am going to give it to you, whether you like what I say or not. You are a witness to what really went on at the manor that day – you are the only witness and the only one who can save that young lad. I can't force you into doing anything you don't want to do, Edna, but you had better think seriously over the next couple of days and I hope you come to the same conclusion that I have – that you've no choice but to tell the truth to the police before it's too late.'

Edna walked slowly down the path and made her way back to the manor, her mind in a whirl. Should she go to the police and cause an uproar in the village or should she wait until the court decided? If the court found him innocent and he was let off, everyone would be happy and she would keep her job. But what if he was found guilty!

The date for the commencement of the trial had arrived and due to the huge interest in the case the courtroom was crowded. From the public gallery people watched in anticipation at the scene in front of them. The weather was unseasonably warm for late spring and as Joe stood in the dock beads of perspiration formed on his forehead and started to trickle slowly down his face. He took out his handkerchief and mopped his brow. He glanced around the court, his eyes coming to rest on Daphne. She was sitting in the front row with her husband by her side. Their eyes met briefly but then she turned away to speak to her husband, who nodded his head before looking up at Joe.

The case had been dealt with quickly and now the tension in the room was electric as they all waited for the jury to return with a verdict. The large, wooden clock on the wall solemnly ticked the minutes away – the jury had been out for just over two hours now. Joe stood patiently. How much longer did he have to wait?

It was twenty minutes later that the side door opened and the jurors filed into the room. Subdued, they silently took their seats one by one and waited expectantly. The judge coughed. He glanced briefly at Joe, then back to the jurors.

'Have you reached a verdict?' he asked firmly.

'Yes, your Honour,' replied the head juror as he handed the clerk a small slip of paper, which was passed to the judge.

The judge stared at it for a few moments, his face impassive, and then putting it slowly on the bench in front of him he told Joe to stand and face him.

Their eyes met … Joe bit his lip … the tension in the courtroom was almost unbearable as they waited for the pronouncement. Then the judge spoke.

'You have been found guilty of the crime of rape.' The judge paused for a moment and leaned to his right ... slowly he placed a black cloth over his white wig.

A collective gasp of horror swept through the courtroom, and then deathly silence as the judge continued.

'I have no alternative but to have you taken to a place where you will be kept in custody until such a time when you will be taken to a place of execution, and there you will be hung by the neck until you are dead.'

Suddenly a woman's voice screamed out from the balcony. 'But he didn't do it! I was there and I saw what happened. He is innocent!'

The judge called for order in the court and two policemen hurried to the gallery and Mrs Riley was escorted from the courtroom.

Joe felt the room sway and put his hand on the rail to steady himself. He turned his head and stared across the room at Daphne. She looked up with cold, unfeeling eyes and then, holding his gaze for no more than a second or two, she took her husband by the arm and walked coolly out of the side door.

Josie sat stunned as she heard the verdict. She wanted to scream out that he wasn't guilty – Daphne had lied! She had lied to the court and to her God and she had got away with it. But in her heart she knew that the verdict had already been decided before the court hearing and that racial prejudice was the deciding factor. How was she going to tell Hank? How could she tell him that his best friend was going to be hung?

It was now 4.30 p.m. and she watched as Joe was taken

below to the cells and people began to filter out from the courtroom. Josie had arranged to meet Hank by the riverbank at 5 o'clock. It was time she left. Wearily she got up from her seat and walked outside.

The sun was shining while white clouds scuttled across the sky like naughty children at play. As it was late spring, the air had lost its chilly fingers and now was caressing her body with a gentle warmth, but her heart was as cold as ice. Joe was going to be hanged and there was nothing anyone could do to prevent it. But what was that trouble in the gallery all about, when that woman shouted out that Joe was not guilty? Crazy woman! How could she possibly know what went on at the manor?

Hank was already on the seat when she arrived and he jumped up quickly when he saw her and came running towards her.

'Honey, what happened … did they let him off?'

Josie shook her head, hardly able to speak; she just stared at him with large, round eyes.

'For God's sake, Josie, tell me what happened. Where is Joe?' he said, grabbing her by the shoulders.

She burst into tears and flung herself in his arms.

'They're gonna to hang 'im – they took 'im away to the cells and that Daphne was grinning when they took Joe away.'

Hank sat heavily onto the seat and buried his face in his hands. This damn war had screwed all their lives up. Poor Joe – what sort of justice was it in this country when a guy can be accused of rape just because the woman involved was a society dame. Joe's fate had been sealed before he had even walked into that courtroom! But didn't he warn him on that very day that he had left for the manor? He had had a premonition that something bad was about to happen, but he didn't expect it to be that. He turned his head and looked at Josie – she was deep in thought. Then he turned and stared at the dark, swirling river, his mind in a turmoil. He must tell her, he must tell her now; there was not much time left. Reaching out, he clasped her in his arms. The words were almost choking him.

'Josie, I don't know how to tell you this and I really shouldn't – but the fact is we are pulling out tomorrow – I don't know when or even if I will ever see you again. Oh, honey, I can't bear the thought of leaving you.'

She sat rigid and silent. There was a tension in the air that was almost tangible. Hank felt a pain in his heart as he slowly removed his arms from around her body, but still she didn't speak. He had heard that the Brits were reserved but this was ridiculous. Even when he said he was pulling out, she hadn't said a word! It was obvious she didn't care for him.

He looked at his watch – it was time to leave. Reaching out, he took her hand and they walked to the bridge – the army truck was picking him up in five minutes to take him back to camp. He felt an indescribable longing sweep over him – a longing to hold her just one more time, to feel her warm body close to his and her soft lips on his face. In the distance he could see the truck coming towards them – he held out his arms.

Josie hesitated for a moment, then, turning quickly, she started to walk away; she didn't want him to see the tears in

236

her eyes. Hank felt a lump rise in his throat and swallowed hastily as the truck screeched to a halt. He took a step towards it, and then turned.

'I'll write, Josie. I'll write to you when I can.' His voice, muffled with emotion, echoed through the air as her footsteps faded into the distance.

Joe was lying on his bunk in the cell. His unit was pulling out today and he was left behind – left to face death in this goddam country. He got up and paced the floor, his mind going over the events of the past few days. The rays of a midday sun filtered through the bars at the small window and he stopped pacing to look up at the tiny bit of blue sky he could see. He looked down at his hands, his nails that he had chewed until they had started to bleed. He thought of his parents. How were they taking it? His girl-friend, Louella? She'd promised to wait for him – now he would never come back. He would never see his home or his parents again. He could see his mother now, leaning against the old wooden gate as she stared along the dirt track, as she had done so many times before when he was a child, looking for him, always looking. Never again would he see the smile that crossed her face or see her outstretched arms as she waited to greet him when he came into sight.

The distant sound of engines revving up broke through his train of thought. He climbed onto his bunk and leaned over to grab at the bars covering the tiny window. At the camp, the first of the convoy had started their long journey to the coast. They were leaving. Leaving forever. He gripped the bars until his knuckles turned white as he watched the trucks pass the prison gates.

Tears streamed down his face as he screamed out in anguish. 'For God's sake, Daphne, tell them – tell them the truth before it's too late!'

But his words fell silently against the cold, grey stone of the prison walls as the roar of engines gradually faded into the distance. The Yanks had left …

A mile away, Josie was standing on the bridge overlooking the river. She too could hear the sound of the trucks as they left for the coast. She leaned forward and rested her arms on the low, stone wall and gazed down at the river which held so many memories, reflecting on the past, of the times she had spent with Michael.

She remembered the happy times with Peggy when they walked along the riverbank on their way to the Olympia to meet Hank and Joe. Now, one by one, they were being taken from her. A deep sob rose in her throat and almost immediately she felt the first stirring of the baby. It was if it felt her pain and had responded with a sudden movement. Instinctively she placed her hands on her stomach as she rocked back and forth and wondered how much longer she could keep it a secret from her mother. An hour passed and it was time for her to leave the river. As she walked through the town she could sense a heavy, oppressive silence hanging over it – it was as if the Yanks had taken part of the town with them, together with the hearts of most of the young girls. Their vibrant energy had disappeared like the sun behind a cloud and life would never be the same again.

Deep in thought, Josie made her way through the town heading towards the prison. She had made a promise to Joe that she would visit him today. How would she cope? How was Joe coping? What could she say to him?

Joe sat gaunt and pale-faced on his bunk and barely looked up as the warder unlocked the cell door to let Josie in. She stood for a few minutes and stared at him; this wasn't the Joe she remembered, that full-of-life guy who was so much fun to be with. He looked a beaten man who was just waiting to get this ordeal over with. Josie sat next to him on the bunk and put her arm around his shoulders. He turned his face towards her and looked with unseeing eyes; it was as if he knew she was there but, at the same time couldn't quite comprehend what was going on. She wondered if, maybe, they had given him some drugs to help him cope! They sat in complete silence until the sound of a key in the lock made her look up. The door opened and the warder stepped inside.

'Joe, the governor wants to see you in his office straight away.' He took Joe by the arm, then turned and smiled at Josie. 'You, Miss, just take a seat in the waiting room for awhile. Shouldn't take very long.'

The governor watched as the warder ushered Joe into his office. With a slight wave of his hand he dismissed the warder and waited until he had left and the door closed behind him. Then, pointing to a chair opposite him, he asked Joe to take a seat.

'I have to inform you,' the governor said as he settled himself more comfortably in his chair, 'that new evidence has come to light which seems to prove that you were not guilty of raping Mrs Benson and, under the circumstances, an emergency session of the court has been convened where the new evidence will be presented to the judge. If he agrees that you have been wrongly accused, then steps will be taken to procure your release from prison.' The governor peered over his spectacles at Joe and smiled. 'In the meantime, Joe, you will be moved immediately from the condemned cell to another one which you will probably find a little more comfortable.'

Joe sat mesmerised, unable to quite take it all in. What was this new evidence?

Had Daphne finally changed her mind? He felt someone tap him on the shoulder – it was the warder.

'The young lady is still waiting for you, Joe. Visiting time is all but over now but you can have five minutes together. That'll be long enough to tell her your good news.'

Chapter 11

D-Day, 6th June 1944

Hank watched the dawn break over northern France as the warship ploughed its way through a choppy sea to reach the Normandy beach. It had been a miserable night; the ship was full to capacity and there was barely room to move. He struggled to stand up; his heavy combat gear felt damp and cold from the early morning mist. The sky was dotted with hundreds of planes and gliders carrying troops who were to be parachuted inland of Utah Beach, while in the distance he could hear the thud of exploding bombs being dropped from German planes as they desperately tried to halt the invasion.

Hank stretched his legs and then crouched down again; he could see the beach in the distance and he knew there was very little time left. Maybe five minutes! Just five more minutes and then they would be storming the beaches. Images of Josie flashed before him and he felt the pain in his heart. It had been over two months now since he had seen her. Most of that time the regiment had been in training for the invasion and there had been no time for dwelling on memories.

Bursts of machine-gun fire, intermingled with the

screams of wounded soldiers, echoed through the morning air as the troops made the final stage of their journey on coastguard assault vessels, which would take them closer to the beach. He slid his legs over the side and felt the coldness of the sea rise up to his thighs. Holding his rifle high above his head he waded desperately through the water, while all around him his buddies were falling like flies, to be washed away on the ebb of the tide. He reached the beach and the machine-gun fire became more intense as units of German soldiers, hidden in the sand dunes, opened fire on them.

In front of him he saw a mound of sand and ran towards it, looking for cover. Suddenly, he came face to face with a young German soldier. Hank quickly raised his gun and aimed straight between the soldier's eyes and fired.

'That's for Peggy and Andy you German bastard,' he screamed. Then, as if in slow motion, he saw him fall to the ground and for a few moments everything seemed surreal as the screams of the wounded and the unstoppable sound of heavy machine-gun fire moulded together and transported him into Hell.

He didn't see the gun that was pointed at him. There was just this searing pain that suddenly stabbed him in the back and he fell across the body of the dead soldier. Through the comforting darkness that was swirling around him he heard a voice. It seemed to come from a long, long way ... 'It's okay mate, we'll soon get you patched up.' He had the sensation that he was being carried, but then the darkness closed in on him.

The summer sun beat down mercilessly from an azure sky as Josie made her way wearily back to her lodgings. It was three o'clock in the afternoon and she was on her way home from work. It was hard, physical work but she didn't mind, at least it gave her some money at the end of the week, money that paid her rent and put food in her mouth. She had managed to rent two rooms at the top of an old Victorian house on Bath Road just over a month ago, and it was about that time that she got a job working in the canteen of a building site just over a mile and a half away. Reaching the house she climbed the twenty-five stairs to the attic and gratefully opened the door.

The rooms were small and barely furnished and as she looked around she felt a sinking feeling in her stomach … was this what her life was to be? She sat down on the hard-backed chair by the small window and gazed out across the rooftops. In the distance she could just see the outline of the hospital where her baby would be born in three months time and her thoughts turned to Hank. His last words came back to her as clearly as if he was standing in the room: 'I'll write, Josie, I'll write.' But that had been four months ago and there had been no letter!

She got up and went into the kitchen to make herself a cup of tea, but when she opened the tea caddy all she saw was the dust from the tea leaves sitting on the bottom and there were no coupons to buy any until next week. It was so much easier when she lived with her mother, she thought, sighing heavily, and somehow the rations seemed to stretch much further when they were at the manor house. She looked in the cupboard to find something to eat but there was nothing to make a sandwich with and her ration of two ounces of butter had been used up yesterday. She opened the cheese dish and found that it was empty. On the top shelf she found a tin of beans ... Josie shrugged her shoulders. Well, that would have to do for dinner tonight. She went back and sat in the chair by the window, suddenly feeling very lonely and lost.

The sound of a voice from downstairs broke through her reverie and she quickly jumped up from her chair and ran to the door. She could hear her landlady, Mrs Kirlpatrick, calling her from the bottom of the stairs.

'Are you in, Josie?' The soft twang of an Irish accent echoed through the house.

'Yes, Mrs Kilpatrick. Wait a minute and I'll be down,' Josie replied as she grabbed a pair of shoes. Mrs Kilpatrick was waiting in the hallway, a couple of letters clasped in her hand.

'Your mother has been here this afternoon, Josie, but she couldn't wait until you got home from work, so she left these letters that came for you at the school where she works.'

Mrs Kilpatrick handed the letters to her and she took them with trembling hands. Who on earth could be writing to her? Who would be writing to her at her mother's address? She looked at the envelopes and recognised Lucy's handwriting on one of them, but the other one looked different somehow.

'Thanks, Mrs Kilpatrick, thanks a lot. I'll go upstairs and read them.'

She took the stairs slower this time; she was nearly six months pregnant and stairs were getting to be a bit of a problem. She lowered herself gently into a chair and studied the envelope that she didn't recognise. Could it be from Hank? With trembling hands she ripped the envelope open.

Dear Josie,

    It seems such a long time ago when we said goodbye on the river bank in England. I couldn't tell you then that we were going into combat. I think about you a lot and hope you are okay. I miss you so much honey and the days are so long here. Of course, you don't know where 'here' is, do you? Well, I am in a military hospital about twenty miles from Reading. Don't worry babe, I'll be okay, but I really would love to see you. Do you think you could visit me sometime soon? The address is at the top of the letter. I really, really need to talk to you. I had a surprise yesterday. Guess what! I had a letter forwarded on to me from France and it was from Joe. He couldn't tell me much because of the censor – even then they had blanked out most of the words – but he seems to be okay and we are going to keep in touch. We will meet up someday, somewhere, sometime ... who knows!

    All my love
    Hank xxxx

For a moment she sat motionless; she felt as if a part of her old life had come back to her and she didn't feel alone any more. As Josie looked again at the letter and specifically at the top where the address was, she could see that the hospital was in Wokingham, about twelve miles from Reading. It would not take too long to get there by train. She would go soon ... as soon as she could get some time off work! Happily, she put the letter on the table then turned her attention to the one that was obviously from Lucy.

Dear Josie,

I hope you are keeping well and looking after yourself! When is this war going to end and let us get back to a normal life? Well, at least the Germans are on the run now and our boys are chasing after them, so maybe next year it'll all be over.

I have some exciting news to tell you – I am engaged to be married! What do you think of that? You must come and be my Maid of Honour and Molly can be a little bridesmaid. She'd like that wouldn't she? Anyway, I have been dating this fellow called Douglas, who works at the Westlands Aircraft factory in Somerset, the same as I do. Well, he took me out on Wednesday night and, guess what, he has asked me to marry him! We have decided on a Christmas wedding and I have been wondering, Josie, whether you could spare a few of your clothing coupons to help me get a new outfit. I wish we could get hold of some extra food so we could have a reception but I guess that's out of the question.

Please, please write and say yes! I must go now, I'm on nights this week and it's time to go to work.
Lots of love
Lucy xxxx

The temporary shed-like building lay sprawled over the tranquil Berkshire countryside like a huge snake. Josie looked at it with anxious eyes as she tried to find unit number 16; that was where Hank was! She felt very nervous as she walked towards it and was glad that she had chosen to wear her loose-fitting long dress, which, she hoped, to some extent would help hide the fact that she was pregnant. Hank would know as soon as he saw her, though.

Pushing open the thin, plywood door she nervously stepped inside. In front of her was a long, narrow room with single beds placed on either side. Dozens of pairs of eyes focused on her as she started walking slowly through the room, her eyes darting from bed to bed looking for a familiar face – looking for Hank. Then from the far end of the room she heard a voice calling her.

'Josie, Josie, up here, the third bed from the end.'

It was Hank! A hand was weakly lifted to greet her and she ran towards him as tears filled her eyes. She looked down at his body, which seemed to be almost entirely encased in plaster – just his arms and head were free. He looked so thin and exhausted, as if everything was an effort, but on his face was a wonderful smile. She sat on the chair that had been placed at his bedside and leaned over to give him a kiss on the cheek. He grasped her hand and held it tightly and then his eyes widened as he saw her swollen belly and he knew that Josie was pregnant!

'Honey!' He had tears in his eyes now as he struggled to come to terms that soon he was to become a father. 'When did you know? When is the baby due? Hell! It is mine honey, isn't it?'

She nodded her head silently and smiled. He couldn't stop talking and questioning her. 'Say, babe, what did your mother say when you told her, I'll bet she's as mad as hell at me, isn't she?'

247

She put finger on his lips. 'Ssch, I want you to tell me what happened to you, Hank. Are you badly hurt?'

He pulled a face, then tried to cover it up with a smile, but she could see the hurt in his eyes. 'I took a bullet near my spine, Josie. I killed this German soldier. I was so mad at them for what happened to Peggy and Andy, I didn't notice this other German creeping up behind me, and then there was this noise. It was so loud and then I couldn't stand up anymore and I fell to the ground. Two British medics were nearby and they took out that guy and then they took care of me.'

'Wot do the doctors say then? Are you gonna to be alright, Hank? Will you be able to walk again? Please tell me you will be alright.'

They were both crying now and dozens of pairs of eyes watched silently at the drama unfolding in front of them.

Hank patted her on the arm. 'They tell me that I'll be okay, honey, but it is going to take a long, long time before I can walk again. I am going to be here for a few weeks more and then I am being shipped back to the US.' He paused for a moment or two, then looked up with a twinkle in his eyes. 'Will you miss me, Josie? Will you be sorry to see me go?'

She couldn't speak. Suddenly she realised how much she would miss him and now he would never know his own baby! He had come back into her life and now he was leaving again. Life was not fair! It just was not fair!

He beckoned her to get closer to him. She leaned forward and he took her face in his hands and gazed longingly into her eyes.

'Marry me, Josie. Please, honey. Let's get married before

they send me home. We can have the padre marry us here next week – then when I am back in the States they will send you over when you've had the baby.'

Her heart raced, her mind was filled with so many questions. What would her mother say? She suddenly realised that she had to get her mother's permission to get married because she was under-age! Her mother still didn't know she was pregnant because Josie hadn't seen her for quite awhile.

She turned and looked down the ward at the sick and wounded soldiers, then she looked back at Hank. He was watching her anxiously – she had to put him out of his misery. Bending down she kissed him on the lips.

'I will, Hank,' she said softly, 'I will marry you just as soon as I can.'

His eyes lit up as he shouted at the top of his voice. 'Hey, guys, she's just said she will marry me. We're going to get married here – next week and you are all invited to the wedding.'

His words resounded around the ward as a chorus of cheers and whistles filled the air. Hank looked up at her with a grin. 'You're going to be a GI bride, Josie – what do you think of that?'

'Yes, me and a million others, Hank,' she replied thoughtfully. 'Me and a million others!'

As she walked away from the hospital she realised the enormity of what she had just done … marriage would mean leaving behind her family and friends – travelling thousands of miles across the sea to a whole, strange new world. She would be leaving behind the river, where so many memories of Michael were held. Could she do it? Could she leave everything that was familiar and dear to her? She needed an answer and she needed it now!

The train pulled into Reading Station and Josie had made up her mind … she would go straight to the river, but this time she would walk the mile and a half to the 5-bar gate where she had stood with Michael on their first date. She would find the answer there. The feeling was so strong she couldn't ignore it.

Dusk was falling when Josie reached the gate. Folding her arms she rested them on the top bar and watched as stars began to form in the sky. Gradually the twittering of birds became silent and a hush settled over the riverbank, leaving just the gentle murmur of the river as it made its way downstream. She felt a presence – a feeling that Michael was here with her. A shiver swept through her body as she looked around. Then her eyes became focused on the willow trees that swayed gently beside the river … she gave a gasp of surprise … standing by one of the trees she thought she saw him! He was smiling at her and nodding his head, and in that moment she knew that the answer had been given to her. She would marry Hank and it would be the beginning of a new life, a new family for her. It was time to move forward. But no matter where she went in the world, memories of Michael would live in her heart forever.